Nantucket BLUE

LEILA HOWLAND

HYPERION
LOS ANGELES · NEW YORK

Copyright © 2013 by Leila Howland

All rights reserved. Published by Hyperion, an imprint of Disney Book Group. No part of this book may be reproduced or transmitted in any form or by any means, electronic or mechanical, including photocopying, recording, or by any information storage and retrieval system, without written permission from the publisher. For information address Hyperion, 125 West End Avenue, New York, New York 10023.

Printed in the United States of America

First Hyperion paperback edition, 2014

10 9 8 7 6 5 4 3 2 1

V475-2873-0-14015

Designed by Marci Senders

Library of Congress Control Number for Hardcover Edition: 2012035121

ISBN 978-1-4231-6139-4

Visit www.hyperionteens.com

For my parents
and for Jonny

One

EVEN WITHOUT HOLLY HOWARD AND DORI ARCHER, WHO'D been suspended for drinking on campus, we were supposed to win that game. The sun was high and white, and the breeze carried the scent of sweaty, shampooed girls and a whiff of the fresh asphalt from the school's newly paved driveway. The sky was bright blue with three marshmallow clouds. It was such a perfect day for a lacrosse game in Rhode Island that it was hard to imagine anything else was happening anywhere in the world. I wiped my forehead with my arm, blinking my eyes against the sting of sunscreen. My cheeks were hot, my ponytail was tight, and my legs were aching to sprint.

We were playing Alden, our school's rival for the past hundred years. It used to be all girls, like us, but went coed fifty years ago. They'd been pretty weak all season because Hannah Higgins, Cat Whiting, Sarah McKinnon, and basically all of their strong seniors graduated last year, giving the Rosewood School for Girls a chance to break a ten-year losing streak. We'd kicked their ass when we played them at an away game; kicked everyone's asses all season long. Our girls' varsity lacrosse team was, for the first time in a decade, undefeated, and yet here we were, tied on our own turf with three minutes left on the clock, the ball in Alden's control as they tossed it around, calling out code words for plays: "Princeton," "Bates," "Hobart," "St. Lawrence"—probably where the seniors were headed in the fall. Some of them should've studied a little harder.

For a moment there, it was hard to care. It was kind of hard to care about anything the last week of school, with classes, APs, and exams behind us, and summer so close, I could almost taste it. (What does summer taste like? Iced lemonade and fried clams.) The only things left were Founder's Day, Prize Day, and watching the seniors graduate.

But all it took was a glance to the sidelines to begin to care, and care a lot. The silver bleachers, which usually glared as the sun hit the empty metallic seats, were filled with girls in variations of the school uniform. Siblings from the lower and middle school spilled onto the grass in front of them. Parents sat forward in their collapsible spectator chairs. As usual, mine were not among them. My mother was correcting papers in her fifth-grade classroom, and my father was at his office in the English department at the

Rhode Island School of Design, or maybe helping his new wife, Polly, and her adopted Ukrainian son, Alexi. Nina, my best friend Jules's mom, was usually there in jeans and one of her cashmere sweaters. They were gray or ivory or aqua—the colors changed, some had a belt or a ruffle; but this spring, Nina liked wraps, and she brought them back from New York in glossy shopping bags with ropey handles. That's where she was now, I remembered. New York.

The principal, former women's golf champion Edwina MacIntosh, was there in her favorite maroon suit, tortoise-shell glasses, and tightly permed hair. Teachers who don't come to games were there. Even Mrs. Hart, the ancient English teacher, was there in her panty hose and pumps, one hand on her hip, the other gripping the strap of her beat-up black pocketbook as she peered over her beak at the action.

More important, guys were there. The boys' lacrosse teams had finished their season last weekend. There was a whole group of Alden guys watching, including my future boyfriend, the delicious Jay Logan. Jules hated it when I used "delicious" to describe anything but food, but that day he was nothing if not a sugar cone of melting sea salt and caramel gelato. He was wearing worn-in jeans and a red T-shirt. His hand swept his chestnut-colored curls from in front of his eyes. I've had a serious crush on Jay Logan since the eighth grade. I have a Jay Logan playlist on my iPod with the fifteen songs that remind me of him. The Jay-Z song from when we fast-danced in a group at Dani Gold's bat mitzvah; the Elton John one that was playing in CVS when I saw him with his mother the summer after freshman year and he asked me what kind of shampoo I was buying; the Coldplay song I played over and over after that time we talked for almost ten minutes at a Brown ice hockey game, etc.

For the first time, Jay was starting to notice me. He'd paid me undeniable attention at Joey Rivera's post–Spring Dance party last weekend. He followed me onto the girl-dominated sunporch, where pink wine coolers matched pedicures and shades of glittering lip gloss. He didn't have to stay there with me, our legs touching on the sofa, for an hour and a half when the guys were drinking beer and playing video games in the basement, a mere staircase away. He didn't have to rest his arm behind me, making it impossible for me not to lean against his boy body, making it so easy to feel comfortable in the crook of his arm.

Now he threw his head back, laughing at something his buddy Chris said. I wondered if I could make him laugh like that, if he was the kind of guy who believed that girls could also be funny.

"Get in the game, Cricket," Miss Kang, our coach, called from the opposite sideline. I snapped out of my Jay Logan haze and turned to see my teammate Arti Rai, ambidextrous and MVP defensive player for two years running, hurtling downfield like an Acela Express.

"Out of the way, Joy," Miss Kang called. Joy Gunther, who always had a bud of snot in her left nostril and had only been promoted to varsity because Holly and Dori had been suspended, shrieked, covered her head, and backed out of the way.

I broke right, flying past three of the red-clad Alden girls, my stick in my right hand only. I'd practiced running one-handed catches in the park last summer. By September I was able to pluck the hard orange ball out of the air as effortlessly as catching an apple falling from a tree.

Arti issued one of her signature clean, powerful passes, and it landed with a satisfying weight in my crosse. I drew my stick close to my body, pivoted, and sprinted down the field so fast I could feel the flesh of my cheeks flattening. The bleachers erupted in applause. I heard cowbells, whistles, and cheers. I saw Jules out of my peripheral vision, wide open and angling for a pass. I tossed it to her, and of course she caught it. We always made the connection. The Alden defense flocked to her, freeing me, and she passed it back.

I was in the twelve-meter fan when I decided it was a good day for a bounce shot and propelled rapidly toward the eight-meter arc, then changed my mind, thinking I'd better make it an upper-left-corner drop down, when a metal stick slammed my jaw and a cleat perforated my shin. In two dark seconds, I was on the grass, eating dirt, my hands scraped and flat, my stick flung three feet away from me. I heard a collective gasp.

"Yellow flag," the ref called. *Red flag*, I thought. But before I had time to spit dirt, someone was next to me, smelling sweet and pink, like baby-powder deodorant or girlie body spray—the kind that comes in a can.

"Don't even think of going after Jay," a raspy voice said.

I lifted my face, holding my breath, afraid that if I inhaled, I'd start to cry, out of shock or pain or both. I turned to see Nora Malloy crouched in a posture that from a distance would suggest concern, but up close was that of a puma about to pounce. From the intensity of her glare, you'd think she was someone I not only knew well but had severely wronged. In reality, we'd probably spoken a total of four times in our lives, and one of those times was when I asked her where the bathrooms in the Alden Sports Center were.

Nora Malloy was a junior at Alden, and I guess she liked Jay so much that she was willing to disfigure the competition. Up close, her prettiness was magnified. I had seen Nora in a bikini last summer at First Beach. It's not every girl who can pull off boy shorts. You need a bubble butt and lady legs for that. While I had nothing to complain about in the body department, I was closer to a girl than a woman. I'm built like my mother, who even at forty-four is still more girl than woman.

I drew my shin to my chest. No skin had been broken, but I could feel a warm prune-colored bruise blooming on my bone.

"Hey, you got that?" she asked. "Stay away."

"Whatever," I said, removing my mouth guard and wiping my mouth. *Whatever?* Ugh. Why don't clever comebacks ever come to me in the moment? They only come later, when I'm in the shower or about to fall asleep, or stopped at a stop sign alone in my mom's Honda Civic, without a witness. Then the comebacks crackle in my brain like static electricity on freshly dried socks.

I touched my lip with my tongue. Please don't be a fat lip, I thought. Not tonight. Rumors were circulating about a party at Chris's house, a party where Jay would be. We'd so carefully laid the groundwork for a kiss at Joey Rivera's. I was determined to get one before Jay took off for Nantucket for the summer.

"You okay, Cricket?" Jules said from her position a few feet away. I nodded and stood, dusting off my knees, the crevices of which were packed with mashed grass. I tentatively put weight on my leg. It hurt, but I was going to be okay. The crowd clapped.

"Hey, Nora," Jules said in a stage whisper, "I heard you did some laundry at Joey's house. I'm curious, how many *loads* did he have?" Nora whipped around, speechless. I covered my swelling mouth with my hand.

"Damn," the goalie muttered under her breath.

Jules just raised her eyebrows, unblinking. Jules had so many comebacks on the tip of her tongue it was a wonder she could close her mouth. Where, I wondered, did she get the balls?

Miss Kang arrived with an ice pack and the first-aid kit.

"Are you all right?" she asked. I nodded, aware of the little granules of dirt in my teeth.

"I'm *really* sorry," Nora said in a syrupy voice.

"Four meters, sixteen," the ref said. Nora retreated to the twelve-meter mark.

Miss Kang tilted her head sympathetically. "You want to come out of the game, Thompson?"

"No way," I said, even though my lip and shin were both throbbing.

"That's the spirit." She looked at the clock. "Fifteen seconds. Okay, here's what's going to happen. You're going to go left, jag right like hell, and pop it in the lower pocket." She turned to the ref and nodded, then jogged backward off the field, smiling at me until she faced forward and strode to the sideline, her short black ponytail sticking straight out from the back of her head. I love Miss Kang.

"Yellow ball," the ref said. "Find your hash mark, number four." I did this, nodding at Jules as if to pass. The whistle blew. I cradled the ball, jogging calmly to the left before springing right, straight across the goal, snapping my stick so fast I heard the whoosh. It bounced high just as the goalie slid low, and the ball skimmed the upper-left corner of the net. It was downright elegant.

"Yes," I said, jumping in the air to high-five Jules. Arti Rai picked me up and swung me around. Miss Kang had dropped her clipboard and was running toward us with her hands raised in triumph. I'd scored my third goal of the game and won the first championship for Rosewood School for Girls in ten years.

"Good game, good game, good game." Our teams filed past each other in a single line. From ten bodies away, Nora bore holes in me with her eyes.

Nora. She'd been given all the raw materials for an enchanted high school existence: a pretty face, a body that just wouldn't quit, athletic ability, genuine confidence, her very own yellow Volkswagen bug with a bud vase on the dash. And that raspy voice that oozed sex, that was like a cherry on top, like finding a ten-dollar bill in jeans you haven't worn in a month. But she didn't know how to manage the attention that came with being popular. Obviously, in order to be popular, you need to be the kind of person to whom attention is naturally given. But then you have to manage it.

Nora's downhill journey started last summer when she'd had sex with Paul Duke, a real garbage can, as Jules said, but a popular one. He was known to hide in closets while his friends made out with girls, then jump out once the girl had her pants off. After he had sex with Nora, he'd told everyone the color of her pubic hair ("burnt sienna") and imitated the moans she'd supposedly made in a three-minute comical opera, whose crescendo was aped by underclassmen after they scored ice hockey goals.

In an effort to get back at Paul, she had sex with Matt Baldwin without him even being her boyfriend. Matt wouldn't talk to her the following Monday at school. Treated her like the plague. As if this weren't enough, she did it again with John Dwyer, a sophomore, on an overnight science trip. By September she was known as Nora the Whora. Even I knew she'd done it with a freshman on top of Joey Rivera's laundry machine last weekend at his party. For a junior girl to go after a freshman guy, that was bad. That was desperate.

It didn't have to be that way. There was another path.

A few years before, a shy but very big-boobed senior named Jenna Garbetti started to get a reputation. "Can't get any? Call Garbetti," the saying went. Instead of looking for validation in all the wrong places, she cut her raven locks into a flattering bob, quit going to parties for a couple of months, studied really hard, and took a silk-screening class at RISD. By April, she'd won some art award and been accepted to Yale. In other words, she turned the wrong kind of attention into the right kind of attention, and by the Spring Dance, she was back on top. Last year, when the senior girls asked me to hang out in their lounge with them and they actually listened to my stories, when I found out Greg Goldberg and Liam Hardiman had an argument over who would ask me to the Arden Spring Fling, when even teachers started telling me that I looked like the girl on the bicycle in the Maybelline commercials, I promised myself that if I started to attract the wrong kind of attention, I'd use the Jenna Garbetti method: lie low, look good, and learn.

"Good game, good game, good game." Nora and I were three bodies away, then two, then one. When it came time to shake, I put my hand out, but she turned away, leaving me hanging.

As usual, Arti Rai's mom had brought us mini bottles of Gatorade and made us chocolate cupcakes, this time with peanut butter frosting. As the team gathered around the bench, giddy and hungry, I hung back and made eye contact with Jay. He was standing with the Alden kids, but he was looking at me. He smiled and drew a line across his neck to suggest he couldn't possibly leave the Alden camp to congratulate the enemy without risking his life.

I laughed at his pantomime, which he dropped immediately when Chris caught on to his traitorous ways. He shrugged at Chris as if nothing had happened, then looked over his shoulder at me and winked. I was about to wink back when Edwina MacIntosh drew herself up to her full six feet and shook my hand. We called her Ed behind her back.

"You have star quality, Cricket Thompson," she said, nearly crushing my hand with hers. Sometimes she wasn't aware of her own strength.

"Thanks, Miss MacIntosh," I said. I've been going to this school since kindergarten, so Ed and I are not exactly strangers. Hell, I'd been here longer than she had. Both my mother and grandmother were Rosewood girls, too.

"Judy, wait one moment," Ed called with a finger in the air as the ref walked by.

"So you know how that party was supposed to be at Chris's house?" Jules said, handing me a cupcake and starting in on her second. Jules has her mom's brown ringlets, ski-jump nose, and strong, slim legs. She also has the metabolism of a cheetah.

"Yeah?"

"Well, there's been a change of plans," she said with a

full mouth. "I guess Chris's parents decided not to go to the Cape after all." She planted her stick in the ground and leaned against it, a makeshift chair. She crossed her ankles.

"So where is it?" I asked, peeling the cupcake wrapper and watching as the Alden crew filed onto their bus, painted the same red as their uniforms.

"Nora Malloy's," she said, and licked frosting from her fingers.

Two

"I'M KIND OF SCARED." I SAT UP ON THE TWIN BED CLOSEST to the window—the one that had pretty much become mine in the last few years, since my parents' official divorce—and pulled up the leg of my jeans to show my bruise. "Nora did this in public. Who knows what she's capable of on her own property."

"Oh, please. There's nothing she can do to us," Jules said, one arm folded over her bare stomach as she stood in front of her closet in her underwear and bra, considering what to wear. I heard her brother, Zack, come up the stairs and turn on the TV in the den. I loved being at Jules's house. It was big but not too big, buzzed with a mild, pleasant chaos, and smelled faintly like her mom's perfume. And Jules's room was my favorite. It had dark wooden floors and big windows with white, floaty curtains. It was painted a deep but calming blue. Jules called the color "Nantucket blue" because she said it was the color of the ocean on a clear day in Nantucket.

"Besides, it's so clear that Jay likes you," she said, rifling through her closet. I flopped back on the bed and grinned. I drummed my fingers on the pale-yellow coverlet as I smiled wildly.

"Do you think I'll lose my virginity to Jay?" I asked, biting my lip to hide my smile, not wanting to jinx anything. Jules and I were both virgins, although she'd come very close last summer with some boarding-school guy.

"It's possible," Jules said. "But don't do it right away."

"Oh my god, no. Six-month rule," I said. Jules and I decided that six months was the perfect amount of time to go out with a guy before sex. With that kind of time, you would know you weren't being used. I lay back on the bed and stared at the ceiling.

"I just thought of something bad," I said. "What if Jay turns out like his brother?" Jay has an older brother who was just like him in high school: gorgeous, popular, athletic, but he quit college, got arrested for drunk driving, and now lives at home and works at the bagel shop. And he can't drive, so I always see him walking places with big circles under his eyes. I could picture him so clearly. "He's such a loser."

"Cricket," Jules said. "That's mean." But she was smiling. This was the thing about Jules. I could always say what

I was really thinking to her and she wouldn't stop liking me. Actually, I got the feeling when I said stuff like this, stuff you can think but really shouldn't say, it made her like me more.

"Sorry, but it's true," I said. "He looks sad all the time. I feel bad going into the Bagel Place."

"I know what you mean. I hate it when he's working there. I can't just be myself when I order a bagel."

"I hope it doesn't run in the family, because I think Jay and I should get married someday. I mean, after we've both been to college."

"Can I be your maid of honor?"

"Of course." I sighed. "I can't believe I won't see him again for like, *months*!" He was leaving for Nantucket soon. So was Jules. Everyone was going somewhere for the summer. The Cape. Martha's Vineyard. Arti was going to an arts program in Innsbruck, Austria. Even Nora Malloy was going on an Outward Bound trip. She was going to scale Mount Rainier (and probably a few of her fellow mountaineers).

"You never know what can happen," Jules said, considering a pair of white jeans.

I wasn't looking forward to spending another summer in Providence babysitting Andrew King. I'd be setting up the baby pool in the King's driveway while everyone else was somewhere fabulous. But my family just didn't have enough money for a summer place or a European vacation. I could just see myself filling up that damn plastic pool with the hose in the heat of the midday and then stepping on its edge to let it drain when the streetlights came on.

The sound of a trumpet blasted into the room through the speaker in the ceiling.

"Guess my mom's home," Jules said. Nina had just discovered a South African jazz musician after she'd read about him in *The New Yorker*, and was listening to his new album on repeat like a teenager to the latest pop star, blasting it through the house's surround-sound system. We broke into the dance we'd made up to this now very familiar tune. Jules air-trumpeted and I twirled around her.

Jules and Zack made fun of Nina for her obsessions, but I loved how she'd focus on something—a poet or a film director or even a color, a particular shade of orange—then leave some corner of their house changed by her discovery: an oversized book of Mexican art in the front hall marked with neon Post-its, a William Carlos Williams quote stenciled in the downstairs bathroom, a vintage John Coltrane poster in the den, a yellow ceramic bowl filled with apricots on the dining room table.

Just last week she'd asked me to read aloud to her from a Jonathan Franzen book she couldn't put down while she cooked dinner. I was sitting cross-legged on their kitchen counter. "What would I do without you, Cricket?" Nina said when I finished a chapter. She was chopping onions. "No one else in this house will read to me."

Mr. Clayton was at work. Zack was studying for an exam. Jules was watching *Splash* in the den. She's obsessed with '80s movies.

"I love this guy," I said, flipping the book over to look at the author photo. "I love how he described the real estate lady in her jeans. And the way he talked about her haircut!"

Nina blinked away onion tears and looked at the author photo. "I bet he looks pretty excellent in jeans." She sipped her wine, then put the glass down and crushed some garlic. "Okay, keep going."

I smiled and turned the page.

I was pliéing around a barely dressed Jules to the flute solo in the South African jazz song when Zack opened the door. "Hey, Mom's in her dashiki." He strode in the room but stopped at the sight of Jules in her bra and underwear. "What the hell are you two doing? Jesus! Why didn't you warn me?"

He ran out.

"You should knock," Jules called after him, howling with laughter.

"I didn't know you were in your freaking lingerie. You've scarred me for life," he yelled from the hallway.

"At least she wasn't wearing a thong," I said, leaving Jules to get dressed, and shutting the door behind me.

"That doesn't make me feel better," he said, retreating into the den. I followed him. He sat on the sofa, his head in his hand. "In fact, great. Thanks for the image."

"What you saw was no different than a bathing suit."

"Oh, yes it is," he said. "I don't know how and I don't know why, but it is." The right corner of his mouth turned up. He put his feet on the coffee table. Crossed his ankles. "I have to make an appointment with the worry doctor now." The Claytons had moved here four years ago from New York. From what Jules had told me, Zack had been an anxious kid with thick glasses who'd seen a psychiatrist, his "worry doctor," during most of elementary school. Most people were embarrassed about therapy, but Zack owned his time in the chair—"It's not a couch," he said, "but a comfortable black leather chair and ottoman, very nineteen seventies"—and was happy to discuss it with anyone who asked. He'd stayed back a year when they had moved here, and now he was a funny, slightly under-the-radar freshman at Alden with plenty of friends and boldly framed glasses he wore with confidence.

"Nice game today, by the way, Cricket." I hadn't even noticed he was there. "And, yes, I'm aggressively changing the subject. You were awesome out there."

"Oh, thanks," I said, and plopped next to him on the sofa.

"You're so fast, like an animal running from whatever's above it on the food chain."

"Are you calling me an animal, Zack Clayton?" I smacked him with a needlepoint pillow of a crab.

"Hey, the crab is a lover, not a fighter," he said, taking the pillow from me and placing it behind his head. "I just meant that you looked like a prairie dog fleeing a jackal."

"I'm a prairie dog now?" He nodded. I looked around for another pillow, but by the time I'd spotted one, he'd grabbed it and was holding it in front of his face in self-defense.

He lowered it and said, "But who says being an animal is

bad? Personally, I think we should honor more of our animal instincts."

"If I ever catch you two following your animal instincts, I'll puke twice and die," Jules said, emerging from her room wearing jeans and a delicate cardigan over a loose, low-necked T-shirt.

"I wasn't flirting," I said.

"Who said anything about flirting?" Zack was smiling, eyebrows raised. I looked at him in shock.

"Busted," Jules said. Zack hugged the pillow and tilted his head back in a silent laugh.

"Don't be a cocky bastard, Zack," Jules said, and then turned to me. "Just so you know, he has a fungus on his back. There is literally a fungus among us."

"Hey, that cleared up," Zack said, adjusting the bill of his baseball cap. "And it was just on my shoulder."

"Hope you've been wearing flip-flops in the shower, Cricket," Jules said.

"Dinner's ready," Mr. Clayton called from downstairs.

Jules looped a long necklace over her head. "I wonder what Mom brought me from the city." I hopped off the sofa and followed her down the narrow back staircase.

Nina wasn't in a dashiki. She wasn't there. It was Mr. Clayton who'd put the South African jazz guy on the stereo. He was in his suit, phone cradled under his chin, as he unloaded some salads from a paper bag with the familiar Providence Pizza insignia. The pizzas were on the table.

Zack had opened the box and was pulling out a slice when Mr. Clayton handed him the phone. "Your mom wants to talk to you." Zack took the phone.

"Mom's not coming home?" Jules asked Mr. Clayton. Mr. Clayton said that no, Nina had a terrible headache and was so tired from a day of shopping with her friends that she'd ordered room service and was going to stay an extra night in the city, which I'd learned from hanging around the Claytons meant New York.

"But I thought we were going to . . . ?" Jules whispered something to Mr. Clayton, and he whispered back. Zack gave the phone to Jules, and she took it into the dining room to talk to Nina. Jules peeked around the corner, signaling for me to join her. She pulled the phone away from her mouth and said, "We want to know if you want to spend the summer with us on Nantucket?" I shrieked and wrapped my arms around Jules with such force we fell backward onto the cushioned window seat, and she dropped the phone. I felt her stomach tighten with laughter under my weight.

I'd heard a lot about Nantucket from Jules. I'd seen pictures of the Claytons suntanned, barefoot, and happy at their house with two benches out front facing each other, the big wraparound side porch, and the backyard that looked like an English garden, with bunny rabbits and butterflies. I'd heard the names of Nantucket places, which, together, sounded like a secret language: Shimmo, 'Sconset, Sankaty. Miacomet, Madaket, Madequecham. Cisco, Dionis, Wauwinet. I'd heard about moonlit, all-night parties on the beach, watching the sunrise with kids named Parker and Apple and Whit. I'd seen photos of a candy-striped lighthouse and a cobble-stoned town so safe that parents let their children wander free. I'd held Nina's jam jar of Nantucket sand as white and fine as sugar. I'd stared at the framed poster in Jules's bed-room of little sailboats with rainbow-colored sails so long that I could practically feel the salt wind on my cheeks.

"Is that a yes?" Nina's voice was tiny from the pinprick holes in the phone. I picked the cordless off the floor.

"Yes," I said. Then I remembered. "I guess I need to ask my mom."

"I already talked to her, sweetheart. She said it was up to you."

"Are you serious?" I squeezed Jules's hand. "Thank you, thank you," I said into the phone. No forced weekends with Dad and Polly and Alexi. No Saturday nights watching *Real Life Mysteries* with Mom, or worrying about why she was going to bed at eight thirty. Instead, Jules and I would get jobs and go to parties and stay out all night. I'd practically live in my bikini. I'd have sand in my shoes all summer, I'd go to bed with hair stiff from swimming in salt water, and I'd always be able to smell the ocean. I'd walk to town on cobblestoned streets. And Jay would be there. I felt pretty certain now that this would be the summer we'd fall in love.

Nina started to hang up, when out of nowhere I told her that I loved her. I blushed, cringing with embarrassment. Who says this to someone else's mom? I'd meant it, but I hadn't meant to say it. I was just so happy.

Nina didn't even pause. "Aw, I love you too, Cricket. And you're going to love the island. Once you spend a summer on Nantucket, a little piece of you will stay there forever. Now, tell everyone I'll call back later. I'm going to lie down. I'm not feeling so great." We hung up.

I had no idea that I'd chosen my words so well. I had no idea how important it was that I'd said what I did. Because by the time we'd pulled into Nora's driveway and marched past her pumping the keg, by the time Jules and I found Jay and all those guys reclining on the deck chairs around Nora's pool, by the time I'd told Jay I was going to Nantucket and he said that was "the best news," Nina was gone.

Three

HOTEL HOUSEKEEPING HAD FOUND NINA'S BODY. SHE'D HAD an aneurysm. (A freak thing; it can *just happen.*) She died not long after eight o'clock, about the time we'd hung up the phone. Mr. Clayton didn't tell me any of this that bright morning when I'd woken up earlier than Jules.

I'd been up for hours. While I was waiting for Jules to show signs of consciousness, for her eyes to blink open, her fists to uncurl, for that sudden intake of air that signaled her release from the depths of slumber, I made a list of the top five reasons I liked Jay. *First, he's beautiful.* He has big dreamy eyes and the best boy butt I've ever seen. *Second, he's such a talented athlete.* He looks like some kind of warrior on the lacrosse field. He's graceful and powerful at the same time. I think part of my attraction is some kind of primitive response to his potential ability to hunt food while I gather berries. *Third, I like the way he stands.* Okay, I know this is weird, but there's something about it I just love. I can't explain it. *Fourth, he has a cool family.* His mom is so pretty, with her long red hair that's always a little messy in a way that makes her seem young, and his dad has cool old cars. Even though his brother is having a rough time, I bet he still has greatness in him. You can kind of see it when he's walking around. His walk is still confident, even if some other part of him is shattered. *Fifth, Jay always sticks up for his brother, so I know he's a good guy with a real heart.* I know he'd be a great boyfriend.

At eleven o'clock, I finally kicked the covers off. I was hungry. I remembered dinner last night and grinned. The Nantucket invitation hadn't been a dream, had it? No, it was real. It was real, and it was all ahead of me, sparkling like a distant city.

I hesitated at the top of the stairs. Usually, I'd hear kitchen sounds: the fridge opening or closing, the cutlery drawer sliding on its rails, newspaper pages turning and snapping, bare feet padding the blond planks of the wood floor. Usually, I'd smell coffee, cinnamon swirl bread in the toaster, maybe bacon, and feel the warm currents of energy that Nina emanated in the cotton pajama bottoms and Brown University T-shirt she slept in. But on that morning, the house felt the way the world does after it's snowed all night: quiet, muffled, absent of sound. The air smelled like nothing. I went down anyway. Maybe they'd gone out?

I was so certain I was alone that I was talking to myself, replaying what Jay had said to me the night before. I was sitting on his lap in a lawn chair. "Do you even know how cute you are?" he'd asked, speaking into my neck, bouncing me slightly on his knee. "Do you?" I wouldn't be able to tell anyone this without sounding like I was bragging, without it sounding stupid and possibly sexist. Edwina MacIntosh dedicated a section of her yearly "Critical Eye" lecture on gender and the media to slides of women in magazines acting sexy in little-girl poses. Those pictures were really messed up. I'd felt a little guilty when I'd sat on Jay's lap like that, like I was disappointing Rosewood School for Girls. I couldn't tell anyone that it had made me feel shy and pretty and powerful all at once.

Also, I couldn't believe we hadn't kissed. He and his friends started playing some drinking game, and none of them were hanging out with girls. Still, I reminded myself with a grin, he'd asked for my phone number. I'd watched him enter it into his phone.

It wasn't until I'd pulled the bread out of the fridge that I'd turned and seen Mr. Clayton, a cup of to-go coffee in front of him, sitting as still and silent as the stone Abraham Lincoln in the memorial we'd visited on a class trip to Washington, D.C. He was fish-belly white. He was holding something. It was wrapped around his fist. A bandage? A pillowcase? He lowered his hand to his lap.

"You need to go," he said, and swallowed. His voice was low and serious and not the one he used to talk to his kids. Or to me.

I instinctively knew not to ask questions. I nodded and walked silently up the stairs two steps at a time, stuffed my feet into my tied sneakers, and walked out the front door with my half-packed overnight bag. I was confused, just following directions, aware that it was hot, almost the middle of the day, and I hadn't yet brushed my teeth or had a sip of water. I had a two-mile walk to my mom's house. Also, I'd left my cell phone plugged into Jules's wall.

When I got to the mailbox on the corner I realized that Mr. Clayton had been holding the T-shirt Nina slept in. He'd been pressing it to his face when I'd walked in the room. *Those red eyes. The strange, wobbly voice.* He'd been crying. And that's when, with no other evidence, I'd wondered if she'd died. I stopped, touched my fingers to my lips, and closed my eyes against the sunshine. A freezing darkness rushed through me, like I'd capsized, like I was attached to an anchor that was pulling me to the ocean floor. But it couldn't be true. It was horrible to even think it.

I let myself into the house. Mom's sad, solitary breakfast plate was in the sink, peppered with crumbs, next to her solitary coffee mug, the one that spelled out "teacher" in letters made by rulers and apples. Mostly we ate off of paper towels or from the plastic containers of the supermarket deli, using so few dishes that she only ran the dishwasher on Sundays.

It hadn't always been like this. There had been a time when I'd passed plates of cheese and crackers at the impromptu dinner parties she and Dad had. I would play waitress until my bedtime, when I'd fall asleep to the smell of roast chicken and the sounds of the party wafting through the heating vents. Mom would check on me before she went to bed, and said that sometimes she'd find me giggling in my sleep. I used to think it was because the last thing I'd hear before I drifted off was her laughter.

We always made a game of cleaning up in the morning in our pajamas. She'd make a big pot of coffee, Dad would buy a dozen doughnuts, and we'd see how many plates we could wash in the span of an '80s song. Barefoot, her toenails painted red, and high on coffee and sugar, Mom sang all the lyrics in perfect pitch. I remember watching her sing Bon Jovi with her hair down, and wondering why she wasn't famous.

But that was a long time ago, back when there was color in her cheeks, and her hair was long, and she got dressed up for school even though the other teachers wore jeans and sneakers. That was before the parties stopped and the fighting started. It was before I heard swearing through the vents instead of laughter. It was before Dad moved out and the house filled with silence: heavy, hovering, raincloud silence.

The phone rang, startling me out of my memory. I had a feeling it was Jules, but I couldn't find the phone. It wasn't on its base, and I had to follow the electronic beeps around the living room until I finally found it between the sofa cushions on the last ring. "Hello?"

"Hi, it's me," Jules said.

"Jules?" She didn't sound like herself.

"Hey," I said. "Are you okay?" There was a pause. My stomach dropped. I sat on the edge of the sofa. "Jules?"

"My mom died," she said. Her voice was flat and clipped. "She had an aneurysm in New York." She said the word like she'd known it her whole life.

"A what?" I asked, breathless.

"It's when the head bleeds, on the inside."

"Oh my god," I said, and lay down, shocked that Jules was defining the medical term. I closed my eyes. My throat cinched. My stomach hurt. "Jules, that's terrible. I'm so, so sorry. I can't believe it." I waited for her to cry or scream or say something, but I couldn't even hear her breathe.

"I love you," I said. "And if you need anything, anything at all, just call me, okay?"

"Thanks," Jules said. I gripped the phone, pressing it to my face. I didn't know what else to say. After a few more seconds of silence she said, "I need to go now," and hung up.

I ran up the stairs and crumbled into my mother's bed. I couldn't remember the last time I'd cried to her. I'd been stoic during the divorce—locked, lights off, like a school on Christmas. I'd been all politeness and competence. It was too dangerous to cry in front of her. It was what she wanted from me, to openly admit defeat, to hop aboard the sadness train, to check in with her at the broken-down Casa de

Divorce, and I wasn't going to do it. But this was different.

"I loved her," I said, breathing raggedly.

"I know you did," Mom said. I hung my chin over her shoulder, my whole body shaking, my breath ricocheting in my ribs. "Poor Jules," she said. "Poor, poor Jules."

My mom let me skip Founder's Day and Prize Day, even though I'd won the Anne Hutchinson Achievement in History Prize and the Chafee Citizenship Award. I could collect them later, Ed said. I went to graduation, where the seniors stood on the stage in tea-length white dresses. I sang "Simple Gifts" and "And Did Those Feet in Ancient Time" with the choir, as I had at every other school commencement. It actually made me feel a little better. Neither my mom nor my dad is religious; I guess those school songs, which I'd sung for eleven years now, were the closest things I had to prayers. Jules wasn't there.

I wanted to call her, to go over to the Claytons', climb into the twin bed, eat a box of Munchkins with her and Zack, and watch movies. I wanted to sit in the backyard on the striped cushions and listen to South African jazz. I wanted to drink a glass of Nina's red wine and cry with the rest of them. But my mother insisted that I stay put; said I needed to give them time alone to grieve as a family. She used her teacher voice. I knew she was right, but who else would understand? Who else was feeling like this? We sent a plant. I was jealous of the plant. It got to be with them.

On the third day, I made them lasagna. I found a healthy

recipe online (they need healthy food, I thought; they need vitamins), but the whole-wheat noodles were gooey in the middle and crunchy on the ends, and the thing didn't hold together. "We can't take this," my mom said, sticking a spatula into the congealed mess. Tomato-colored water leaked out the top. We picked them up some cookies and a loaf of Portuguese sweet bread. But Jules wasn't there when we dropped them off. Her grandmother had taken her to the movies. I slipped upstairs to get my phone. I don't know what I was expecting, but Jules's room looked the same as it always did. My phone was plugged into the wall. There were three texts from Jay in the last three days.

#1 Hi!

#2 Heard about Mrs. Clayton. I'm so sorry. (This was followed by a missed call, but no message.)

#3 Leaving for Nantucket tomorrow. See you there?

The memorial service was at the church near Brown University, the one Nina liked to go to every now and then because they had a good choir. It was an old New England–style church, pretty in a simple way, without pictures of Jesus or stained-glass windows. Nina had dragged Jules and me to a choral concert there once last spring, and the church had seemed almost spacious, but there had only been about twelve of us in the audience. Now it was packed with people, and it felt small and cramped, especially without any air-conditioning. Kids were using their programs to fan themselves. There were hardly any seats left when Mom and

I arrived. We found room in a pew a few rows back from the Claytons, on the opposite side of the aisle, next to some people I didn't know but who I guessed were from New York. I could see the sides of Zack's and Jules's faces as we all stood to sing "Morning Has Broken."

"And now I want to give her children a chance to speak," the minister said after delivering her eulogy. She had the gray hair of an old lady, but the smooth, tanned skin of a young one. "Jules?"

Jules walked to the front of the church and stood behind a plain wooden podium. She looked blank. Her lips were pressed together so tightly they were colorless. She seemed someplace else; I'd seen this expression when she checked out of math class. She scanned the crowd, gazing into some kind of middle distance for what felt like a hundred seconds too long.

"Um," Jules started. I watched her eyes dart to Zack, but his eyes were closed, his shoulders were shaking, and tears streamed down his face and dripped from his chin. I'd never seen a boy cry before. That's one of the things about going to an all-girls' school your whole life: it's hard to believe that boys are people too.

"Hi," Jules said, and waved a weird, stiff hand at the crowd. Her eyebrows rose. Oh my god, she was now biting her lip because she was trying not to *laugh*. It was happening. I'd heard about that happening to people at funerals, and now it was really happening to Jules. There was a long silence. A baby cooed. A few people whispered. One corner of Jules's mouth twitched upward. She looked like she was in physical pain. Breathe, I thought, as her face turned red. She needed oxygen or she was going to pass out.

I stood up.

"Cricket?" my mom whispered.

"She needs me," I whispered back and slid past her, out of the pew. Maybe my mom was the type to disappear into herself when things got rough, but I wasn't.

It couldn't have been more than ten paces from my pew to where Jules was standing, but it felt like it took forever to get there. I could feel everyone looking at me as I walked down the aisle. My ears were hot, and my feet were sweating inside my too-tight flats. I locked eyes with Jules. Her head tilted and her brow pinched as she watched me approach. For a second I wondered if I was doing the right thing, but leaving her standing there alone, suffocating in front of everyone, was not an option. Not for her best friend.

"It's okay," I whispered when I finally reached her. She looked at the ground and took a big gulp of air. I turned to face the crowd.

"The last time I saw Nina," I said, "I was over at Jules's studying for exams. I was really stressed out." I could hear myself speaking, like an echo on a cell phone. Then without meaning to, I started to focus on a pleasant-looking dad type with foppish hair and wire-rimmed glasses. There was something kind about him, like a beloved English teacher. His head tilted. "And she was in the backyard, painting a

big fish, like applying paint to an actual trout or something."
The man smiled, his eyes squinting behind his glasses.

"She was making these fish pictures. And she was barefoot, one pant leg was rolled up, and her hair was doing that thing where it kind of stands up on one side." At least ten people laughed. Jules walked back to her seat. My mouth was dry, but I kept going. The story seemed to be telling itself. "And she had that look on her face. The one she got when she was really into something?" A horse-faced woman with a headband nodded. "That look that meant she was ready for anything, ready for action, ready for life." That last word hung in the air. My breath caught. "And before I knew it, I had a cold fish in my hand and she was teaching me how to use a trout to make a print, which was actually fun— gross and messy and fun. I forgot all about my exam. We made five and left them drying in the basement." I wiped my eyes with the back of my hand. "I don't remember what happened to the fish."

"So *that's* that smell," Mr. Clayton called from the front row. This time almost everyone laughed. Except Jules. She was slouched, her hands in the lap of her black crepe dress, her face as still as a doll's. I tried to make eye contact with her, but she was staring at the ground. Zack looked right at me, though. Something about the way he was smiling, crying with his eyes open, urged me to keep going.

"And that was the thing about Nina. She looked at a dead fish and saw an art project; she'd look inside a refrigerator and find nothing but hot dogs and mayonnaise, and she'd throw them together and make you feel like you'd had the best meal of your life." I was gesturing wildly with my hands— they seemed to have a life of their own. "She looked at you," I choked, "at me, and saw someone to love." The man with the wire-rimmed glasses dabbed his eyes with a Kleenex. "She was the best, and I'm going to miss her so much," I said. I walked quickly back to my pew and slid in next to my mother. I looked at Jules, but she didn't turn around.

"You know, it's not healthy to be handling raw fish like that," Mom said, as she handed me a tissue. "You could've gotten sick."

I looked at her in disbelief. How could she have chosen this moment to criticize Nina? How could she have missed the whole point of that story? If I hadn't been crying, I would've screamed.

After, the church parlor was crowded. I knew a lot of the people—parents from school, people I'd seen around Providence. Practically our whole class was there, gathered in a corner, a cluster of navy and black dresses. Arti waved me over, but I didn't want to join them. They hardly knew Nina, and they certainly didn't love her. They wouldn't know how I was feeling. I didn't want to talk to anyone but the Claytons. While my mother talked to the woman with the yellow dogs from the yellow house on the corner, I studied a bulletin board of community announcements and ate a crustless egg salad sandwich and a handful of wet red grapes. I was hungrier than I'd been in days. In fact, I couldn't remember the last time I'd had an actual meal. I was reading a flyer advertising a playgroup for toddlers when someone tapped me on the shoulder.

"I know that you're drawn to the neon-pink paper, but you can't join that group," Zack said. He'd dripped Coke or coffee on his tie.

"Why not?" I asked.

"Too old." He shrugged. "And you have to be potty-trained, so there's that." His exhausted smile pained me.

"I'm working on it," I said. "Every day."

"Thanks for what you said about Mom," he said.

"Really? I was a little worried that maybe I shouldn't have," I said.

"No, it was good," he said. "It was funny. And sweet."

"Thanks," I said, taking in a sharp breath. "Where's Jules?" I asked. The reception was so packed that I'd lost sight of her. I'd figured we talk, finally, when it had thinned out a little.

"She just left," Zack said, and shrugged his shoulders. "She's on her way home. You might be able to catch her."

As soon as I stepped out of the church, I saw her down the street, three blocks away. I jogged in my flats, which were murdering my pinkie toes, and caught her as she was about to turn up her street.

"Hey," I said.

She gasped. "You scared me."

"Do you want to go and get some iced coffee or something?" I asked as I caught my breath. Little trickles of sweat ran down my back. "We could go to The Coffee Exchange."

"Um, no. Not right now."

"Later, maybe?" I licked my upper lip. Summer was here early.

"Sure," she said. I walked with her up her street. "Only thing is, my cousins are here, so I don't know what we'll be up to. Hey, I saw that Jay called you."

"Yes, but that's not important right now. You are." I put my hand on her shoulder, where it hung awkwardly as she walked fast and I tried to keep up. "Jules, are you okay?"

"Yeah," she said. We stopped in front of her house. I wanted to ask her if she'd been about to laugh up there, if she'd been sleeping okay, if she wanted to collapse in my arms the way I had in my mother's. I wanted to peel back the clear plastic curtain that seemed to be hanging between us so I could touch her. I wanted some proof that she was still herself. I wanted her to cry.

"Is it okay that I stood up there and said that stuff?" I asked.

"Yeah, it was great," she said. "I was freaking out. I'm just tired."

I sighed with relief. "Well, just so you know," I said, feeling a little shaky, "this summer, I'm there for you no matter what. We don't have to go to parties. We can stay in and watch '80s movies. We can go for walks on the beach every day. I'll do whatever. Just whatever makes you feel better. You're my best friend and I'm here for you one hundred percent." Anyone could come up with those words. Where were the right words?

"Thanks," she said, and crossed her arms. "I'm going to change out of this dress. I feel like a freakin' pilgrim."

"Okay," I said. She stood on the bottom step in front of the closed door. "I guess I'll head back to the church and find my mom. Call me, okay?"

I was standing in front of the mirror, brushing my teeth, when Jules called the next morning. I spat and picked up. "Hey!"

"Hey," she said, sounding like her old self again. "What's up?"

"Uh, not much," I answered. "How are you doing?"

"Oh my god, it's so crazy in this house," Jules said.

"I can't imagine," I said, and looked out the window. Frankie, the neighbors' beagle, was curled under the one patch of shade in their backyard. It was going to be another hot one.

"My little cousin is sleeping in my room, and she wet the bed last night, all the way down to the mattress. It stinks so bad in here. And my grandmother ironed all my jeans stiff as a board. With pleats. I'm not kidding."

"Well, that sucks," I said, surprised at how normal she sounded. "I was thinking maybe we could ride our bikes out to Bristol?" Bristol is a little seaside town with coffee shops and a cool antique store. Jules and I liked to look at the stacks of old photographs in back of the store.

"Not today," she said. "My whole family is here."

"Oh, right. I just thought, you know, it would be peaceful out there. Anyway, that reminds me, should I bring my bike to Nantucket?"

"Actually, that's what I was calling to tell you. You can't come with us anymore."

"Oh," I said, as I watched my face pale in the mirror. "Okay."

"It totally blows, but my dad said only family in the house this summer."

"Of course. I understand. Of course." I sat on the closed toilet seat and hung my head. How could I be thinking of myself? I burned with shame. "I totally get it."

She sighed and added, "But you can get your babysitting job back with the Kings, right?"

Four

THE FIRST TIME I THOUGHT OF GOING TO NANTUCKET BY
myself, I was about to pick up the phone and call Deirdre
King, mother of Andrew. I'd already typed in her number
on my phone and was staring at it on the screen. My lip
curled. Why, I wondered, was I doing it? I hated that job.
Last summer, Andrew was obsessed with the word *boobies*.
He'd say "boobies," then punch me in the boob. It really
sucked. Especially when Mrs. King found it funny, which
maybe it was if it wasn't *your* boob. I didn't want to play the
straight man for Andrew King's comedy act again. I hung
up the phone. I won't do it, I thought, falling back on my
bed. *I won't.*

I started to think of other babysitting jobs, ones that

provided housing, ones that I heard paid twenty bucks an hour or more. Ones on Nantucket.

A little seed was planted.

The second time I thought of going to Nantucket by myself, I was sitting on the front porch, texting with Jay. It was supposed to have been my night at Dad's, but Alexi wasn't having a good night, so none of us was having a good night. Polly had adopted him from an orphanage in the Ukraine when he was three years old, and he'd had a pretty rough time there, which I guess is why he sometimes had these fits. Alexi loved the Beatles, and that night, after the fifth time of listening to "Yellow Submarine," I was going a little insane, so I changed the song. I put on James Taylor, one of Dad's favorites, but it set Alexi off. He started rocking on the floor, kicking his heels and wailing, even after I'd switched it back. Polly had to make him feel better, which meant that Dad had to make Polly feel better. I slipped out the back door without even touching my grilled steak. Dad was too swept up in the chaos to convince me to stay. He just waved good-bye and blew me a kiss.

At least it was peaceful at Mom's, I thought as I read a text from Jay. He'd gotten a job as a lifeguard out there on Nantucket, at a beach called Surfside. I started thinking about my almost-kiss with him and the moment when he'd pulled me onto his lap. I was thinking about sitting in a lifeguard chair with him in my new plum-colored J. Crew bikini with a ruffle. I was thinking about kissing him in the sand.

The seed burst from its husk and sprang green spindly roots.

The third time I thought about going to Nantucket alone, I was at the Brown University Bookstore. I was looking for my summer reading books when I saw a T-shirt just like Nina's. My heart cramped. I held my breath. I couldn't be away from Jules all summer. The Claytons might need alone time now, but in a week or so Jules would want me there, she'd need me. I wouldn't be in their house, so I wouldn't be a burden, and they'd still have their privacy. But I'd be close by. Ready to pitch in. Ready to load the dishwasher or run to the store for milk. I'd be ready to whip out a board game when that famous Nantucket fog rolled in. I'd make silver dollar pancakes for everyone. I'm good at that. I had an image of me setting the table.

But the vision was quickly replaced by one of Nina with the colorful place mats that she brought home from Mexico last spring. I could see her hands laying them on the table. I could see the wavy silver cuff bracelet around her wrist. I could see her eyes squinting in a laugh as Jules and I tied the matching napkins on our heads like bandannas. It made me miss her so much I felt like I'd been kicked. I held my breath until the sadness subsided.

I bought all my summer reading books except one (they didn't have the collection of Emily Dickinson poems for Mrs. Hart's class), and stopped to get a Del's from the cart on the corner. I handed over the dollar bills, soft and crinkled from a whole day in my back pocket, and took the cold little waxy dish of frozen lemonade. One lick woke up my mouth, chilled my sinuses. It would be *fun* to go alone. I was going to be eighteen in eight weeks, an official adult with the right to vote and join the armed services. I'd have my own paycheck and spend my money as I chose. I'd go to that café I'd heard Jules talking about, the Even Keel. I'd develop a croissant and coffee habit. I'd go running on the beach every morning and cool off in the ocean afterward. Maybe, in the evening, I'd carry a sketch pad. My whereabouts would not be known at all times, and this idea filled me with space: a pleasant, light-filled space.

I'll be like a college student, I thought as I stopped in front of a café popular with Brown students. The plastic bag of books strained and started to cut off the circulation in my hand. I switched my grip and peered in the window. A girl in a sundress with a purse slung over her chair was scribbling in an artist's notebook. I should wear dresses more. I need a notebook like that, I thought, when a cute guy walked in, kissed her, and sat down with a couple of drinks. As he touched her knee under the table and they clinked glasses, the idea of going to Nantucket by myself bloomed like a tropical flower.

I had to go.

Five

THE HORN SOUNDED, THE FERRY LAUNCHED, AND MY summer swung open like a saloon door. The engine hummed under my metal seat. I placed my duffel bag on the seat to save it—I had a good one, front row—and leaned on the cold, sticky railing. The breeze was soft, persistent, cool but not cold. I zipped up my hoodie and looked at the ocean. Farther out it was a deep blue, but right here, right under me, it was beer-bottle green and brown with flashes of gold. I lifted my face into the late afternoon sun and inhaled the salty Atlantic air.

The ferry was crowded with families. They seemed to own the place. Nearby, a little boy resisted the hugs of his mother, wrestling out of her arms to press his face against the grating. A girl in a hot-pink Lilly Pulitzer dress tried to climb up the viewfinder, begging her parents for a quarter. Kids in polo shirts darted around the seats, wanting to be chased. The parents were dressed in clothes as vivid as their children's. Grown men wore kelly-green pants stitched with yellow whales. The women were in an unofficial uniform: white jeans, bright-colored tops, and Jack Rogers sandals— I recognized the brand instantly because Jules had a pair in blue and another in pink. Six young moms talked in a circle; they looked like a fistful of lollipops.

"Uh-oh, here come the Range Rovers," said an old man with a weathered face and a light, sensible windbreaker, as a madras-clad couple walked past with monogrammed tote bags that looked freshly sprung from L.L. Bean. Their three blond kids wore T-shirts that said *Nantucket*.

"Why do they have to wear T-shirts that tell the world where they're going?" the old man's wife said, shaking her head. "I don't wear a shirt that says *New Hampshire* when I go there."

The old man saw me eavesdropping and leaned toward me. "To us, it's home; to them, it's *Nantucket*," he said with a tight jaw and an over-the-top snob accent.

I laughed and nodded as if I were a native, too. Then I made a mental note not to buy a T-shirt with *Nantucket* written on it. I didn't want to piss off the locals.

"Avery, come back here!" Here was the mother of the Lilly Pulitzer girl—in a skirt that matched her daughter's dress.

"No!" Avery stuck her tongue out at her.

"Avery, if you don't get back here right away," she stammered, "Theresa will get very mad at you." Disgust flashed across the face of a short, round Hispanic woman before she remembered herself and leaped to coax the girl off the viewfinder.

"Why would you want to be a servant?" Mom had asked when I'd accepted the live-in babysitting position it had taken me less than twenty-four hours to be offered.

All it took was a morning on the Web site for the local Nantucket newspaper, *The Inquirer and Mirror*, and a few e-mails before a woman named Mary Ellen called my cell asking if I'd be available to start on Monday. She was the house manager—basically a butler—to a wealthy family in Boston who was already on Nantucket. She'd heard of Rosewood. She actually knew Miss Kang from college. If I could hop on a bus and meet her that afternoon in Boston, and if my references checked out, I'd be on a ferry Sunday. I met her in a crowded Starbucks on Newbury Street.

"Oh, you're perfect," she said when we spotted each other. "Caroline is going to flip over you. And you can swim?"

I nodded. *Obviously.*

"And please tell me you drive. Do you drive?" I nodded. *What seventeen-year-old doesn't drive?*

She told me that it paid eight hundred dollars a week for eight weeks. Eight times eight was sixty-four! For a half a second I thought I was going to be making sixty thousand dollars (math is my worst subject), but when I got to six thousand four hundred dollars it was still an awesome amount of money.

"It's not easy, though. You're on from the minute the kids get up until they're dead asleep. If they wake up in the night, it's your problem."

I nodded, grinning. Eight hundred *a week*! It turned out the father was the famous national news anchor for CNN, Bradley Lucas. He seemed a little old to have kids who needed a nanny, but he was famous. Mom would definitely let me go now. There were three girls, and three nannies rotating shifts around the clock. She told me that one nanny, a local Nantucket girl, hadn't worked out and they were "in a pickle." Then she bought me an iced tea, took a map of Nantucket out of her purse, and drew a path in blue pen from where the ferry would drop me to the house on 25 Cliff Road. At the bottom she wrote her phone number.

"Should I have the Lucases' number as well?" I asked.

"No," she said, chuckling to herself. "You need anything, call me. My cell is on all the time." She gave me money for the ferry ticket and an extra fifty for "my time," and told me that she'd be out there in a week.

I was thrilled when I told my mom. But she wasn't.

"Babysitting again?" Mom asked as she ate the last bite of moo shu pork from the carton. "I thought you hated babysitting."

"I don't hate it," I said. "I just don't *love* it." Mom leveled me with a look as she sipped her wine. "I want to go to Nantucket, and there's no other way. Besides, I'd be a servant here, to Andrew King."

"That's different," she said. "You wouldn't live with the Kings. You don't want to live in anyone's home. It's beneath you. They'll think they own you." She finished her glass of white wine and poured herself another. "And what if that news anchor is creepy? He's too smooth, and he has that hairpiece."

"If he tries anything, I'll call the Law Offices of Snell and Garabedian," I said, using the name of a criminal law firm whose ad, which featured two meaty guys holding up a golden set of scales in front of a wall of law books, was on every bus stop bench. Mom laughed. I could count the number of times she'd laughed this year on one hand. "Besides, Mom, you did it."

My mom had spent one summer on Nantucket when she was my age. She'd worked at a hotel on the beach. I found a picture of her on a little sailboat in a blue bikini, grinning, a pointed foot dangling over the edge. The wind is sweeping her blond hair across her freckled cheek, and she's laughing at whoever took the picture.

It's pretty crazy how alike we look. For a minute I'd thought it was me. How could I have forgotten that day? It looked like the best day of my life. It only took a second to register that the picture was small and square with a matte finish; it was taken a long time ago. On the back it said *Nantucket, 1984.*

"I wasn't by myself. I was staying with family, with my

aunt Betty," my mother said. "It can be really snotty out there, honey."

"Can I stay with Aunt Betty?" I cracked open my fortune cookie: *Surprise doubles happiness.*

"She died in 1993." Mom sat up a little and tucked her hair behind her ear. "And she also read my diary, which infuriated me. But you'll be all alone. I don't want you to go. You're only seventeen. What if something happened to you?"

"I'll be eighteen in August. And what could be safer than Nantucket?" I asked. "It's not exactly the Gaza Strip. And I won't be alone. I'll have the Claytons and the other nannies."

"The Claytons," Mom said. "What is so fascinating to you about those people? From the way you follow them around you'd think they were the Kennedys." She took another sip from her glass. "Some people thought Nina was a little weird, you know. Last month I saw her in a turban on Thayer Street. I was like, really? A turban?"

"Mom!" I said, feeling my face get hot. "How can you say that right now?"

"You're right," she said. "Sorry." She didn't sound sorry, and she was speaking in a near whisper, a trick she used with her students when they got rowdy. When she lowered her voice, they lowered theirs. But it only made me louder.

"She was a bohemian," I said, my hands curled into tight fists. "That turban was for yoga."

"People don't wear turbans to yoga, Cricket," she said. I could tell that the second glass of wine had worked its way through her system.

"Yes, they do," I said, my voice shaking. "For a special kind of yoga in New York. And Nina wasn't weird, she was just . . . herself." I choked on the last word. Tears filled my eyes.

"Okay, okay." Mom looked me in the eye and took a deep breath. "I'm sorry. I shouldn't have said it." She meant it this time.

"And I don't follow them around," I said quietly. "They're like family."

"I'm going to go take a shower," she said, then sighed and headed up the back stairs.

"Wait, so can I go to Nantucket?" I shut my eyes and crossed my fingers as I awaited her reply.

She paused on the creaky stairs. "I'll think about it."

While she was taking one of her half-hour showers, I packed my bag. I was going to get her to say yes if it killed me. As I put the summer reading books in my suitcase, I decided to check the bookcase in the hallway, where Mom kept her old school books. I was looking for the Emily Dickinson collection. She had had Mrs. Hart, too. Sure enough, there it was. Had the summer reading really not changed in all these years? I plucked it by its spine. It was a little dusty, and the font on the cover was different, but it was the right book.

A little later, when I thought we'd both cooled off, I went into her room. Mom was lying in bed reading her mystery novel.

"Well?"

"I'm still thinking," she said, and turned the page.

I took the novel from her hands, marked her page, and placed it carefully on the nightstand. I sat on the edge of her bed and looked in her eyes.

"Mom, it's very lonely for me here," I said.

"Oh, but we have each other," she said, and took my face in her soft, light hands. She turned out her lower lip.

"I want more than that," I said, pulling back sharply. Anger crept up my throat like a poisonous spider.

"Cricket," Mom said quietly, and shrank back into her pillow. "I love you too, you know. I love you more than the Claytons do."

"I know, Mom. And I love you. I love you so much." Her eyes brightened. "It's just that—" *It's just that you shouldn't take me down with you. It's just that I want a life, even if you don't. It's just that you're like a ghost, a strong ghost, barely here but holding on to me too tightly.* I drew a deep, calming breath. "All of my friends are away for the summer on an adventure, and I want an adventure, too. It's been a hard year for me, Mom, with Dad and Polly getting married." Mom leaned closer. I was talking about it. I was *going there*. "I need to get away from it, so that I can move on from this—" *Say it*, her eyes begged. "Divorce." There. "I need to move on. We both need to. I don't know if I can do that in Providence. And I don't know if you can, either."

She took a long breath, relaxing a little more deeply into her pillow. She folded her hands in front of her and looked out the window. "Okay," she said.

"Really?"

"You can go."

"Thank you," I said, and hugged her. "Thank you."

Nantucket emerged between the sea and the lavender sky like a make-believe village. White church spires peeked above lush treetops. Sailboats dotted the harbor. On a sandy point, a lighthouse flashed green. When the boat docked, people on land waved to friends and family on the ferry. I didn't mind that no one was waiting for me. I had it all planned out. I hadn't told Jules. I was going to surprise her. *Surprise doubles happiness.* As I stepped onto the busy dock, the lowering sun left a path on the water. It had followed me here like a spotlight.

Six

I IMMEDIATELY WANTED TO CHANGE OUT OF MY SCRUFFY jeans and hoodie and into one of two nice outfits I'd brought to Nantucket. Maybe I should've told Jules I was coming. She might've warned me that a different league of people existed here. No wonder she read those beauty magazines all year. Everyone was pretty here. And I could see them all. It wasn't like walking around Providence, where I didn't notice much because I was busy doing my own thing. There was something about being alone in a new place that pushed the world a little closer, like when I put on the huge reading glasses from the kiosk in CVS to make Jules laugh.

Even the old lady in the powder-blue sweater carrying one of those basket purses was the prettiest old lady I'd ever seen. She had white-gold hair and eyes the color of a

Tiffany box. Nina had given Jules a necklace from there for her sixteenth birthday, and Jules returned it to its original box every night when she took it off. It was a bean-shaped pendant. It was delicate and grown-up, and I liked to try it on when Jules was in the shower.

Nina, I thought, and for a second I swore I smelled her perfume.

I walked passed an ice cream store with a line around the corner, a bookstore, the Whaling Museum, and an inn with three rocking chairs on the porch. Everything was quaint, preserved, one of a kind, looking like it wouldn't ever change and couldn't exist anywhere but here. The sidewalks were brick. The fire hydrants were tennis-ball yellow. With my duffel bag slung over my shoulder, I walked past a row of fancy restaurants bustling with a spiffy dinner crowd, and a quiet art gallery where a woman stood ballerina-like in the doorway, smoking a cigarette.

I turned up Cliff Road, which was exactly where the map said it would be. The street sign looked hand-painted. Maybe that's what they make the prisoners in the Nantucket jail do, I thought. Instead of making license plates, they had to hand paint the street signs. Instead of orange jumpsuits, they were issued fisherman sweaters.

Three guys rode by on bicycles, calling after each other in an undecipherable boy language. None of them wore a helmet, and two were barefoot. The smaller one stood on his peddles, coasted, and gave me a double take. I smiled. The bicycle ticked. Where were they going?

I reached a mailbox with the Lucases' address on it. Tall hedges surrounded the house, so I couldn't see it until I lifted the latch of the wooden gate and turned to walk down the driveway. The house was huge. It was definitely bigger than Sophie Toscano's house, and she was the richest girl in our class. She got dropped off at school in a Rolls-Royce. This place seemed to exceed the boundaries of a house; it was an *estate*, closer in size to the mansions my parents and I used to see in Newport. We sometimes drove around town on a rainy day. We'd go to Sue's Clam Shack for bowls of clam chowder and then visit Ocean Avenue, pretending to pick out the house we were going to buy.

"Welcome home," my dad would say as we slowed down in front of a glorious shingled place with a wraparound porch and a stunning view.

"Honey, why didn't you tell me? I would've brought our suitcases!" my mom would say. I'd laugh from the backseat and point out my bedroom window—always in a turret, if there was one.

This house, this mansion, was alive with the sounds of a party. I heard peels of laughter and music. Jazz—was it live? In the driveway was a Nantucket Catering Company van and a line of SUVs, most of them Range Rovers, just like the old man on the ferry had said, and a few older-looking Jeeps, the bumpers plastered with beach permit stickers. As I made my way up the stone path lined with lanterns, I heard the murmur of adult conversation, the exclamations of dressed-up ladies, the clinks of silverware and glass. I could feel the ocean in the air.

I rang the doorbell. After a few minutes, no one answered. I opened the door and walked inside.

"Hello?" I called into the entryway. All the lights were on. And there was no sign of people living here. There were no family photographs, no kid drawings on the fridge, no tiny stray socks. It was a house-hotel. "Hello?"

A girl in frog pajamas popped up from behind a sofa, clutching a blanket.

"Hi," I said, and dropped my bags. "I'm Cricket."

"I'm Lucy," she said, hiding behind her blanket.

"I'm the new babysitter," I said.

"Another one?" she asked, peering at me from behind her blanket. I nodded, smiling. She held the blanket over her nose and mouth and narrowed her eyes at me.

"Are you a robber?" I asked.

"Yes!" she said, her eyes widening. "I'm going to rob you!"

"Uh-oh," I said, and cowered dramatically. She giggled. "Robber, I think we should find your mom so that I can introduce myself."

"Okay," she said. "Come on." She led me through a palatial kitchen and out to a large, crowded patio with a bar and a live jazz band playing "Moondance." Nearby, a college-age girl in a Nantucket Catering Company apron grilled shrimp kabobs. A waiter passed a tray of fizzing cocktails, each glass topped with an impaled twist of lime. The ocean sparkled darkly in the distance. The sun was gone now, and a band of deep pink glowed on the horizon. The breeze carried the sweet smell of honeysuckle and beach grass.

There was a small rectangular pool bordered by eight trim recliners. A group of women sat on them, looking adoringly at a broad-shouldered blond man. His bold hand gestures seemed to be conducting their laughter like an orchestra. Bradley Lucas! I thought. Telling funny stories! Twenty feet away!

If I'd felt a little messy and underdressed when I stepped off the ferry, I was now officially in Oliver Twist territory. The men wore Nantucket Reds—I recognized the salmon-colored pants because Jules had teased Zack when he wore his to the Spring Dance, even though I think she was secretly proud of him—and the women swished like tropical fish in silky, brightly colored summer dresses.

"Which one is your mom?" I asked Lucy. The only woman with any mom pudge was the one crooning into the microphone in a fringed vest and scuffed flats. Lucy pointed to a tall woman who stood on coltish legs in a short white dress and very high heels, conversing with a man in seersucker pants and a fedora.

"Mommy!" Lucy called. Mrs. Lucas's head turned. Her ponytail, which looked like it had been gathered and fastened by a professional, brushed the air. Her brow furrowed.

"Lucy, why aren't you in bed?" Her eyes widened as she

took me in and strode toward us. "Caroline Lucas," she said, and extended a narrow, bejeweled hand. She blinked.

"Cricket Thompson," I said, and shook her hand.

"She's the new babysitter," Lucy said. "Another one!" She smacked her head with an open hand like a cartoon character.

Mrs. Lucas put a hand over her mouth. The band transitioned into "Killing Me Softly." Usually, I love that song, but for some reason my stomach sank.

"Let's go inside, shall we?" She gestured to the sliding glass doors I'd left open. "Come on, Lucy. You need to be in bed."

"But it's not even dark out," Lucy said, and hopped inside.

"Who's your grown-up tonight?" Mrs. Lucas asked.

"Sharon."

"Go find her."

"She's asleep," Lucy said. "Snoring!"

"Well, wake her up," Mrs. Lucas said.

"I'm so frustrated, Mommy," Lucy said as she traipsed upstairs, dragging her blanket behind her.

"I've made a terrible mistake," Mrs. Lucas said to me. I could smell the cocktail on her breath as she exhaled and placed one tan hand on a boney hip and the other on her temple. "I'm completely overstaffed. Mary Ellen was hiring in Boston and I was hiring out here and we didn't communicate very well and now I've got babysitters up to my eyeballs. They're packed to the rafters in the cottage," she said, laughing. "I've got one on an air mattress above the garage." Her laughter trailed off as she took in my expression. "Mary Ellen didn't call you, huh?"

"No."

"Well, I apologize. I'll talk to her about that. But I can't keep you. I just don't need another babysitter. I have backups for the backups." She tilted her head. "But you can still catch the last ferry back. Those things run until ten o'clock, at least." She checked her watch and tapped it with her perfect red fingernail. "Oh yeah, you've got plenty of time."

"But I'd still need to catch a bus back to Providence," I said. "There won't be another bus by the time I get back to Hyannis." As if this were my biggest problem, as if disappointment weren't hovering over my heart like a bee over a slice of watermelon, as if my dream weren't fading into nothingness, a Polaroid picture in reverse—there goes Jay in the lifeguard chair, there go my rainy afternoons watching movies with Jules, my morning runs on the beach, my eight hundred dollars a week.

"Right, how stupid of me," she said, shaking her head. "You'll need a taxi." She walked to the kitchen island and opened a drawer. She swayed a little as she counted out some cash. She handed me three stiff hundred-dollar bills. "That ought to get you home with a little extra." She hiccupped. "Now, do you want me to have someone drop you at the ferry, or can you walk from here?"

Seven

I CONSIDERED MY OPTIONS AS I LEFT THE LUCASES'.

Option one: catch the ten o'clock ferry. I didn't want to go back home. If I did, Mom would pretend like we were having a great girls' weekend all summer even though we were both miserable; she because she missed Dad, and I because I wanted to be with other kids. She promised we would go on trips to Newport and Block Island but would always come down with a headache when it came time to get in the car. She would get that look in her eye like I was betraying her every time I went to Dad's house. It was a soft, pleading look that made me want to wrap my arms around her and comfort her and, at the same time, sprint away from her as fast as I could. I nixed the thought before I'd even reached the end of the driveway. I couldn't give up yet.

Option two: go to Jules's house. "It's right in town," she'd told me. "A five-minute walk to the Hub." The Hub, Jules told me, was a little store where she bought all her magazines. "They also sell postcards, little things, Tic Tacs, gum, Nantucket key chains, crap like that. Oh, and also, there's no CVS on Nantucket, no Target, no Costco, nothing even close."

She went on to tell me that no one locked their doors at night, people left their keys dangling in the ignitions of their Jeeps, and everyone bought their bread from a bakery and their vegetables from a farm, not the supermarket. She'd made Nantucket sound like a foreign land whose customs I might have difficulty comprehending. It bugged me. It was only one state away. My mother had spent a summer here. I'd been to Cape Cod a bunch of times. And there was a farm stand in Tiverton that Mom, Dad, and I used to go to in the summer for blueberries, tomatoes, and Silver Queen corn. I wasn't a total ignoramus. Still, I'd packed two big boxes of tampons just in case they were scarce out here, or really expensive, like in Russia.

I had her address memorized, 4 Darling Street, and could picture the house perfectly. The Claytons' Christmas card every year was of the family standing in front of the blue door with the scallop-shell knocker. A gold "4" hung above them, as if counting the perfect family: mom, dad, sister, brother. In last year's card, Nina is looking up and laughing. What would the picture be like this year? Would they still stand in front of the door? I felt another kick of sadness, right in the stomach. I was realizing that loss has a kind of violence to it.

When I got closer to town I took out my map and, straining my eyes in the darkness, found the Claytons' address. Insects thrummed in the nearby yards as I traced my finger over the route.

I passed back through town and crossed the busy, cobblestoned Main Street. Jeez, was there a beautiful-people factory out here? A breeding ground for J. Crew models? The older ones walked in close teams of two and four, the younger ones in looser packs of six or eight. The uneven sidewalk was illuminated by glowing, old-fashioned street-lamps. The shop windows were decorated with sea-motif jewelry. Gold starfish earrings lay in pools of green silk, and diamond-crusted anchors hung on velvet necks.

The windows of the interior-design stores were so warm and inviting I wanted to crawl inside and curl up in one of their nautical tableaus, bury my toes in the knotty rugs, and fall backward into the plump pillows. How funny would that be, I thought, if Jules walked by in the morning and I was sleeping in the bed of a shop window?

I turned onto Fair Street, about to head toward Jules's, when I heard my mother's teacher voice in my head telling me that Jules said I couldn't stay with her, and I needed to respect that. I couldn't just drop in unless I had a place to stay for certain. A church bell rang, and I counted the low gongs. It was ten o'clock. I paused, dropped my duffel, and looked at the map. I was four blocks shy of Darling Street, standing in front of an inn. It was white with dark red shutters and a front porch, and had a carved, gold-lettered sign.

Option three: the Cranberry Inn.

The door was unlocked. The lobby, with the bookcases, worn oriental rugs, and clusters of sofas and armchairs around a fireplace, looked like a living room. A man with a ponytail and goatee sat behind an antique desk, reading a paperback with one of those dark, manly-man covers. A pair of drugstore glasses sat on the end of his nose. He was sitting cross-legged in an armchair in what looked like pajama bottoms or maybe karate pants. The string of a tea bag hung over his mug. He sipped his tea and turned the page quickly, his eyes darting to the top of the next page.

"Excuse me, are there any rooms available at the inn?" I asked. Oh god, I was actually saying a line from our fifth-grade Christmas pageant when I played Mary!

The man jerked his head up, eyes wide, startled for a second, then laughed a little.

"I didn't even hear you come in," he said as if he knew me. He held up the book. "People leave these mysteries behind, and I can't put them down. They get me every time." He shook his head, disappointed with himself, and waved me over. "Come on in. I'm Gavin." He glanced through the open door behind me. "Are you with your parents?"

I shook my head.

"A solo traveler," he said. "Nothing like traveling alone to get to know yourself. Sit down. Have a cookie." He gestured to a table with a pitcher of water and a plate of chocolate chip cookies. I took one. He tilted his head and consulted his reservation book. "We have one room. It's the Admiral's Suite."

The kitchen door swung open, and a girl walked through with a tray of fresh glasses. She stacked them next to the pitcher of water.

"Oh, great," I said, covering my mouth as I swallowed. I was hungrier than I'd realized. "I'll take it."

"It's three ninety-nine." He sighed and added, "Plus tax."

"Oh," I said. "I can't do that. I'm not exactly on vacation, I'm looking for a job." I needed my three hundred dollars to last at least two or three nights. I sank a little lower in the chair. I was tired for the first time since I'd woken up at five a.m., wired with anticipation.

"Give her Rebecca's room," the girl said in a thick accent. Was she Irish? "Can't charge more than a hundred for that, can you?" Was she his daughter? She was a little chubby, with pink cheeks and a sunburned nose. She pushed a black curl back behind her ear and gestured to me. "Poor thing looks knackered."

"Rebecca won't mind?" I asked, wondering who Rebecca was.

"She's halfway to England by now," Gavin said.

"I got my cousin a job on Nantucket, and she quit after a week 'cause she missed her lug of a boyfriend." I wasn't sure if this was funny because of her accent, or even if it was meant to be a joke, but I laughed. "And he's a right wanker."

"I'm looking for a job," I said, sitting up and tapping

the table with my palms. "And I need one that comes with housing."

"Well, this works out perfectly, then, doesn't it?" the girl said, a hand on her sturdy hip. "You get a job, Gavin doesn't have to go on the great chambermaid search, and I don't have to share a bathroom with a freak of nature. You're not a freak of nature, are you?"

"Nope." I shook my head. Chambermaid? It sounded like a job from another century, like a charwoman or a scullery maid. Would I be churning butter, cleaning chimneys, beating rugs with a broom? Who cared? I'd have a job and a place to stay for free on Nantucket.

"We don't even know her name," he said to the girl, then put a hand to his chest and turned to me. "Excuse us, what's your name?"

"Cricket," I said. "Cricket Thompson."

"Amazing," Gavin said. "I was noticing, really *noticing* the crickets earlier. I thought to myself, Ah, the song of the cricket, the song of summer."

"See, it's a sign," Liz said. "I'm Liz, by the way. Not Liza, not Lizzy, and"—she shot Gavin a look—"definitely not Lizard."

"Nice to meet you, Liz."

"What do you say, Gavin?" she asked.

"I'm interviewing someone tomorrow," he said. "But I don't see why I couldn't interview Cricket as well. Come back in the afternoon, say around three?"

"Okay," I said, and shook his hand. "Sounds great."

"Wait, who are you interviewing?" Liz asked.

"Svetlana," he said.

"Svetlana . . . *the cow?*" Liz asked with a look of horror. She sounded dead serious, so I tried not to laugh.

"She has good references," Gavin said.

"She flirted with Shane in front of my face at The Chicken Box," Liz said.

"It's not your decision, Liz," Gavin said, now sounding officially annoyed. "See you tomorrow, Cricket?"

"Yes," I said, and smiled. I felt too awkward to ask about Rebecca's room again. "I'll see you then."

I gave him my cell phone number, picked up my duffel bag, and walked out the front door. As soon as I hit Main Street I sat on a bench in front of one of the beautiful shops, wondering where I was going to spend the night now. My phone rang. I prayed it was Jules and that she'd invite me over right away. But it was my mom.

A part of me didn't want to pick up. I'd have to tell her that the job didn't work out and I was considering sleeping on a park bench. It would show that she had been right and Nantucket was a bad idea. It would be evidence that I wasn't the independent girl I worked so hard to be. But the other part of me, the tired part of me, with a blister forming on my left foot, a growling stomach, and no idea where I was going to sleep tonight, wanted to talk to her.

"Mom?"

"Honey? What happened?" She had always been able to tell by the way I said even one word if something was wrong. If Mom had a superpower, it was her hearing. When it came to me, her ears were as keen as a wolf's. It was no use lying to her.

"Well, the babysitting job didn't work out," I said.

"Oh, I'm sorry," she said. "You must be really disappointed."

"Yeah," I said.

"But do you remember when Andrew pooped in the minivan and you had to clean it up? Or when he insisted you play Transformers . . . for a week?"

"Yes. That minivan was disgusting."

"So, you hate babysitting, remember?"

"I guess I do."

"So, this is a good thing. That family's letting you spend the night there, at least?"

"Not exactly," I said.

Her voice dropped an octave. "What do you mean? Where are you?"

"Before you freak out, here's the good news. I have a job interview at an inn tomorrow. And I have a fifty percent chance of getting it. Maybe even like sixty percent."

"To be what?" she asked.

"A chambermaid."

"A maid? No, no, no. And where are you staying tonight? It's late!"

"I don't know," I said.

"Well, where are you *right now*?"

"I'm in town," I said, taking in the cobblestones, the

misty evening air, the books nestled in the display of the bookstore across the street, the elegant well-dressed couples holding hands, "and it's perfect."

"Here's what I'm going to do," she said as if she hadn't even heard me. "You're going to sit tight. I'm going to call around, find a place for you to stay, and pay for a room with my credit card. I wonder if the Jared Coffin House is still there."

"Thanks, Mom." I felt cool relief wash through me. With a good night's sleep and at least another day out here, I knew I could make something work.

"Then tomorrow morning, first thing, you'll get on a ferry back to Hyannis. I'll pick you up, and you'll spend the summer with me. Just us girls."

Now I had wolf ears. I could hear her smile. Her relief laced through my disappointment with delicate, painful stitches. Just as I was about to protest, I got another call. It was a Nantucket number.

"Mom, hold on one sec," I said, and switched lines. "Hello?"

"Cricket, it's Liz. Where are you, you daft girl? You fled."

"I'm in town," I said. This was good news. I could feel it.

"Well, come on back! I convinced Gavin to give you a try tomorrow. I told him if you were a disaster, he could hire Svetlana and I wouldn't say a word about it."

"That's great," I said, smiling. "That's so great. Thank you!"

"So, don't be a disaster!"

"I won't," I said. "I promise. See you in a sec."

I switched back to Mom. "Mom, I just got the chamber-maiding job!"

"What? Just now?"

"Yes! I can stay on Nantucket!"

"As a maid?"

"Yeah, but so what? It's better than babysitting, right? And this place is really cute. It's called the Cranberry Inn." I picked up my duffel bag for the zillionth time that day and headed back toward Fair Street. "If you saw this place, I swear you'd love it. It's cozy and old-fashioned and they make cookies every afternoon. Google it." I waited for her to find the Web site. "You could even come and visit."

"It looks like a really nice place," she said. I had to give her credit. She was trying. "Okay, now, if you change your mind, I'm right here—"

"I'll call you when I get settled—okay, Mom?"

"All right," she said, and hung up.

I turned up Fair Street, picturing Mom turning in for the night with a mystery novel, a glass of tepid tap water by her bed, and the picture of my father she still kept in the drawer of her bedside table. I knew she had nothing to do tonight or tomorrow night or the night after that. As Liz opened the door for me and led me to a tiny room with rose wallpaper, a window with peeling paint, a twin bed, a sink, a dresser, and a slanted ceiling, I tried to tell myself that it wasn't my fault my mother was alone.

"We start tomorrow at six a.m. sharp," Liz said.

"Got it," I said, and dropped my duffel bag on the floor of my new room. I'd wait until tomorrow to ask what exactly being a chambermaid involved and how much I was going to be paid. Now that I had it, the job seemed like a small deal compared to the real purpose of my Nantucket adventure: to be there for Jules, and maybe, just maybe, fall in love with Jay Logan. I splashed some cold water on my face, slipped out the front door, which Liz promised was always unlocked, and walked to Darling Street. It was 10:43. Hopefully, Jules was awake.

Eight

AS I WALKED TO THE HOUSE, I IMAGINED LIFTING THE scallop-shell knocker—Jules's eyes huge at the happy surprise—how she might do that little jump-flutter-kick thing, then link her arm in mine and pull me to the two-seater swing on the porch, another spot well documented in the Clayton family photos.

I got there in no time at all. The house was exactly as I'd imagined it. Rose-covered trellis, soft inviting lawn with a garden, bushes with big flowers lining the front of the house, a wraparound porch with beach towels hung over the railing to dry, two bicycles leaning against the garage, a wood-paneled Wagoneer parked in the driveway (the land yacht, Zack called it).

I knocked. Jules answered the door right away. Her hair was up and she had on makeup.

"Ta-da," I said, and stretched out my arms.

"What?" She blinked. She wore new earrings. Dangly ones.

"It's me, Cricket," I said. I wondered if in her grief she'd forgotten who I was.

"I know," she said. "What are you doing here?"

"I'm living here. I got a job and a place to stay and everything!" I said, holding my arms open like Jules might jump into them. But she just stood there in the doorway with a blank face. I put my hands in my pockets. "I'm a chambermaid." God, it sounded so weird.

"Oh." She stepped outside and shut the door behind her, switching on a light that hung above the door. "Where?"

"The Cranberry Inn?" Jules shook her head, didn't know it. "It's so close. It's practically around the corner."

"Wow." She smiled, but it looked like it hurt.

"So this is the famous Nantucket house," I said, taking a few steps backward. The damp grass brushed my ankles. The light bulb buzzed inside its glass walls. Dark moths fluttered around it. The sky above was filled with stars. I breathed in the night air. "It's beautiful."

She nodded and sat on one of the benches. I sat across from her, tucking my hands under my thighs. She was quiet, so I just started talking. I told her about the bus ride to Boston and the Lucas kid. I told her about Gavin in his hippie pants, and Liz's accent. I told her about my room at the Cranberry Inn, the slanted ceiling, the tiny dresser and the little window, the front door that was never locked. I told her that it took me less than five minutes to get to her house from there. I talked so much my mouth was dry; she didn't say anything back.

"I completely understand why you can't have any house-guests this summer," I said. "I mean, of course. But I figured this way I could be here for you. If you need me at any time, you just call out my name, that kind of thing."

"Thanks," she said, staring past me. She crossed her legs and pulled out a cigarette. I tried not to act surprised. We'd only smoked once before. It was in her basement. It felt terrible, like breathing exhaust from an old school bus, and it made me nauseous and lightheaded. Nina smelled the smoke from the garage, where she'd been doing one of her projects—something with a sawhorse. She ran into the basement saying *no*, *no*, *no*, and waving a broom in a way that was unintentionally hilarious.

Later, she'd sat us down for a serious chat, showing us pictures on the Internet of black, shriveled lungs and faces so wrinkled they looked like they were made of corduroy. I hadn't had a cigarette since then, but Jules was smoking like she knew how, tapping her finger on the end so that ash fell like snow into a Coke can. The beach towels on the porch rail stirred in the breeze.

"Want one?" she asked. I shook my head.

"Where's your dad?" I asked.

"At the Club Car." I nodded as if I knew what this meant. I heard someone laughing inside the house—a girl.

"Who's here?" I asked.

"Zack and this girl."

"Who is it?" As far as I knew, Zack hadn't ever really had a girlfriend. There was Valerie, a French girl he'd met on a ski trip to Vail, but after a few weeks of video chatting, she'd sent Zack a dramatic e-mail and moved on. He wouldn't eat french fries for a month, and all French words were banned from the house, including *omelet*, *perfume*, and *champagne*.

"This girl out here," Jules said. She dropped her cigarette into the Coke can. It hissed.

"Cool. Hey, have you seen Jay?" I asked. "He said he was a lifeguard at Surfer's Beach."

"Surfside," Jules said. "And, yeah, I saw him last night."

"How'd he look?" *Was he with anyone? Did he ask about me?*

"Hot," she said with a quickness and certainty that made me want to remind her how much I liked him.

"I can't believe how close we came to kissing at Nora's. It was amazing."

"Must be something about a whore's house."

"I can't wait to see him. I don't know if I should text him, or if it's better for me to just run into him."

"I'd wait to run into him," she said.

"You think?"

She nodded. "Anyway, I'm really tired. I think I'm going to hit the sack."

"Well, all right," I said, standing up. I hadn't had a puff of the cigarette, but I had that lightheadedness anyway. I turned to head down the path that led back out to the street. "So I guess I'll see you tomorrow?"

"Sure," Jules said. I opened the gate to leave.

"Are you hacking butts again, Jules?" I turned around. Zack was leaning out a first-floor window. He squinted in my direction. "Hey, who's that?"

"It's Cricket," I said, and waved. Seconds later, the screen door was snapping shut behind him. He was barefoot and his hair was sticking up, like he hadn't taken a shower since he'd come home from the beach. Jules stepped out of the way as he walked toward me in a half jog. Had he grown an inch in the last week?

"What are you doing here?" He gave me a quick, hard hug. He smelled like sunscreen and salt water. "I thought you weren't coming. I thought you had a babysitting job in Providence. When did you get here? Are you staying with us?"

"No, remember what Dad said?" Jules said, standing several feet behind us. Zack looked confused.

"I got here tonight. I got a job at the Cranberry Inn, and I'm staying there."

"Oh, I've seen that place. Don't they have famous muffins?"

"I don't know," I said, smiling at the thought of Zack keeping up with the Nantucket muffin gossip.

"What?" he asked.

"Nothing."

"Are you coming to the party in 'Sconset tomorrow?"

"What party?"

"It's not a party," Jules said. She was now silhouetted in the doorway, and I could see Nina in her shape so well that I felt a light pressure on my chest. "Just a few kids who come every summer, getting together." I wondered if this meant that Jay would be there. I had a feeling it did.

"Fine. We'll call it a mixer," Zack said to Jules. "I didn't know you had such a penchant for precision."

"Don't be a dick," she said.

"Penchant?" I asked with raised eyebrows.

"I'm a Word Warrior," he said. That was the SAT vocabulary-building program everyone had. Zack took a pen from his pocket. Then he took my hand, uncurled it, smoothed it, and wrote on my palm: *15 Sand Dollar Lane.*

"I don't know where that is," I said.

"Just take Milestone Road."

"Can I walk?"

"No. I'm getting a ride from work. But text Jules. She'll take you." We turned to her, but she was gone.

Nine

"EVERYONE EATS BREAKFAST IN THE GARDEN, EXCEPT when it rains," Liz said as she expertly pulled silverware from the dishwasher and wiped it with a checkered dishrag. "Then we put them in the dining room."

"Got it," I said, and sipped my coffee, the first cup from the percolator I'd just been shown how to set up and get started (fill with water, twenty scoops in the filter, plug it in, flip the switch). I sipped some more, hoping I'd start to feel more alert soon. Liz pulled a stack of little bowls from the dishwasher and handed them to me. "There's some jam in the fridge. Put it in these ramekins."

"Okay, no problem," I said, noting the new word *ramekins*, which sounded like a species of rambunctious munchkins, and took another gulp of coffee.

Gavin took a fresh batch of blueberry corn muffins out of the oven, and their scent made my cheeks pucker with desire and my stomach growl so loud that he and Liz laughed. Gavin gingerly plied a muffin from the tin, placed it on a saucer, and slid it down the counter with just enough force that it landed right in front of me. "You might want to let it cool," he said. But I couldn't wait. I tore off the crusty top, smeared it with butter, and stuffed it in my mouth. I hadn't finished the last bite before I took another.

"Come on, piglet," Liz said, "we have to wipe down the chairs in the garden."

I ate another bite, grabbed a clean rag from the stack under the sink, and followed Liz outside. Eight wrought-iron tables with matching chairs sat nestled in dewy green grass, awaiting sweethearts. They were surrounded by hedges, roses, and bushes that looked like they had blue pom-poms on them. A gray rabbit hopped across the lawn and into a bush with pink berries, right next to the window I'd propped open with the Emily Dickinson book.

"You didn't have any visitors last night, did you?" Liz asked as she wiped off the tables.

"No," I said. Gavin emerged with some clippers from the back door and was headed down the brick path, past the gurgling fountain, to the rosebushes, no doubt to make an arrangement for the buffet table. "What do you mean?"

"Don't scare her," Gavin said as he passed, smelling faintly of patchouli oil.

"It's only fair that I warn her about Mr. Whiskers," she said.

"Do you have a cat here?" I asked.

"Better. A ghost," Liz said. "An old sea captain with a great, bushy beard." She stuck out her chin and gestured as to the bigness of the beard.

"I've worked here eight years and I've never seen him," Gavin said as he inspected a rose for clipping. *Huh. I thought Gavin owned this place.*

"I don't believe in ghosts," I said. I never have. It always seemed like there was too much in real life I was supposed to be afraid of: drunk drivers, rapists, unwanted pregnancy, HPV, undercooked chicken, toxic shock syndrome, and a bad reputation. I just couldn't add the unseen and paranormal to my list. Besides, there was always someone with one eye open sliding the thing across the Ouija board, someone's brother outside the tent making the footsteps or wagging the flashlight under his pimply chin.

"But he's heard the ghost," Liz said. "Heard the door latch opening and closing."

"Could've been the wind," Gavin said, moving on to the pom-pom flowers.

Liz looked up from the chair she was drying. "Opening a latch?"

"Liz, if you scare away Cricket like you did Rebecca, I won't hire anyone else. You'll be stuck doing this alone."

"Twice the tips for me, then," she muttered.

"Have you actually seen this ghost?" I asked Liz.

"No, but one of the guests saw him. Standing by the stairs in an old-fashioned mac, he was."

"That's a raincoat to you and me," Gavin said.

"He looked in her direction," Liz continued, "but it was more like he was looking *through* her, and then he turned around very slowly, and as he walked up the stairs she saw he was floating, for"—she slowed down her speech—"he had no feet."

"Ew," I said, a little creeped out. "But wait, was she high?"

"Good question," Gavin said. "Yes, probably. Also, Liz didn't hear this story directly. It was told to us by the woman's friend, who was stoned out of her gourd at breakfast."

Liz waved him away. "Anyway, I was in a gallery on Main Street, and they were doing a portrait show about old Nantucket."

"Don't tell me," I said, wiping the heart-shaped chair backs. "There was a picture of a bushy-bearded captain."

"Don't worry about the backs," Liz said. "You just need to do the seats. Anyway, yes. And under it was a grim account of how he'd fallen overboard, his legs tangled in ropes. He thought he'd seen a mermaid and was calling out to her. I'll spare you the details, but I will tell you this." She folded her arms, pausing for dramatic effect. "Lost his feet at sea."

I laughed aloud.

"Fine, don't believe me," she said, and inhaled sharply, her nose in the air. "But don't come crying to me when you bump into a gimpy, transparent sea captain on your way to the loo."

Gavin turned to Liz, a bouquet in his hand. "It's almost seven, we have two couples trying to make the seven-thirty boat, and you still need to set up the creamers and the napkins. Could you *try* to focus?"

Liz plucked a rose from the bouquet and stuck it behind her ear, turned on her heel, and sashayed inside.

"Don't listen to her," Gavin said. "Nantucket is full of people who know someone who's seen a ghost, but I have yet to meet anyone who actually has."

"I'm not worried," I said, checking to make sure the address Zack had written was still on my hand after handling the damp rag, and thought, At least not about ghosts.

Ten

BY THREE O'CLOCK, I WAS READY TO THROW IN THE
cleaning rag. Vacuuming was no big deal—kind of satisfying
to push the heavy thing (it was mustard yellow and dated
back to the 1900s) across the floor and leave those stripes
on the carpets. And dusting was a piece of cake. Changing
the beds wasn't so bad, either; people had been sleeping in
them for two days at the most. But I hated cleaning the
bathrooms. There were certain smells, certain unmistakable
dribbles and marks that inevitably evoked mental pictures of
what had left them. The more I tried to block the pictures,
the faster and stronger they came on. A few times, I thought
I was actually going to barf.

And on the seats, in the bathtub, on the floor, and in the
sink was hair. Hair, hair, hair! It was everywhere, and nine

times out of ten, it was not the kind that grows on the head. I couldn't help but wonder what people did to shed so much in this region. Were they combing it daily, letting the hair just fall where it may? Did everyone do this but me?

The best part was checking the little tip envelopes on the dressers. Liz had drawn cartoon pictures of whales on them, with smiles and water spouting out their blowholes. Usually there were just a few dollars inside, but sometimes there was a five or a ten. We'd made nineteen bucks apiece in tips, and on top of my twelve dollars an hour, I'd made almost a hundred bucks in one day. It was no eight hundred a week, but it wasn't so bad, either. Liz warned me that the tips today were especially good; we'd had a lot of turnovers.

"Don't get too used to it," she said. "Usually we're lucky to get ten apiece."

We locked the last door at three o'clock, and flipped a nickel we'd found in the hallway for the first shower. Liz snatched the nickel in midair and slapped it against the back of her hand. "Heads, I win," she said. After her shower she was going to see her boyfriend, Shane, who worked at a bar on Jetties Beach. "He's twenty-three. An older man," she said as I followed her down the back steps to where our rooms were. "A tall, dashing Irishman who gives me free whiskey sours, calls me 'sexy delicious,' and reads Yeats in his free time."

Liz had a definite swagger. She was not a skinny girl; her boobs were big and unwieldy, and she had mom thighs with cellulite. She was wearing short shorts and a baby T anyway. She sauntered down the steps like a perfect hottie even though her pudge was poking out the top and bottom of her shorts. I felt a little rush of admiration for her confidence. I hated to admit it, but I couldn't imagine not caring what people thought about how I looked. It almost scared me to contemplate it.

"Shane sounds rad," I said, using a classic Jules word. We passed through the hallway where the supposed ghost liked to hang out, pausing in front of our bedroom doors.

"He's an absolute dream," Liz said, and went into her room.

I wondered what Jay read in his free time. I didn't know much about Yeats, but I knew it was impressive that Shane read him. If Shane called Liz sexy delicious, I bet they were having sex. It was too ridiculous a thing to say to someone if you weren't. I wondered if Jay and I would be having lots of sex by the end of the summer. I wondered what he'd call me. Was I sexy delicious? I worried I wasn't. Partially it was the word *sexy*, which just seemed funny, not real, not connected to an actual way of feeling.

"You want to meet me at the beach later tonight?" Liz asked, poking her head into my room without knocking. "It's really fun."

"Thanks," I said. "But I'm going to a party."

"Suit yourself," she said. "But Shane has friends." I doubted I'd be interested in anyone over eighteen.

When Liz was done, I took a long shower, using so

much soap that it was a mere sliver at the end of twenty minutes. Then I took a two-hour nap.

I texted Jules twice and she didn't respond. She's busy, I thought for the first hour, wondering if she'd gotten her job back at Needle and Thread, one of the high-end boutiques on Main Street. She's definitely mad at me, I thought around seven o'clock, when she didn't respond to my second text. I walked to the pizza place near the ferry because I wasn't sure what else to do for dinner. After I finished my pizza, I called her. I felt desperate, a feeling I hated. Jules didn't pick up. "Can I get a ride to the party with you?" I said to the dead air of her voicemail.

It was almost nine by the time she texted me back.

There's no room in the Jeep.

I felt a flash of anger, could almost hear it, like a sizzling pat of butter on a skillet. What the hell, I thought. She's blowing me off so hard that I'm getting windburn. There was another text:

Sorry ☹.

I gave the phone the finger, then took a deep breath. You're thinking like a desperate person, I said to myself. You're thinking like a Nora. Maybe there really is no room in the Jeep.

Besides, I didn't do anything wrong, I told myself as I clasped a necklace around my neck and squeezed into my nice jeans. I unpacked a green tank top that had once made a random guy stop me on the street to tell me my eyes looked like emeralds. I pinched my ears with delicate gold hoops.

I blew out my hair and swiped on shimmery lip gloss. I dusted my cheeks with some blush.

No room in the Jeep, no problem. Gavin had said it would be fine for me to borrow one of the inn's bikes as long as a guest wasn't using it, and 'Sconset was only six miles away by Milestone Road. It would probably only take me a half hour at the most. I chose a blue bike with a big basket. It looked kind of old, but it was the only one with a low-enough seat. As I rode the bike out of the garden, Gavin waved to me from the kitchen window, where he was cooking ratatouille for his chiropractor girlfriend, Melissa, a glass of red wine in his hand.

The moon was so bright, I had a shadow. There was something freeing about the whole thing, about getting myself there without waiting for someone to take me, about the air, which felt soft and smelled like hay, and listening to the invisible insects. Jeeps and mopeds sped past me, some of them blasting music, but there were long stretches of road that were quiet, just me, my breath, my shadow, and the sound of the wheels whirring on the pavement. The best part was that I wasn't afraid of being alone at night. This is why people come to Nantucket, I thought. So they don't have to be afraid at night.

I coasted around a rotary; 'Sconset was its own little town with a coffee shop, market, and the smallest post office I'd ever seen. I was in front of some kind of country club, the flags out front snapping in the wind. I remembered that I needed to bear right to get to Sand Dollar Lane. It wasn't long before I found it. It was pretty obvious where the party was, from the sounds of kids talking. The conversations were clear even a few houses away.

I hopped off of my bike and walked it down a driveway. My legs were wobbly and I was thirsty. My heart was beating fast, snapping like that country club flag, and my pretty green tank top was sticking to my back. I wished I'd brought a sweater. I wanted to cover up. As I was looking for a good place to put the bike (against the house? Inside the half-open garage?) I stumbled, my ankles suddenly soft as custard, and dropped the bike. It bounced off of a rock. Shit. I picked it up and placed it gingerly against the house. Pull it together, I thought, and applied more lip gloss. You're fine.

I heard Jules's laugh, her unmistakable "ha," and a chill went through me. I should've gotten back on the bike and turned around, because I actually did know then, the way you just know sometimes, what was about to happen. You didn't need a worry doctor to know that's what jelly legs are all about. But for some reason, even though it was blasting as loudly as a mattress commercial, I just couldn't hear the truth. So I straightened up and walked right into that party, practically begging for it.

Eleven

A LOUD TEXTURED BELCH CAME FROM THE FRONT PORCH. It was so specifically disgusting, I could practically taste it.

"So, you're trying to say that there's a truth with a capital *T*," the guy on the porch said to his friend as he watched me approach. He was overweight, with a flat, smooched face, but he wasn't acting like it. He was sitting there like some kind of million-dollar man. It's not fair. Guys can embrace their fatness as a unique personality trait, but we girls have to sit on the very edge of chairs in our shorts so as not to reveal the back-of-the-leg cellulite we feel bad for having even though everyone does. Well, everyone but Jules.

"Absolutely, dude," Fitzy said, as cool and lean as a racehorse. He was wearing '80s-style sunglasses even though it was ten o'clock at night. "How else do you explain the commonality of instincts for good and bad across wildly divergent cultures?"

I climbed the three stairs onto the porch. There was a bottle of Jim Beam between them, a pair of empty shot glasses, and plates with sandwich remains.

"I'm Oliver," the fat one in the Deerfield Academy shirt said with a little chin nod. Okay, so I guess this was his house.

"Uh, hi," I said. I stuck my sweaty hands in my pockets. "I'm Cricket."

His eyes widened, full of thoughts. "I've heard about you. You know a friend of mine, Jay Logan."

"Yeah," I said, shifting my weight, glad I'd worn my good jeans. "Is he here?"

"I know he's anxious to see you." Oliver laughed. "He should be here any minute. In the meantime, have at it." He opened the door and I stepped through.

Some sort of rap music was playing. . . . But wait, it wasn't rap. It was more mellow and sophisticated. And I heard un–raplike instruments. I wanted to find out who it was so that I could download it. This could be part of my summer sound track. I could add it to the Jay playlist.

Jules was right. This wasn't a big party. There were maybe twenty people here, and from the way they were lounging, leaning in door frames, draped on the furniture, on one another, I could tell they were all friends. I felt just a little foreign, like I was from Canada, or California.

Jules was sitting on the sofa holding a beer. She was wearing a little dress, and a Jack Rogers sandal dangled from her foot. She was tan, like she'd been at the beach all day. She also looked skinny—not anorexic or anything, just a tiny bit too thin. Actually, it was kind of the perfect amount. The pounds Jules had unnecessarily dropped made her features clearer, her cheekbones elegant. She looked older, that's what it was. Why hadn't I noticed last night?

Her Tiffany necklace dropped over the ridge of her clavicle and sparkled off center. She tried to cross her legs, but her crossing leg fell short. She swung her head back in a laugh. It took that extra effort for her to pull it back up, like the three pounds she'd lost had gathered in the ponytail spot. She was already drunk.

"Hey, Jules," I said as I took a seat on the sofa between her and another girl, who I recognized almost immediately as Parker Carmichael. She had long, shampoo-commercial hair. I'd seen pictures of her at Jules's house, and Jules talked about her sometimes. She was one of those horse girls who won jumping contests and had rock-hard thighs. Also, she was one of *the* Carmichaels, the big political family. The sofa felt a little snug for three people, but it was the only place to sit.

"Hey," Jules said, and took another sip of beer. She made eye contact with Parker, then flapped her hand around to introduce us. "Parker, Cricket; Cricket, Parker."

"Hi," we said at the same time with zero enthusiasm.

"So, is Zack here?" I asked, filling the awkward silence.

"Still working," Jules said, and wrinkled her brow. "How'd you get here?"

"I rode my bike," I said, and shrugged, sensing that I was the only one who'd arrived on two wheels. I'd worn sneakers because I always wore sneakers when I rode a bike. It was the safe thing to do. But all the other girls had delicate shoes and pedicured feet. My dirty white Converses didn't match the rest of me, which was kind of dressed up. And I was still a little sweaty. My bangs were sticking to my forehead. I felt the opposite of drunk. "So, where can I get a beer?"

"Kitchen," Jules said, not even looking at me. She stood up, put a hand on her hip. "Hey, where's Ginny? Is she on the trampoline?" she asked no one in particular.

"I think she's with Fitzy," Parker said. "Showing him those bodacious ta-tas." Parker and Jules burst into laughter.

"Seriously, they got so big this year," Jules said. "I've got to go get another look at them." She staggered forward, but her foot caught on the carpet. I leaped to catch her, but not fast enough. She fell backward and landed on the floor with her dress around her waist. Parker was nearly dry-heaving with laughter. Jules was laughing so hard she couldn't even sit up. She pounded the floor with her fists. I yanked her dress down over her freckled thighs.

"Nice thong," Parker said. "Leopard print." Now a couple of guys leaned in from the kitchen. Since when did Jules wear animal-print underwear? Or thongs? We'd read an article in one of those magazines about thongs and fecal matter, which had scared, well, the shit out of us.

"My bodacious cha-cha," Jules said, laughing so hard she was drooling.

"Jules, you need some water," I whispered. "You're really wasted."

"That's some good police work, Captain Cricket," Jules said, slapping me on the knee, then using her grip on my leg to hoist herself up. Parker rode a fresh wave of laughter and wiped tears from her eyes.

"Whatever," I said, stinging, and made my way to the kitchen to find a beer. This was an old house. It had wooden walls, low ceilings, and small, old furniture. There was a group of guys at the table. They had men's voices and men's hands. They were concentrating on a card game. Poker, I think.

"Do you have a bottle opener?" I asked, a cold beer in my hand.

"It's a twist-off," one of them said without even looking at me.

"Oh. Thanks." I twisted the top off and wondered what my next move would be now that I had the beer. I was about to make my way back out to the front porch when I saw that Jay had arrived. He looked gorgeous, with a new haircut and a tan that had a little bit of sunburn in it. He had such a nice body. He didn't have a girl butt or anything, but unlike a lot of guys, he actually had one, and you could totally see it in his jeans. And he wasn't too tall, just the most perfect height for kissing on my tiptoes.

Also, he had muscles. I bet when he was in his lifeguard bathing suit, he had those diagonal lines that go from his hips down to his you know what. I almost called out to him, but I thought it would be better if he noticed me first, so I pretended to read the calendar that was hanging on the wall, figuring he'd definitely be coming this way for a beer. I was so excited to see Jay walking toward me, but when he saw me, he looked away with disgust, and moved past me to get a beer.

"Hi, Jay," I said, biting my lip to try to restrain a smile. He didn't seem to hear me. "Jay?"

"Don't talk to me, bitch," he said.

I was so stunned I couldn't move. I had never been called "bitch" before. With anger behind it, that word has knuckles. It has nails. Jay grabbed two beers and stepped past me, careful that not even our shirts brushed.

"Wait," I said, finding my voice and following him down the hallway toward the back door. "What is this about?"

He turned around so fast that I jumped a little. "You think my brother's a loser?" His face was red. His eyes were hard. He was squeezing the beers so tightly I thought the bottles might break.

"No," I said. My heart was pounding. My cheeks burned. Jules had told him that I'd said his brother was a loser for having a DUI and working at the bagel shop. He was looking at me with such intensity I couldn't lie. "I mean, I'm sorry. I didn't mean it."

"Who says shit like that?" He glared at me like I was

lower than dirt. I looked at the floor, grabbed my stomach. I felt dizzy and sick. I opened my mouth to speak, but nothing came out. He took a step backward and shook his head. "You know what? Forget it. I don't care what you think. I don't even want to bother getting angry at someone like you. It's not worth my time." He turned around and kicked open the back door with his foot. It slammed shut behind him.

Twelve

"CAN WE TALK?" I ASKED JULES. "OUTSIDE."

"Whoa. Sure." She stood, straightened her dress, and followed me out the door.

"Someone's in trouble," Parker sang, slapping her knees.

Jules turned to face her. "If I get killed out there, her name is Cricket Thompson and she's like, a really fast runner. So you may need to hop into the Jeep if you want to catch her. They call her 'Wheels' back in Provy."

I led us to the top of the driveway, where I thought we'd be out of earshot.

"You told Jay what I said about his brother?" I asked.

"It just kind of came out," she said.

"But I didn't actually mean it. You know I was joking. I like him, Jules. I really like him. You know that."

"You have to admit, it was a really mean thing to say," Jules said.

"But I was saying it to *you*. In private. I wasn't trying to be mean. You say mean things all the time. How could you tell him something like that?"

"Sorry," she said, not meaning it *at all*, and threw her hands in the air.

"And why are you acting like this?" I asked. "Saying that thing about police work? I was trying to help you. All I've tried to do is help you."

"I don't need your help," she said.

"You were making a fool out of yourself," I whispered.

"No. Those are my friends. I've known them forever. I've known them longer than I've known you." She crossed her arms and looked up at the sky, eyelids fluttering in frustration.

"She was just having a little fun." It was Parker. How long had she been standing there? "Don't you want her to have fun? Don't you think she deserves that?"

"Of course," I said, my voice rising. I clapped my hand to my chest. "I'm her best friend. Of course I want her to have fun."

"Are you a lesbian?" Parker asked, her head cocked, her magazine hair shining in the moonlight.

"Oh. My. God," I said, looking at Jules. "Jules? What the hell?"

"I want you to leave me alone, Cricket. I want you to stop bothering me." *I was bothering her?* The worst part was that she said it in this really calm, steady, grown-up voice. "You need to get your own life."

"Fine," I said, shaking. "Fine. I'll stop *bothering* you."

"I didn't want to have to say it. But you're like, making me, Cricket." Jules screwed her hands over her eyes. "I didn't want you to come here. I told you not to come."

It took all my strength to walk, not sprint, back down the driveway to get my bike. I felt hot, neon with pain, all lit up for everyone to see. My hands were trembling; I dropped the bike and it clanked against the drainpipe. Fitzy stood up.

"Is that chick okay?" he asked Oliver. Then called to me, "Hey, you okay?"

I waved awkwardly, not daring to speak, not risking public tears. My foot slipped twice on the pedal before I was able to push off, turn the wheels, and ride back into the night, alone.

I had wanted to be best friends with Jules since she'd come to Rosewood in the eighth grade. I'd been with the same group of girls for ten years already. I knew their handwriting, whether they chewed with their mouth open, and how they sneezed. So when on the first day of eighth grade, the social studies teacher asked us to find a partner with whom we'd be working for the next six weeks, I immediately turned to Jules, the new girl from New York.

From the moment we drew our time line, to the rap we wrote about Roger Williams, the founder of Rhode

Island, I liked the way I felt around Jules—like I was tipping backward in a chair, on the edge of falling. We thought that this was the best thing about an all-girls school. You could write a rap about Rhode Island history and not worry about what guys would say or if they thought it was lame. We decided it was funny, so it was funny.

It was Jules who made me cool. I'd been just a middle-of-the-pack girl before Jules. It was she who told me I was pretty, who convinced me to grow out my hair and cut my bangs and taught me about plucking my eyebrows and what a big difference the right pair of jeans could make. It was she who laughed hardest at my stories so that the other girls started laughing, too. It was Jules who told me to try out for varsity lacrosse as a freshman. "You're the only one in our class who's good enough," she'd said. And she was right. After a year of her looking at me like I was the prettiest, funniest, coolest girl in our class, I started to believe it, too.

As long as she was near me.

Thirteen

"AND THIS IS WHY MOST AMERICANS WON'T DO THIS JOB," Liz said as I turned in disgust from the dirty toilet in the honeymoon suite. "Or Brits, for that matter."

"But here we are," I said. "Confronted with skid marks."

"I can't believe these people are on their honeymoon." Liz shook her head and we promised each other we would never allow such things in our future marriages. "Once you let them see you pee, it's all downhill," she added. I nodded in agreement. I couldn't imagine letting a guy see me pee. Disgusting. Friends, yes. Boys, never.

I used a clean rag to wipe down the sink and thought of the young couple who had been smooching all through breakfast. The man had muscles you could see through his T-shirt, and the woman had perfect white teeth. "You'd think they'd have at least closed the seat," I said.

"Must be true love," Liz said, and snapped on the extra-long, yellow latex gloves. "Go tackle the bedroom. I've got this loo, but you have to get the next."

"Deal," I said, and went to plug in the vacuum cleaner.

For the past week, I'd been consumed by what had happened with Jules. While I was emptying the dishwasher, vacuuming the rugs, or tucking crisp sheets under the corner of a mattress, I was reviewing the scene, obsessing over each word, slowing the fight down, trying to get a grip on it, hoping to figure out exactly where it all went wrong. I'd expected her to call me with an apology, but there hadn't been a word.

The biggest question in my mind was . . . why? Why had Jules told Jay what I'd said about his brother? If she didn't want to hang out with me for some crime too great to be named, if I was *bothering* her, fine, okay. But to go and ruin my chance with Jay?

I tried to picture the moment she'd done it. Had she exaggerated my comment for a crowd, or had she said it to him with a sisterly pat on the arm, her voice low and dripping with concern, like, *Oh, Jay, this is something you should know*? I put the blanket the couple had left in a tangled heap on the floor back on the bed, but decided to vacuum around the clothes that were strewn everywhere. Was true love really this messy? Wait a second, I thought as I picked up a still-damp towel with my thumb and forefinger and dropped it in the laundry bag. Had Jules been flirting with

Jay? Oh my god, why hadn't I thought of that earlier?

This wave of anger, just like every other, was dragged back out to sea when I remembered that her mother had died. Her *mother. Died.* Even though she drove me crazy sometimes, the thought of losing my own mother made me feel like I had a dry cleaning bag over my head. But still. What the hell had I done except try to be good, except offer to help, except try to be there for my best friend at the worst moment of her life?

I switched on the TV to give my mind a break. Liz said it was fine as long as Gavin was out and we kept the volume way down. I thought I'd stumbled onto some local Nantucket channel when I saw Bradley Lucas standing in front of a big Nantucket house. Isn't that nice of Mr. Lucas, lending his talent to the local station, I thought as I bent to find the switch on the vacuum. But after a few seconds I realized this was no local TV station, but CNN. This was national news. As the shot widened, I saw other news vans in the background and a small crowd of people.

A banner ran at the bottom announcing the death of William "Boaty" Carmichael, the Massachusetts senator whose family vacationed here. He was famous for his boyish good looks and his weird nickname. He was also Parker's uncle. He was around my parents' age, with a baby face and blond curly hair. I remembered during one election season when my mother was driving me home from an away lacrosse game, somewhere near Boston. We passed a sign with Boaty Carmichael's picture on it.

"I'd vote for him," I said, prying some dirt from my cleats. "He's so handsome."

"That's no reason to elect a person," my mother said, a look of horror on her face. She saw a clump of dirt that had fallen from my cleat and added, "Stop that. This is my car, not a stable."

"I still think he's cute," I said, releasing my foot to the floor and tossing the hunk of dirt out the window.

"Really, Cricket? I'm sending you to an all-girls' school and you think it's a good idea to vote for a man *based on looks*? Do you know anything about him? About his policies?" She stepped on the accelerator.

"Mom!" I said, gripping the door as the driver of a silver minivan slammed on her brakes to avoid hitting us. "That was a stop sign."

Now I looked at the clip of him on the TV, shaking hands with the less handsome people of the world. He looked like such a great guy the way he made eye contact, smiling so vigorously his curls shook. As he leaned in to listen to a liver-spotted old lady, his blues eyes crinkled with friendliness.

"Liz, come here," I said.

"What happened?" Liz looked around the room to see if I'd broken or spilled something.

"On the TV. Senator Carmichael died. Heart attack."

"You're kidding," she said, and grabbed the remote off the quilt. She turned up the volume. "They're out by the family compound. Poor Boaty."

"You knew him?" With her swagger and that accent, Liz seemed capable of knowing senators, of knowing anyone she wanted to.

"He came here at least once a summer. Big muffin fan. Rhubarb was his favorite." She shook her head. "What a shame. He has those two small children." As if on cue, an old clip of the young family flashed on the screen, probably from the night he'd been elected. They were all dressed up and waving on a stage. I could see bits of Parker in them. I could see her toothy smile, the high cheekbones, and the big round eyes, all of which made the family seem part of a Disney movie. The Carmichael family possessed features that should have added up to beauty but somehow fell short. All except Boaty.

Now Parker and Jules would be more bonded than ever. I felt like curling up in the bed, pulling the sheets over my head, and taking a nap. And then I remembered that this was probably where the honeymooners were having sex all night long, so I leaned forward and put my head in my hands.

"Don't take it so hard," Liz said, patting my back. "His brother will surely take his place."

Fourteen

LATER, I RODE THE BLUE BIKE THAT BY NOW HAD SORT OF become mine into town, where faces were downcast, heads were bowed, and hands were shoved into brightly colored pockets. All the children tucked closer into the sides of their parents. My mother's dislike of Boaty Carmichael was a buffer against all the solemn, complimentary chatter, making me feel like less of a Nantucket person than ever. "A loss for the whole country." "On his way to the White House." "Nantucket's son, *America's* son." I was afraid if anyone looked at me for a second too long they'd be able to tell that my mother hated the guy.

I saw a short dress in the window of a boutique. It was a slim, silk, one-shouldered number with a thin gold belt around the waist. It filled me with hope, and I decided to try it on to cheer myself up. I went into the store, which was empty except for the saleslady, who looked pale despite her tan. She held a tissue to her lips as she watched the TV, the same loop I'd seen earlier, reviewing the same news.

"Can I try this on?" I asked. She nodded vaguely in my direction, her eyes glued to the TV, then dabbed her reddened nose with the shredded tissue. I felt like a criminal for smiling.

Once in the dressing room with the canvas curtain closed, I slipped the dress over my head. The cool silk kissed my skin and skimmed my body. It hit my mid-thigh, flirting with being too short but staying, somehow, classy beyond a doubt. I peeled off my sweaty socks and slid my feet into a pair of strappy gold heels that were under the bench, waiting for me. The high waist made my legs look longer, and the deep emerald green brought out the blond streaks in my hair, which I took out of my ponytail and shook to my shoulders. The one bare shoulder was the secret, the reveal. I look like I could be on TV, I thought, turning to see the back. I look like I could be famous. If I wore this dress it would be impossible for anyone to make me feel bad. Powers would shift.

I checked out the price tag dangling beneath my armpit. Four hundred and ninety-five dollars! That was more than a week's pay. I thought about how difficult my first week had been. My elbows were sore from scrubbing, my hands felt rougher from the various cleaning chemicals. My summer earnings were the only money I had all year for trips to the movies, clothes that weren't uniforms, and my cell phone bill. But I wanted this so badly that my wanting began to grow a life of its own. I unzipped carefully, leaning forward and rounding my back to pull the dress over my head, trying not to touch the silk too much, afraid to matte its gloss. I sat on the bench to think.

The bell that hung over the front door rang faintly.

"Hi, doll," said the saleslady. Her voice was surprisingly rough: a smoker, a drinker, or maybe a yeller.

"Hey, Nan." That voice I knew. It was Jules. It was her *talking to a grown-up she didn't like but had to be nice to* voice. I went pale, stuck my hands in my armpits, felt lightheaded. I lifted my bare feet from the ground onto the little bench, my toes as cold as frozen peas. As much as I wanted to run into her, as much as I wanted to force her to face me, as much as I wanted to ask her why she'd done what she'd done and said what she'd said; as much as I wanted to scream and cry and really have it out with her, I couldn't seem to move from this shell shape. I felt stupid for being here all by myself and trying on a dress without an occasion. What would I say I was shopping for? Next year's Spring Dance? I could smell my deodorant. I could smell Formula 409 in my fingernails.

"I just came in for my check," Jules said. "Anyone come in today?"

Of course: this was where she worked! I glanced at the price tag on the dress where the name of the store was printed in pink: Needle and Thread. How had I not noticed? How had I not put it together?

"There's someone in the dressing room, with the Chloé dress, I think."

"Great dress," Jules said, under her breath. They whispered something to each other that I couldn't make out. Then Jules sighed, and I imagined one hand was on her hip, because that's usually how she stands when she sighs like that. From the silence, it seemed like they were watching the TV.

"Can you believe this?" Nan asked, and blew her nose.

"It's so sad. You know Parker Carmichael is my best friend." My stomach twisted. I clutched my knees. Parker wasn't her best friend! Parker didn't know how worried she got about her skin, that she went to the dermatologist sometimes once a week for treatments to prevent a relapse of the acne that had plagued her for a semester our freshman year. Parker didn't know that even though Jules had the quickest comebacks, trying to conjugate French verbs could make her cry with frustration. She didn't know that she had a team of tutors and even then couldn't get above a B in pretty much anything; that she had failed her driver's-ed test three times. Parker didn't know that she actually had hooked up with Jeremy Stein sophomore year at the Winter Ball, even though she denied it so much and so often that by now even she believed it hadn't happened. No one knew that stuff but me.

"Oh, poor girl," said Nan.

"Are you going to close the shop this week?" Jules asked. I could hear the hope in her voice. Jules liked having a job but hated the working part.

"In July? Are you kidding me?" Sadness vanished from the woman's voice. "I'll see you tomorrow."

Jules thanked her for the check, and I heard the bells jingle softly.

I waited a few minutes, soundlessly got dressed, left the dress on the hanger in the dressing room, and fled.

I hopped on my bike and cruised out of town, in the opposite direction of Jules's house. It was hot—the air thick with future rain—and sweat prickled my upper lip. I followed one of those hand-painted-looking signs to Jetties Beach, where I thought maybe I'd find Liz. But when I got there, there was a group of kids my age, the girls with their arms slung around each other. Was Jules among them? I couldn't risk it. I turned around and headed up a cobblestone hill bordered by a wall of golden moss.

It didn't matter how good my grades were or that I'd made varsity as a freshman; it didn't matter how carefully, how perfectly, I'd managed my popularity; it didn't matter that I'd measured and doled out my flirtations like teaspoons of sugar—never too much to be a tease, always enough to be sweet. Jules was able to take my happiness away from me with one swift betrayal. My social life had slid from good to bad like a hockey puck across a rink. It wasn't fair. I wanted to take her to friend court. I wanted to sue her. But I could see the faces of the jury when it was revealed that her mother had just died. *Died.*

I coasted on a quiet little cul-de-sac, peering over

hedges, looking at the huge estates, all of them with their flags at half mast. I was wishing I were that kind of rich, the kind where people have to respect you, because that's what money does. It makes people shut up. It means you live in the big house, throw the cool birthday parties, belong to the country club that has its own jokes, its own dances; take awesome vacations, go skiing enough to get really good at it, own the best clothes, get the green dress.

I was thinking about how being rich was protection, armor, authority, a cushion, a parachute, something to fall back on when the rest of your life sucked. I was pedaling slowly and looking at the biggest house on the street, gazing upward into its turret, pretending I lived there with a three-hundred-and-sixty-five-degree ocean view, a telescope, and a Jacuzzi, when a huge black Navigator peeled out of nowhere, swerved to avoid me, and screeched to a halt an inch from my body. I froze, wincing, shutting my eyes against the spray of gravel and the heat from the car's engine. A big mean man with fat baby cheeks and a white baseball hat leaned on his horn. The sound moved through my muscles, pulsing the marrow in my bones.

"Get out of the street," he said, shaking a fist at me, his complexion ruddy with anger.

I got off my bike and jogged it to the sidewalk. I let the bike fall on the grass and sat, my head in my hands, waiting for the man to drive away. I wouldn't look at him, but I could feel him looking at me, his anger like a scorching ray of sun.

"Fuckin' idiot," he said. My legs were shaking. My throat was dry. I was past crying. "You tryin' to get yourself killed? Stay on the sidewalk."

"You slow down, Mr. Big Shot!" shouted an old woman in tennis whites walking an even older-looking standard poodle, one hand cupped around her mouth like a megaphone. She had wobbly knees on legs so tanned they looked like they'd stepped on the tennis court in 1975 and never stepped off. "New Yorkers," she said, eyes narrowed, catching his license plate as the car turned down the hill. Her mouth was pinched, like she'd just chewed a lemon. And I wasn't sure if she was talking to the poodle or me. "Well, you're okay," she said. I nodded quickly. "He was completely out of order. You're not *supposed* to ride your bicycle on the sidewalk."

As she walked past me on her long, old, freckled legs, her proud standard poodle strutting beside her, I wondered how it was that on this tiny island off Massachusetts, with its candy-cane lighthouse, church bells on the hour, daffodils, and ice-cream cones, nowhere felt safe.

Fifteen

I COULDN'T SLEEP THAT NIGHT. MY NERVES WERE JANGLING from almost being hit by that Navigator. There was a fluttery, unsettling lightness in my body that made me want to hug myself just to feel my own weight. The pillow was too squishy and the sheets were scratchy against my skin. I tried counting the roses on the wallpaper, but I couldn't get past ten without my mind wandering back to Jules or Jay.

Earlier that day, I'd bought a chutney-and-cheddar sandwich from Something Natural, a place Gavin said was the best on the island. The thing was so huge it was like two sandwiches, and I'd only been able to eat a quarter of it, saving the rest for later. That sandwich seemed like the best thing in the world around 2 a.m., when my stomach remembered about lunch and dinner and was demanding both. I walked quietly into the dark kitchen and opened the refrigerator, which Gavin kept gleaming and clean. Where was my sandwich? My perfect, delicious sandwich, full of such odd flavors I almost couldn't believe I liked it. I'd put it right here, I thought, touching the empty shelf as if the sandwich were only momentarily invisible. I opened the crisper and the meats-and-cheeses drawer, mystified in the cold breath of the refrigerator.

Behind me, the floor creaked, though softer than when Liz was marching around the kitchen—almost as if it were bending under the weight of cat or a child. It creaked again, even more softly, as if it weren't really being stepped on but moved over. Oh my god. I heard breathing. I froze, my feet nailed to the floor. A cool, silvery sweat lined my body. *I don't believe in ghosts*, I told myself as I stared ahead. But the chords of my neck were as stiff as cables. My heart was thwacking. I let go of the fridge door and told my feet to *move*. My eyes shifted to the kitchen door, which had swung shut behind me on my way in, and I wondered if my lead arms would be able to push it open as I took my first giant step toward it.

"Hey, didn't mean to scare you," said a voice.

I flung my hand on the light switch, an act of bravery worthy of getting my picture in the paper. My other hand rested on my jumping heart. I turned to see a guy with messy brown hair, a crooked smile, and a wrinkled shirt sitting at the kitchen table. His back was to me, and he was twisted around in his seat, chewing. A pair of crutches leaned against the table.

"I'm George Gust," he said, wiping his mouth with a napkin. He looked too old for college but too young to be a dad. "Are you staying here, too?"

"I work here." I leaned against the wall and took deep breaths. "Sorry, I thought you were a ghost."

"Is this place haunted?" he asked, completely serious.

"Supposedly. I don't believe it, though."

He raised an eyebrow, like, *Sure you don't.* "Well, I apologize again. I thought at first you were sleepwalking, and you know how they say you should never wake up a sleepwalker? Anyway, my bad." He wiped his hand on his jeans and extended it. "I didn't catch your name."

"I'm Cricket Thompson," I said, taking his hand and catching a full view of his plate. "And you're eating my sandwich."

Sixteen

"I HAVE A WHOLE MONTH TO MAKE THIS UP TO YOU," George Gust said as he swallowed the last bite, explaining that he was staying in the annex, a little studio cottage in the backyard, for all of July and probably August, too. We sat there talking for at least a half hour. He seemed to have a lot of talking in him, and I wasn't exactly dying to get back to my rose-covered chamber. He was writing a biography of Senator William "Boaty" Carmichael. He'd sold his idea to a big publishing house over a year ago and had been taking his sweet time. But with the latest news, his editors were pushing for a draft by the end of August. He was staying at the inn to do research and to write his ass off.

"I don't know how I'm going to do it," he said, his forehead crimping. "Especially with a broken leg."

"But you don't write with your leg." I grabbed one of Liz's beloved key-lime-pie-flavored yogurts (or, as she said, "yah-gurts") from the fridge. She loved this stuff. I thought it tasted like whipped soap, but it was pretty much my only option tonight. Luckily, it was her day off tomorrow and she was at Shane's, so I'd have time to replace it before she noticed.

"But everything takes me twice as long," the man said. "Buying a cup of coffee is like a half-hour adventure. And I need to interview people. I can't drive. It sucks." He shook his head. "Are you a night owl, too?" He crumpled the butcher paper the sandwich had been wrapped in into a ball.

"Not usually. Can't sleep."

George aimed the paper ball toward the garbage. It landed next to the dishwasher. "I've never been good at that," he said. "I've never been the guy who makes the basket with my trash unless I'm right next to it."

"And this bothers you?" I polished off the yogurt and washed the spoon.

"You know, it kinda does. I'd really like to be one of those guys. Everyone would say, 'he shoots, he scores,' and I'd feel like a big deal just for throwing something out."

I took five steps backward, assumed a basketball pose, and tossed the empty yogurt container directly into the bin.

"You're one of those guys," he said.

"One of those girls." I picked up his paper ball and handed it back to him. "You need a loose wrist." He rolled his wrist around. "Now, you've got to look where you want it to land." George narrowed his eyes at the trash can. "Just kind of put yourself in that place."

"In the trash?"

I laughed. "Yup."

"I'm there," he said. "It's not pretty, but I'm there." He lifted his arm to throw.

"Okay, now keep your eyes on the can and trust. Trust that your arm knows when to release." I was pretty much quoting Miss Kang directly. He reared back his arm, took a breath, and shot.

"He shoots, he scores," I said as the butcher paper landed in the trash.

"Look at that." He clapped once, smiling broadly. "Thanks!"

"You just needed a coach," I said, and shrugged. He stood up, balancing on one leg as he grabbed his crutches.

"What I really need," he said, as he hobbled toward the stairs and used the butt of his crutch to push the door, "is an intern."

Seventeen

"SHE LISTENS TO THE JESUS STATION SO LOUDLY THAT YOU might find yourself converted by the end of the day," Liz said. We were standing at the window, watching Bernadette walk around the inn to the kitchen door. Bernadette was the chambermaid who worked when Liz or I had the day off. She wore a little radio fastened around her waist. It had old-fashioned headphones that covered her ears entirely, lobes included. Today was Liz's day off, and my first time working without her. I already missed her.

I didn't know where Bernadette lived, but she arrived at the inn via an old van with tinted windows. It dropped her off, then rattled away. "She thinks we're lazy, and she's not afraid to tell us."

"I'm not lazy," I said. I had straight A's, excluding math but including physics.

"Well, she thinks so. Oh, and there's one more thing." Liz poured herself coffee in one of the to-go cups we gave to guests who were headed to the ferry. "She doesn't take a lunch break and she'll yell at you if you do. So eat up while you can."

"She can't yell at us for taking a lunch break," I said. "That's like, illegal, I think. Does Gavin know about that?"

"He loves her." She laughed. "It's a love that springs from fear, but he says Bernadette is the only one who gets this place truly clean."

"So why doesn't she work here full-time if he loves her so much?" I asked.

"She refuses to work anywhere more than twice a week. Considers herself freelance. That way she maintains her autonomy." She patted my hand. "Just remember, it's better to work straight through to the end or eat something quick when she's on her cigarette break."

"No lunch break for us, but she takes a cigarette break?" I said with a full mouth of muffin.

"Look on the bright side. You'll be done early. Ta-ta," Liz said, and flounced out the door, twirling her bikini around her finger. I took another slug of coffee as Bernadette walked through the door, took me in, sighed disappointedly, and headed for the laundry room. We had a big day ahead;

almost all the rooms were turnovers. I stuck the rest of the scone in the pocket of my apron.

Bernadette emerged from the laundry room with an armload of clean rags. "Put down your coffee. It's time to work, girl."

I took one last gulp and chucked the rest down the sink.

Okay, fine, I'm lazy, I thought, three hours later, shaking with hunger, covered in a fine mélange of sweat, filth, and Lysol, and on the verge of tears. Bernadette cleaned so hard it was like she saw the devil's face in the toilet bowl and his asshole in the shower drains. She could snap sheets onto beds with one jerk of her long arms—her quick, cracked hands folding hospital corners too fast for me to understand how she did it.

She appeared to be ignoring me, but at the same time I felt like I was being watched by the FBI. I'd leave a room, thinking I was done, and she'd go back in and check over my work. Inevitably, she'd come out of what I thought was a perfectly clean room shaking her head and sucking air through her teeth. I'd missed some scum in the caulking around the tub, grime in the corner of bathroom floors, perhaps a bit of dust along the baseboard.

"You girls are so lazy," she said, checking under a bed I'd just made. "Look under there." I got on my hands and knees to peer under the dust ruffle. A man-eating dust bunny stared back at me. The worst part was that I *had* actually swept under there. "Go on, get it."

"With what?" I asked. I had stopped trying to be nice. "Broom won't work at this angle."

"With the hands the Good Lord gave you."

As I crept on my elbows like an alligator in a swamp, my head brushing the bottom of the box spring, I wondered what the hell I was doing on Nantucket. This job sucked. My best friend and the guy I liked both hated me. I reached for the dust ball, and feeling my own soft arm against my cheek, lay my head on it for a moment. This small, protected part of me still smelled sweet, still felt pretty. I held my breath to keep from crying. I missed Jules, who I wasn't going to be able to tell this story to. Without a best friend to tell stories to, it almost didn't matter if they even happened.

"Get your head out of the clouds," Bernadette said to me, grabbed my ankle, and yanked on it. My elbows burned on the wooden floor. I pursed my lips and twisted my head to keep from literally mopping the floor with my lips. I pushed myself all the way out.

"I'm taking a cigarette break. Here." I handed her the dust monster. I stormed down the stairs, not making eye contact with a sunburned couple, back early from the beach, their eyes full of concern as I stomped past them.

I sat in the shade of the bike shed, on a stone that faced away from the backyard to the hedges, wanting to quit so badly. I shut my eyes. I could do it. But if I did, I'd just be back at home, back with Mom and her white wine, her phone that didn't ring, her furrowed brow, and eight-thirty bedtimes. I'd be back to Dad's new life, to his new house, where the floors were made of eggshells, and Alexi's temper bombs ticked in every corner. In his new family I had to be polite all the time, like he was someone else's dad, which he was now.

It was better to stay here. It was better to try to make things work. I just needed to turn things around. I remembered Jenna Garbetti, the shy, big-boobed senior from a few years ago who had turned around her bad reputation by disappearing from the social scene, getting a new look, and focusing on her studies. If there was ever a time to use the Jenna Garbetti method, it was now.

Lie low, look good, and learn, I said to myself. I was already lying low, I thought. I lifted the twig in the air, pretending to smoke it like a cigarette in case Bernadette was watching. I couldn't lie much lower than this. I just needed to figure out how to achieve the other two. I stood up and moved around the shed so that I could stand in the sun. I saw George coming around the corner on his crutches, a bag from Something Natural in his hand. I dropped the twig.

"Just the person I was looking for," he said. "Your sandwich."

"Mmm, lunch," I said, and took the bag. "I really needed this today."

"Well, good. There's a cookie in there, too." He smiled in a way that made me feel like my old confident self again. "I don't know how you feel about chocolate chip. Bought it on spec."

"Yum. Um, hey listen, so I was thinking"—this took some courage—"that I could be your intern. I have straight A's, except in math, and English is my best subject."

He smiled. "Don't you already have a job?"

"I get off at three o'clock. You said last night that you're not even functional until one."

"That's true. But I can't exactly pay you," he said, his forehead crinkling.

"I just want my name somewhere in the book. Like the thank-you section?"

"That wouldn't be a problem at all."

"We could try it out and see if it works." I shrugged.

"This is called marketing," he said. "You've just sold me." We shook hands.

"I have to go; my cigarette break is almost over."

"You smoke?" he asked.

"No, but don't tell." George looked confused. "Long story."

"Got it. We'll talk later today, then? Iron out the details?"

I nodded. *Lie low, look good, and learn.* I was two-thirds of the way there.

After I finished with Bernadette, who wouldn't even look at me, I went back to Needle and Thread. I peeked in the window of the tiny shop to make sure that Jules wasn't there, and then I bought the dress. It was a whole paycheck, but if I was going to make the Jenna Garbetti method work, I had to go all the way. I carried the bag back to the inn, peeking into the tissue paper a few times to make sure it hadn't disappeared on me. It was twilight, the crickets were chirping, and the air smelled like flowers. Thank you, Jenna Garbetti, I thought. I hoped she'd grown her hair long again, that she was in love with a guy who loved her back, and that her life at Yale was nothing less than beautiful.

Eighteen

THE NEXT DAY WAS MY DAY OFF—MY TURN TO WALK OUT the door in my bikini, with a big Saturday smile on my lips on a Tuesday morning. George, having probably finally crashed when the sun rose, was going to be asleep until at least noon, so I had the whole morning to myself. It's better to have the morning to yourself than the evening. You don't have to feel lonely when you're alone in the morning.

I wanted to go to the beach. I'd already been on Nantucket for ten days and still hadn't gone in the actual ocean. On a run the other night, I'd found myself back on the street where I'd had my brush with the Navigator. I hadn't meant to, but I'd somehow just wound up there. That's when I discovered the path to Steps Beach. I noticed a few people with beach chairs emerging from what looked like someone's backyard. I jogged over. "Welcome to Steps Beach" was engraved on a rock. I followed a leafy path where a few people had left their bikes leaning unlocked against an old twisty-wood fence, and others had shed their flip-flops mid-walk, one in front of the other, staggered like footprints. There was a set of steep stairs that went down to the sand. Then there was one little dune to climb, a mound of low green bushes, tangled roses, sun-bleached, hay-colored grass, and red berries. The path split in two around it and opened up to a field of warm sand and a calm slice of ocean.

Today there were about fifteen people there, all spread out: a few pretty moms playing with their naked babies, a group of old ladies under the shade of umbrellas in their skirted suits, a fully dressed couple, pants rolled up, lying on their stomachs, sifting sand between their fingers. A few people walked in the distance. I lifted my beach towel to the breeze and spread it on the perfect spot, off to the side but not too close to the little fence, and about halfway to the water. I watched a single sailboat glide on the horizon's rim.

That's when I noticed the color of the water. It was a million different shades at once, changing with the few clouds that floated above, darkening with depth, reflecting the deep canyons and sandbar stripes below the surface; but in the distance, in a wide, sparkling, uniform band, was a color peeled from the hot summer sky and chilled by the sea. It was cool and bright, brand new, and yet so familiar. It was the exact color of Jules's bedroom. Nantucket blue.

Would I ever get to sit in her bedroom again? I didn't know. But if I did, it would never be the same, not after our fight, not without Nina.

I sat on my towel, let the sun drip into my bones, and combed the sand with my toes. This was my day off, I reminded myself, my Saturday on a Tuesday. I leafed though the *Us Weekly* I'd bought at the Hub on my way over here, but then decided that I might as well take a crack at Emily Dickinson. Since fifth grade, we'd had to read at least one poem of hers a year. I'd never really understood what made her so famous. What did she really have to write about, hiding alone in her Amherst attic all the time? I unfolded the paper with the list of poems we were supposed to read and opened the book.

It was filled with my mother's familiar loopy handwriting in what appeared to be letters to Emily Dickinson. Mrs. Hart had wanted us to get this special edition because there was only one poem per page, leaving lots of white space for our "thoughts, reflections, and in-depth analysis of this American genius." At first I thought that Mom had just had a lot to say about Emily Dickinson, that she was not only a secret fan of the poet, but some kind of Emily fanatic. But when I looked closer, I saw dates, dashes, *fucks*, *shits*, exclamation points, Aerosmith lyrics—this wasn't poetry analysis. This was her diary. I flipped on my stomach and turned to the title page.

6.30.84

Dear Emily D.,

Since Aunt Betty reads my diary, since she basically admitted it over her third gin and tonic on the porch last night, I've decided to write here, in your book, where Aunt Betty will never look. She told me she always hated your work. Don't take it personally—she's sexist! So, all my secrets will go right here. This will be like putting my pearls in the freezer to hide them from thieves. I feel better already! I need to write down my thoughts because I'm completely busting at the seams, bursting with the best news. After years of loneliness and desperation, I am here to report that I, Kate Campbell, am in the process of falling in LOVE. I can't write his name in case this document is discovered, but I met him today, so I will call him Lover Boy. He is THE ONE. I can feel it. I need to record this, as this is, without a doubt, going to be the best summer of my life. He's not a preppy guy. He's actually kind of a guido. But you know what? I like it! Aunt Betty, if you are reading this, put it down or risk being totally scandalized! Hee, hee, hee.

I closed the book. Took a breath. Opened it again randomly.

I ran into him at the A&P. We smiled at each other and pretended to be chatting casually, but he was totally undressing me with his eyes again. I took off those jean shorts of his with my baby blues. I'll take them off for real soon!

OMG. I flipped again. And this time the book opened to a photo of a guy sleeping on his stomach naked. I put a hand over my mouth. My mother was a slut! And kind of a funny one.

"Hey, what are you reading?" I flinched and looked up to see Zack, dripping wet, a beach towel slung low around his hips.

"Poetry," I said, and slammed the book shut. If Zack was here, then maybe Jules was, too. I squinted and looked across the beach. Was she on her way down? My chest contracted, pulled tight as if by an invisible corset.

"Are you okay?" he asked.

"Yeah," I said, shoving the book into my bag and grabbing a bottle of water. It took a couple of tries for my nervous fingers to unscrew the cap. "Who are you with?"

"No one," he said, smiling at me with bemusement.

"You're alone?"

"Yup," he said. I exhaled and guzzled some water. "That must have been some poetry." He ran his hand over his face, flicked away some water. "You were pretty into it. And now you're . . . kind of a mess."

"Well, Emily Dickinson is an American genius," I said.

"Guess so," he said, and laughed. I laughed, too. Partially out of relief that Jules wasn't here, and partially because I knew I'd sounded so serious about Emily Dickinson.

"I'm going to have to see if they have another copy at the library," he said. Then he took off his towel and wiped down the rest of his body, which I had to admit, was really nice. Soccer player nice. "Are you looking at my nipples?"

"What? Zack. No. So, what are you doing here?"

He opened his arms in a gesture like, *What does it look like I'm doing?*

"I just felt like going for a dip. I like this beach. It's quiet and I know I won't run into anyone."

"Except me," I said.

"I don't mind that," he said, and smiled. "That's a good thing." I jammed my heels in the sand, biting my smile. "What are you doing on Saturday?"

"What's Saturday?"

"Fourth of July?"

"Oh, I don't know," I said. Shit. I kept trying to forget about it. It loomed. A national holiday I was going to have to spend alone. I'd overheard Liz saying something about a party. Maybe I could tag along. "I might be going to a party on a beach. Nober . . . Nobersomething."

"Nobadeer?" His eyebrows rose. I nodded. "Careful. Those things can be kind of crazy. And the police are going to be everywhere this year."

"Police? Well, I'm not sure yet." I buried my feet, patted the sand over them. "What are you doing?"

"Did you meet Fitzy?" he asked. I nodded, shading my eyes with my hand as I looked up at him. "He's having a little party on his dad's boat. That's where Jules and Parker and everyone is going."

"That's cool," I said, trying to sound neutral. I wondered what Jules had told him about the fight, but didn't want to ask. It would've been almost worse if she hadn't said anything at all. It occurred to me that Jules had erased me from her life, that she wasn't thinking of me, that she had so much going on with Parker that she hadn't noticed my absence. That she hadn't actually been affected by it.

"Seems boring to me. I don't know if it's my scene." He looked out at the ocean. "Are you going to go in?"

"I don't know," I said, and stood up. I dusted some sand off my butt, then lifted my arms out to the side, feeling the air. "I'm not quite hot enough."

"Oh, you're hot enough." It took a second for it to sink in. He was smiling in this goofy, adorable way. I opened my mouth, but he spoke first. "I'll race you to that rock out there." I followed his gaze to the top of a rock not too far out.

"Okay." Zack drew a line in the sand with his toe and we struck runner's poses. "On your mark, get set, go!"

We were both grinning like idiots as we took off, though it was clear by the time we hit the water that Zack was going to win. Bikinis aren't exactly made for racing.

Nineteen

"SHANE AND I GOT IN A MASSIVE FIGHT LAST NIGHT ABOUT the Fourth of July," Liz said the next day as we made the beds. "He wants to go do a little backyard barbecue with just a couple of mates, and I want to go to the party on Nobadeer." I'd been asking her about Fourth of July all morning, hoping for an invitation, and she hadn't seemed to pick up on it. "But I really don't mind the fighting all that much because the makeup sex is fabulous."

"That's awesome," I said, as if I had a clue. The truth was that I wasn't exactly experienced. I'd only been to third base once with Greg Goldberg last fall, after we'd dated for three whole months. I hated to admit it, but I hadn't actually felt anything that great. I thought that when a boy touched you it would feel amazing, but instead it was like he was programming his DVR with my vagina. I wondered if something was wrong with me. I could do this to myself, I'd thought, and not in *that* kind of a way, not in a *touching myself* kind of way. I just wasn't into that, either, even though we'd been told in seventh grade by Mrs. Levander, the school's sixty-nine-year-old nurse and self-declared earth mama, that there was *nothing wrong with that*. That we wouldn't go cross-eyed or blind if we touched our "area," no matter what anyone told us.

That's what they told me," she'd said, shaking her head. "And I have twenty-twenty vision. Believe you me, I should be blind as a bat!" She threw her head back in a laugh. All of us were biting our cheeks or doodling in our notebooks with a kind of glazed-over madness.

"Ooookay," she'd said after realizing she was having a moment entirely separate from the rest of us. "Let's see what difficult questions we have today." She drew a question from the "difficult questions" box. It was a shoe box covered with shiny green wrapping paper where we were supposed to put anonymous, sex-related questions.

Mrs. Levander's eyebrows rose and she made an O with her lips. "Here's an interesting one. 'What does horny mean?' Anyone want to share?" We couldn't take it, we all laughed. I laughed hardest, of course, because it was my question.

I was beginning to think that Liz and Mrs. Levander would really get along by the way Liz was going on and on in graphic detail.

"This is the best sex of my life," Liz said as she unfolded

a fresh duvet cover. We had to work as a team to fit the duvet back inside it. Because I was smaller, I was deemed the intrepid explorer, sent inside the cover with the corners of the duvet in hand. "It's cinematic. It's Technicolor. Do you know what I mean?" I thought that British people were all stuck up and only liked to talk about tea and crumpets and the queen.

"Well, I wouldn't exactly know," I said from inside the duvet.

"Wait a second," Liz said. "Are you a virgin?" I froze, sensing this wasn't cool in her book. Liz burst out laughing. "You are! You're a virgin." I felt her grab the corners of the duvet, and I crawled out, my cheeks on fire.

"There's got to be an easier way to do this," I said, patting down my staticky hair. Liz stood on the bed and shook out the duvet in place. I smoothed it out and zipped the bottom.

"Cricket's a virgin," she sang as she jumped on the bed. "I knew it. That explains everything."

"Oh my god, Gavin is like, wandering the halls!" I said.

"You're getting a bit old. How old are you?"

"I'll be eighteen in August."

"Eighteen!"

"That's normal," I said. "It's like, perfect, for a girl."

"Americans." She stepped off the bed with narrowed eyes. "People think British people are prudes, but the truth is that Americans are. And why should it be any different for girls?"

I didn't know why it was different for girls. It shouldn't be, but it was. I hated it when people pretended otherwise.

"We're going to have to fix this by your birthday," Liz said. "I'm going to make it my mission."

"That's okay," I said. Liz ignored me, stuffing a pillow into its case.

"Fourth of July, you'll come with me." At least I'd gotten an invitation out of this whole ordeal. "I'll tell Shane, and we'll get his friends in a lineup. You choose."

"No, no, no, no."

"I'm thinking Colin. His willy is just the right size. Not too big and not too small. It's perfect for Goldilocks!"

"No, no, no, no." God, I regretted this conversation. What I wouldn't give to take it back. "The thing is, and this is actually really important to me, I want to be in love."

"Don't be ridiculous," Liz said, laughing. "You can't expect to fall in love by August."

"Well, I want to at least really like him."

"Do you have any candidates?"

"There was one guy, but"—I shook my head—"that's over."

"Oh! What about that writer fellow?" She wiggled her eyebrows. "An older man knows how to please a woman."

"Gross!" I said, shaking a pillow into its case. "He's married with a pregnant wife."

"You girls almost done in here?" Gavin stepped into the room with a pile of fresh towels. "Sometimes I think Bernadette is right about you two."

"You aren't going to believe what I just learned," Liz said, all lit up.

"Liz." My voice was low. "Don't you dare!"

"Cricket is an eighteen-year-old—" I smooshed the pillow in her face.

"I don't want to know," Gavin said, dropping the towels on the bed and leaving. "And change that pillowcase."

Twenty

"YOU'RE THE BEST," GEORGE SAID, LOWERING THE NOISE-canceling headphones from his ears as I put a six-pack of Coke Zero, peanut butter pretzels, and turkey jerky on his desk—the three items he claimed gave him special writing powers. He was sitting in an old office chair that Gavin had found in the basement, behind his makeshift desk, which was really a card table, on which sat his digital voice recorder, laptop, a few files, four notebooks, and the laser printer his wife had shipped and I'd set up yesterday. The windows were all the way up, the door was propped open, and his good foot was in a bowl of ice water. But it was sweating weather inside the annex. George had started calling it the hot box.

"Crack me open one of those sweet, sweet man-sodas," he said, rubbing his hands together. I laughed, opened a

Coke Zero, and handed it to him. He tipped his head back, guzzled half the can, and then held it up with a big smile like he was in a commercial. "Like a refreshing mountain stream."

"Wait, there's more," I said, and unveiled my big prize: a fan I'd found at the Nantucket Hospital Thrift Shop. It only had one speed, and the blade tips were covered with a layer of dust, but it would take the edge off.

"What? What? Am I hallucinating?" George said as I propped it on his dresser and plugged it in. "I was told there wasn't a single fan or air conditioner for sale on this godforsaken island. The guy at the hardware store laughed in my face when I asked if he had any."

"I found it at the thrift store," I said, getting on my knees to plug it into the circuit breaker. "It was way in the back, behind a framed poster of a whale they were trying to sell for four hundred dollars."

"You're resourceful and intrepid, and I like it," George said, pulling out his wallet and handing me a twenty-dollar bill.

"It was only five dollars," I said, dusting my hands off on my shorts.

"Keep the change," he said.

"Are you sure?" I said, holding the crisp bill. "It doesn't oscillate."

"I like my warm stale air blowing in a steady stream right on my face."

"Okay." I folded the twenty and tucked it in my back

pocket, then handed him a manila envelope from my bag. "And here are the pictures." I'd gone to the Nantucket Yacht Club to pick up some old photographs of Boaty from when he was in his twenties and just married. There was one of him at a clambake, shaking hands and smiling thoughtfully, a golden afternoon glow on his serious face. The people around him gazed at him adoringly. One guy had his hand on his shoulder and was looking at him like he was his favorite son. Boaty definitely had what Edwina MacIntosh would call "star quality."

"He was so popular," I said.

"With most people, yes. But not everyone was a fan. Some people hated him."

"Like who?" I asked. "I mean, besides Republicans." And my mother, I thought.

He pointed to the guy with his hand on his shoulder. "That guy. Tom Frost. Boaty met him out here on Nantucket. Frost was the first person to hire him. He took him under his wing in the state Senate, showed him the ropes, treated him like a son. Tom Frost was gearing up to make a run for Congress. Boaty decided he wanted to do the same. And after five years of friendship, Boaty planted a story about him in the press."

"Oh my god," I said. "What was it?"

"An affair with the nanny."

"Sounds like a soap opera."

"It ruined Tom Frost, and Boaty got elected."

"That's terrible," I said.

"Well, technically, Boaty didn't plant the story. 'His people' did, but one of those 'people' told me Boaty signed off on it," George said. "Some of that is just par for the course in politics, but not generally with people you know and love. Boaty had spent Christmases with the guy."

"Why'd he do it?" I said.

"To win."

I thought that the feeling of wanting to be popular went away after high school. Our parents and teachers were always telling us that "winning" and "being cool" didn't matter. What mattered, they said, was being a good, happy person who did the right thing. Edwina McIntosh gave the same speech every year, in which she took a poem about a man in the mirror and changed the words to be about a girl in the mirror. "The only person who needs to think you're cool," Edwina MacIntosh said, "is the girl in the mirror. The approval you need is your own." So, were they all lying, not telling the truth about what it was really like to be an adult?

"On the other hand," George said as he cracked open another Coke Zero, "Boaty made huge strides in health care reform, and Tom Frost was an old fart. It's all very complicated, which is why it will make a good book, which is why I need to get writing."

"Well, do you need anything else?" I asked.

"I think that's it for today. I'm good to go," George said. "I just need to crank out another, oh, twenty pages, and I'll be right on schedule."

"Good luck with that, and don't forget to drink some water in between your man sodas."

"You're a good influence, Thompson," he said, and I was out the door—where it was a whole five degrees cooler—thinking of the beach, a yellow butterfly of anticipation circling my chest, half hoping, half dreading, that I'd see Zack again.

As I walked back to the beach, I thought about the other day when I'd run into Zack. We stayed in the water for what felt like hours, just talking and swimming around, following the warm patches, until our fingers and toes were puckering. I knew Jules wouldn't like me hanging out with him. And I know it had only been a week of feeling so alone in the world, but a week is actually a long time to feel like that.

I honestly tried to walk away from the Zack situation twice, but the first time he'd made me laugh, pretending to rescue me when a tiny wave pathetically knocked me on my ass, and the second time, right when I'd gotten too cold and come to my senses, he promised me half of his Something Natural sandwich if I stayed. It was turkey with cranberry and avocado. "On sourdough," he added. My teeth were chattering, partially because of the cold and also out of fear of what Jules would say when she found out we'd spent a whole day together.

He looked up. "If the sun comes out in the next five seconds, you have to stay." For some reason, I acted like this was a real rule.

"Five, four, three." We started counting, and by "two" I was squinting into bright sunshine, floating on my back, once again under its spell. We stayed until he had to go to work at Gigi's, the restaurant where he was a busboy. We shared my towel because his was sandy. And then we shared his sandwich.

When I arrived at Steps, I scanned the beach looking for him. He wasn't there. I reminded myself that that was a good thing.

Twenty-one

Zack: Happy 4th!

Me: You too.

Zack: Where r u?

Me: I don't know!!! Not Nobadeer. Some other beach. Cops
at Nobadeer.

Zack: 40th Pole?

Me: Let me ask.

Me: Tom Nevers.

Zack: K. Want me to come get u?

Me: OMG. Yes pls.

Zack: See you in 20. Meet me at shuttle stop.

"I think I'm going to leave," I said to Liz, who was
downing her fourth beer in less than an hour. My first beer

was still almost full and had grown warm in my hand. We hadn't even tried to go to Nobadeer, because the cops had found out about that one. This was supposedly the secret, small, underground one. And yet, it was the biggest party I'd ever been to, even though Shane said it was lame compared to 2010, where there were almost three thousand partiers.

I couldn't tell how many were here now, but there were at least a hundred Jeeps parked on the beach, all of them filled with people in their bathing suits, all of the people getting shitfaced, blasting loud music, and peeing in plain sight. *Shit*, I thought when I accidentally turned my head and saw a gross, chinless guy whip it out to take a leak in the dunes.

"But you can't leave yet," Liz said. "I haven't introduced you to Colin! Where is that wanker? He said he'd be here by now." She checked her phone for messages. "You shouldn't go yet. You should stay and experience this bacchanalia. This is just the type of atmosphere you need to loosen you up—literally!" She laughed.

"Ha-ha," I said. Nearby, a guy in stars-and-stripes swimming trunks threw up in the dunes, and he looked like a real adult, with a bald spot and everything. He wiped strings of vomit from his mouth with the back of his hand. "I really have to go, Liz."

"Suit yourself," she said under her breath. "But you need to relax if you ever want to—" She made a circle with one hand and drove her index finger through it with the other.

"That's gross," I said.

"Wimp," she said as I walked away.

"Tart," I called back, laughing.

"I take that as a compliment!"

I hadn't seen Zack since our meeting at Steps. I closed my eyes as I waited for him at the shuttle stop, remembering how good it had felt to float around with him in the shallow water, how funny it was when he pretended to be the life-guard, how strong he was when he picked me up and then flipped me in the deeper water, how it had finally, finally started to feel like summer.

When I saw Zack coming toward me in the land yacht, I felt a happy relief at feeling known, recognized, under-stood, familiar, the same feeling I used to get at the sight of Jules in the cafeteria when we hadn't seen each other all morning. He pulled up next to me, pretended that he didn't know me, and asked me if I needed a ride. He wasn't wear-ing a shirt. The feeling changed. It transitioned, spinning into a warm glow that spread up to my cheeks and to the last knob of my spine. I tipped back on my heels. Maybe the quarter of a beer I'd had in the sun had been too much. My heart picked up, but my pulse slowed down. Then the feel-ing changed again, into something brighter, something alive and jumping, like a sparkler in my chest, when I slid into the front seat next to him and our thighs touched.

What is wrong with me? I wondered as the engine hummed under the hot vinyl seat. I flipped down the sun visor to see if my cheeks were as red as they felt. They were. And my eyes and lips were shining. Was I coming down with something? It didn't feel like it. This was different. What was this feeling anyway? This need to move? This need to get a little more air, cross my legs, squeeze something? Had someone put something in my beer?

"You okay?" Zack asked, touching my knee. I jumped a little.

"Yeah," I said, shifting in my seat as we took off. "I'm just a little . . ." I was searching for the right word when an image came to me. Mrs. Levander holding the folded-up piece of paper that I'd dropped in the Difficult Questions box. My eyes went wide. Here, years later in the Claytons' land yacht, was the answer to my question. I reached for a bottle of water in the cup holder, opened it, and downed the three swallows that were left. "Thirsty," I said. "I'm really thirsty."

"I guess so. What's wrong?" he asked.

"Nothing," I said, sliding away from him. I wasn't supposed to be feeling this way about Zack. "Um, can we stop somewhere for water?"

"Sure," he said, and turned up the radio.

A few miles down the road, we spotted a water fountain along the bike path, and Zack pulled over. I hopped out and filled the water bottle up, trying to remember if Mrs. Levander had given us any information on how long this feeling lasted and what might make it pass. Besides the obvious.

"Hey, do you feel anything?" Zack asked.

"What do you mean?" I asked.

"There are a bunch of kids who say that there's a ghost here." I noticed a white cross, the kind they put up when someone gets killed on the road. "And they say if you drive by at night, you suddenly get cold when you hit this spot. I guess there was a girl who was killed out here in the '70s or something."

"What is it with Nantucket and ghosts?" I asked.

"There's just a lot of ghosts here," he said. I gave him a look of doubt. "You don't believe in ghosts?"

"Do you?"

"I think there's something out there, I guess."

"Do you think that your mom's a ghost?" Zack took a deep breath, and for a second I wondered if I'd just asked the worst question in the world.

"You mean, do I think she's hanging around, lifting up the chair in that hotel room? Or juggling candlesticks in our dining room?" I laughed. I couldn't help it. He smiled, and I could tell he was imagining something. "Like, when the lights go out at Bloomingdale's, she's thumbing through the racks, making herself a cappuccino in the home goods department?"

"Or lifting almond croissants off the trays at Seven Stars Bakery?" I asked.

"Taking the Mini Cooper for a spin?"

"So it looks like it's driving itself?"

"Really fast, right in the middle of the street?" We both laughed. Nina was a terrible driver. She thought stop signs were suggestions, but would stop in the intersection, surrendering her right of way, confusing everyone involved. Zack crossed his arms and shook his head. "No, Mom's not a ghost." His smile faded and he was quiet, staring at a patch of grass, his eyes still and brimming, like a water glass filled to the very top.

"But she's here," I said, focusing on my own patch of grass. "I feel it."

"Me too," he said, and took several deep breaths. The sun was low. A few distant fireworks went off. The insects were singing. Zack took my hand, weaving his fingers with mine. "Come on, I want to show you something."

Twenty-two

ZACK HELD THE LITTLE ROWBOAT CLOSE TO THE DOCK, AND I stepped in. He handed me the canvas bag with the champagne and plastic cups he'd taken from 4 Darling Street. "Dad hates champagne, and Jules forgot all about it. So that whole case of Dom Perignon in the pantry is for me."

"What's Dom Perignon?" I asked, lowering the bag into the stern.

"The good stuff," he said, untying the line.

"Won't your dad notice it's gone?"

"I don't think he'd notice if the fridge was gone and a white tiger sat in its place," he said, and stepped in. I couldn't help but picture the bizarre image. He slipped the oarlocks into place, slid in the oars, and rowed us into the harbor with long, even strokes.

"Hey, you said *champagne*. Does this mean you've gotten over the French girl?"

"Maybe," he said, smiling. I leaned back, elbows on the edge, and looked up. The sun had set, but it wasn't dark yet. The sky was purple. Above us, a half-moon tipped. We rowed past the homes that lined the harbor; past the squares of lighted interiors; past people sitting on verandas, drinking and laughing. Voices floated out to us on waves, turned to wisps, drifted away. The oars slapped the dark water, slid under and emerged, tilted and weeping as they skimmed the surface. I dropped an arm, let my fingers trace the water. I felt like I could've stayed in the back of that boat all summer and been happy.

"So, you see that McMansion with all the lights on?" Zack asked, taking both oars in one hand as he turned and pointed to a house on a distant cliff.

"Yeah." It was a huge place with a hundred windows.

"Okay, now, you see the one next to it, with only one light on? That's where we're headed. It's the best spot to see the fireworks." He turned to face me again, rowing with effortless strength and confidence. Maybe this was where he got his soccer-player body. The thought made me shiver.

"Here," he said, taking off his sweatshirt and tossing it to me.

"I thought you had a fungus," I teased.

"I told you, it cleared up," he said, splashing me a little with the oar. I wiped up the drops on my leg with the sweatshirt and put it on. It smelled like the beach.

Farther out were some yachts. On one of them, there were at least thirty people, all dressed up like they were set to sail to the Academy Awards. A tall, thin woman with long red hair in a short, sparkling gold dress talked to two men in tuxedos. I wondered if that was Jay's mom. It was hard to tell, but she had the same model-like silhouette. Zack waved. One of the tuxedoed men waved back.

"Looking for Bella Figura?" the man asked.

"Excuse me?" asked Zack.

"Bella Figura!" the man said.

"Bella what?" Zack asked, rowing us closer to the yacht. Now the woman in gold was looking at us. I felt certain she was Jay's mother. Oh god. Had Jay told her what I'd said about his brother?

"Aren't you the one we sent to bring us more wine?"

"No," Zack said. He handed me the oars and stood up, hands on his hips.

"Oh my god," I said under my breath. I hid my face in his sweatshirt.

"On my yacht"—he unfurled his arm, his forehead crinkling as he named the little boat—"*La Principessa*, we only drink Dom Perignon!" Zack said. "Isn't that right, Principessa?"

"Uh . . . yes?" I said quietly. I was afraid to look at the reactions of the fancy party people. Especially Mrs. Logan.

Zack sat down, took the oars, and rowed on. "Hey, why were you hiding?"

"Wasn't that Mrs. Logan?"

"Was it?" He shrugged. "So?"

"So? We know her. And who knows who those people are. Maybe they're important."

"You care too much what other people think."

"Well, it matters."

"No it doesn't," he said, maintaining eye contact. "Anyway, she was laughing."

"Hey, can I row?" I asked, anxious to change the subject and get back the mood of five minutes ago.

"Sure." The boat rocked as we switched spots. "Keep your eye on that buoy." My strokes were choppy and uneven. "So, you don't need to go so deep in the water. Just go right beneath the surface. And you want to keep the oar pretty flat." I did what he said. "Okay, that's better. The tide's coming in. It will be easier on the way back." He lay back, put his feet up. "I kind of like this whole girl-in-charge thing."

"We're not going to get lost at sea, are we?" I asked.

"Not unless you want to." Zack smiled. There was the feeling again. The warmth. The fluttering. The heart buzz. I focused on rowing. A few fireworks shot off from a distant beach. Little gold ones.

"So, where's your family?" he asked.

"Providence. What do you mean?"

"Most people spend holidays with their family."

"Fourth of July isn't exactly Christmas."

"You're a little heavy on that left oar; we're veering." I looked over my shoulder and then used the right oar to get us back on track. "You were at our house on Christmas, too."

"Christmas night, not Christmas morning."

"You were there by two o'clock."

"Whatever." Neither of us spoke for a minute. I was doing the choppy thing with the oars again. I took a deep breath, tried to get them at that perfect angle. "Well, your family is so fun. And my mom, it's like she *wants* to be sad all the time. I'm like, 'Go out, Mom. Please, make some friends. You're not eighty years old,' you know? It's like she's forgotten how to be happy."

"Did she ever know how?" he asked.

"Yes," I said, thinking about when we used to go to Newport together, about sitting on her bed when I was little and watching her put on her makeup. I paused. My hands were starting to hurt. And where had these words come from? I'd never said them aloud before. It was like I was stirring them up from the ocean.

"Want to switch?" Zack asked.

"Not yet."

"Where's your dad? Did he move?"

"He's still in Providence," I said. "He's just really busy. With his new family." Zack raised an eyebrow. There was a weird lump in my throat. I pushed it down, rowed on, my eyes fixed on the buoy. "Well, his wife has this son. She adopted him from an orphanage in the Ukraine when he was three years old. She basically rescued him, which was a pretty incredible thing. She didn't have a husband or anything when she went over there and got him. And he's actually a really cute little boy.

"But I guess he wasn't held as a baby, and he didn't get the proper nutrition, so he has all these problems. Like, every night, he wakes up screaming. He has these nightmares and wets the bed and stays up all night just rocking, and Dad and Polly stay up with him, and then everyone's exhausted the next day. I know he can't help it, and I know Polly and my dad are basically heroes, but sometimes I don't know." I shook my head. "Never mind. Anyway, it doesn't matter, because I'm almost eighteen."

"So?" Zack asked. The lump rose. I swallowed, sending it back to my gut.

"So, I'll be in college soon. Gone." The sky was blacker now, the moon whiter. Silver fireworks shot into the sky. "Look, they're starting," I said.

"Nice," Zack said, looking up for a second before turning his attention back to me. "But he's still your dad, and it sounds like these people make it impossible for you to spend time with him. That must be hard."

"No, I'm glad he has a life. I wish my mom would get one. Once, like, three years ago, when I started to realize that she wasn't getting out at all, I actually signed her up for an online dating site for divorced people. It was called Second Glances." I hadn't told anyone about this, not even Jules.

Zack laughed. "How'd that turn out?"

"It started out good," I said. "I made her a great profile, and I put up this old video I had of her singing 'My

Girl' to me on my birthday. You know that song by the Temptations? She looked so pretty in that video, and she has such a good voice. I knew if guys saw it they'd want to meet her."

"Did it work?"

"Oh my god, yes. So many guys were 'glancing' at her—that's what they call it on the site when someone checks out your profile. And I was 'glancing' back as her, just to keep them interested until I could get her into it. But every time I brought up online dating she was like, 'No way.' And then we were at Whole Foods and we ran into one of the guys. And he started to talk to her and she was like, 'I don't know you.' And he was like, 'Yes, you do. We've been glancing for two weeks now.' He pulled up her profile and played the video right there by the bananas."

"Oh shit," Zack said, laughing. "She must've been so pissed."

"She was. I got in so much trouble. And it was really expensive. It turned out I'd signed her up for a two-year nonrefundable membership. She made me pay for it with my babysitting money." Zack laughed harder. So did I. "Twenty bucks a month."

"When did you finally stop paying for it?" he asked.

"Actually, I renewed the membership last year," I said. "But I didn't tell her."

"What? Why?"

"Well, there's this one music teacher in Newton. He's not the best-looking guy in the world—he's kinda bald and he has a big nose—but he plays the guitar and the piano, and he just seems nice. I keep thinking that if she'd just give him a chance . . ."

"Or a glance," Zack said.

"Yeah," I said, laughing. "Exactly. If she just gave him a glance, she might actually be happy." But when I thought of her telling me over and over again that she wasn't interested in dating, my smile got swallowed up by the sea.

"Let's switch places," Zack said. "You've been rowing a while." The boat rocked again as we switched places. The fireworks were picking up. An umbrella of red light opened above us. There was the faint smell of something burning. A blue umbrella followed with a boom, turning to silver rain. "Oh my god, it's so beautiful."

"And we're almost there," Zack said.

I looked at the house. It was so close now. I hadn't realized how far I'd rowed. It looked spooky, leaning to the left, like one strong wind would blow it over. There was a steep hill that went from the back door to a perfect little horseshoe-shaped beach, a rickety staircase between them. I felt the boat scratch against the pebbly bottom.

"Come on." Zack took the bag with the champagne and jumped out of the boat and pulled it almost all the way to shore.

"Is this public?" I asked as I took off my flats and hopped out. The water was ankle-deep and surprisingly warm.

"No," he said, dragging the boat up onto the beach. "But

I've always thought this little beach would be the best spot to see the fireworks."

"So, this is someone's private land?"

"Yeah, but she won't bother us. She's just some super old lady who barely comes out of her house. She's a famous miser and she has the best view on the island. She should want to share it."

"So, are we like, trespassing?"

"Yes, but whose land really is it?"

"Ah, hers?"

Zack spread out a blanket, secured it with four rocks. "Wrong. It belongs to the children of tomorrow. And they don't mind that we're here. Now, let's open that bub!"

"Who's down there?" said an old voice.

"Oh shit," Zack said, our eyes locking.

"Who's on my property?" said the voice.

"Uh, just a couple of friendly youths," Zack said, shoving the blanket into the bag. I took off my shoes again and stuck them in as well.

"We're really sorry," I said. We ran to the shore and pushed the boat into the water. Above us the sky was in gold and silver hysterics. The old lady searched for us with a high-powered flashlight.

"You're trespassing and it's against the law!" She made it halfway down the stairs, shining the light right on us. For a super old lady, she sure was quick. The boat scraped the sand until it was deep enough to float. The bottom of my shorts were now soaked. Zack hoisted me by the waist and I hopped in. He followed, the boat wobbling. I scrambled to the seat in the stern, pulling my wet shorts away from my body. Zack bit his lip as he fumbled with the oarlocks. He lifted an oar while I guided it into place. Zack rowed us quickly away, out to sea, both of us cracking up.

"Youths?" I asked.

"It's what we are," he said, and then shouted, "Happy Fourth of July!" The old lady said something in response, but we couldn't understand. Above us the fireworks were in a riot. Little rockets of light shot upward and popped open, full of sequins.

"Look," I said as the explosions quick-fired, getting bigger and more dramatic. "The grand finale."

"The Fourth of July, aboard *La Principessa!*" Zack added in an Italian accent.

"Oh! Champagne!" I said, and clapped my hands.

"Yeah, get it."

I unwrapped the gold paper and tried to pull off the wire cage over the top of the bottle, but couldn't figure it out.

"Here," Zack handed me the oars. His knees were outside mine. Our legs touched, his knees squeezing mine. He untwisted the wire and popped the bottle. The cork flew into the water, and champagne spilled over the top of his fingers and all over my lap.

"Sorry," he said, and tried to wipe it off with the bottom of his T-shirt. We were both laughing. The bubbles were cool and tingly on my thighs.

"I'm totally soaked!" I looked up; he was so close. Our cheeks touched.

"You are just. . . ." he said into my ear. My eyes closed, eyelashes like matches striking my cheeks, setting them on fire. He kissed me, long and sweet, on the mouth.

"Just what?" I asked when I came up for air, stunned, heart stomping like a parade, wrists aching from holding the oars.

He seemed unable to finish his sentence with words. He pulled the wet oars inside the boat, wrapped his arms around me, and kissed me again. He gripped my waist. His fingers slipped down the back of my shorts.

"She'll kill me," I said, pulling away. "Literally."

"She'll kill me twice," he said, and pulled me closer.

"That's impossible," I said.

"Not if I turned into a zombie."

"Zack." I removed his hands and placed them on his own knees. I put my hands behind my back and took three deep breaths. "It can't happen again."

"Okay," he said. A warm wind twisted my hair. The boat drifted, and his hands did too, back to my legs, up my arms and neck. We kissed. We drifted and kissed and drifted and kissed as the sky flashed and clapped and bloomed and broke.

Twenty-three

"AW, BLESS, SOMEONE'S BEEN SNOGGING," LIZ SAID THE next morning when I walked into the kitchen, which was warm and fragrant from the baking muffins. Gingerbread, I guessed. Liz leaned against the counter, one blue-nail-polished hand on her mama-sized hip, and the other wrapped around her coffee cup. Her curls looked wild, backlit by the rising sun that shone through the sliding glass door.

"What are you talking about?" I asked innocently, and tied one of the new Cranberry Inn aprons that Gavin's chiropractor girlfriend had stenciled for us and were now part of our breakfast uniform. It was no use. There was a permanent blush on my face. I could feel it.

"Oh, it doesn't exactly take a detective, now, does it? Your lips are practically bruised—" I put a hand to my mouth. "Fess up, Goldilocks!" She pointed a croissant at me like a pistol.

"No," I said, pouring myself coffee. I tried to stop smiling, but the corners of my mouth would not be deterred, even with only four hours of sleep. I was a smiling fool. "I've got nothing to say." I added cream and sugar, and stirred.

"There's no use denying it. You look like you've just lifted the crown jewels. Besides, I saw you on the porch last night." My eyes popped wide. She smiled at me defiantly, rubbing her hands together. "But I could only make out that it was you. I couldn't see the guy. So, was it the writer? Did he lure you to the annex with sweets?"

"No!"

"Well, don't be so coy. Who is he? And more importantly, is he a contender for the big bang?"

"No," I said. "Definitely not." Zack and I had sworn that these kissing attacks wouldn't happen again, that it was probably best if we didn't see each other for at least a week in hopes that our newfound, red-hot attraction would fade. Also, making out with Zack was one thing, but sleeping with him? Forget it. Jules wouldn't ever speak to me again. Not to mention that it was understood that she would lose her virginity first, since she'd come so close last year. It was an unspoken pact.

"Why? What's the secret?" Liz's voice dropped low, her eyebrows arching. "Was it . . . Gavin?"

"Oh my god, Liz. Don't be disgusting!"

"Well, you're acting like it's so scandalous. What am I to think?"

"Okay," I said, folding under the charm of her accent. "It's this guy I know from home. But it's kind of . . . bad."

"All the better, my dear," Liz said, taking the industrial block of butter from the fridge and pulling the special butter knife from the drawer—the one that sliced the butter into pats with a wavy design.

"He's my friend's younger brother." I couldn't believe I was telling her this after the way she'd reacted when I'd confessed my virginity. But I wanted to tell someone so badly, and Liz was pretty much my only option.

"How young?"

"Sixteen."

"Oh, well, what's wrong with that?"

I looked at the timer on the microwave. Gavin would be here in three minutes to take the muffins out of the oven. He was kind of a control freak about his muffins.

"Are you kidding? A *younger* brother? It's like the worst thing a friend can do."

"Don't be ridiculous. People get together with friends' brothers all the time. It's totally natural. Unless your friend has some kind of sick fascination with him. In which case, I suggest you stay far away, lest they try to pull you into their web of perversion."

"It's nothing like that," I said. "I just know she's going to hate me for it. We had this fight." I took the chilled ramekins from the fridge, and Liz placed a fat, wavy pat of butter in each one.

"There's nothing worse than fighting with a friend," she said, her voice soft. "You can be awful to your mum or sister, but they're stuck with you, aren't they? But a friend . . . a friend can disappear. Have you talked since your fight?"

"She won't talk to me," I said. "And I came to Nantucket to spend the summer with her. She told me I was bothering her."

"Well, she doesn't sound like a very good friend," Liz said, putting down the knife and facing me. "That's a terrible thing to say." The protective tone of her voice and the sympathetic tilt of her head felt like a cool balm on the place inside where Jules's words had landed and burned.

"Well, the thing is that her mom—"

"I won't hear it." Liz cut me off. "I don't like the sounds of her, and I say what she doesn't know can't hurt her. I like seeing you all aglow. Suits you, actually."

The oven timer went off, Gavin breezed into the kitchen in his 2004 IYENGAR YOGA RETREAT T-shirt, lifted the muffins from the oven, switched on the singer-songwriter breakfast playlist, and put on the kettle for his second cup of green tea. And despite the tectonic plates that had shifted last night, my morning began just like any other.

Twenty-four

IT WAS ALREADY A ROUGH DAY AT TEN O'CLOCK, AND IT WAS only going to get rougher. Except for the older Australian couple, all the visitors who were here for the Fourth of July weekend were headed home today; all the rooms were turnovers and required bathroom scrubbings, vacuuming, fresh towels and sheets, and, of course, the dreaded duvet covers.

And they'd all decided to eat breakfast at the same time. The backyard, the porch, and even the big wooden table in the kitchen were packed. Liz and I were sweating as we cleared dishes, refreshed coffees, and refilled butters and jams. Gavin was washing the glasses by hand in the sink—no time to run the dishwasher.

"Excuse me," said a sunburned woman, holding a writhing toddler. "How do I get a cab to the airport?"

"We've got cards on the reception desk," Gavin said. "Pat's Cabs. Pat's the best. Normally I'd call for you, but I'm . . . in up to my elbows." He laughed because he literally had suds up his arms. Not amused, the woman disappeared into the living room.

I was about to show her where the cards were before I headed outside with the coffees when someone tapped me on the shoulder. I turned, expecting Liz, but instead found a tall middle-aged guy in Nantucket Reds grinning at me like I was his favorite movie star.

"If you aren't Kate Campbell's daughter, then my name is mud," he said, leaning forward, anticipating my reaction.

"I am her daughter," I said.

"Paul Morgan," he said, putting out his hand to shake mine. But I just shrugged, nodding toward my full hands. He squeezed my shoulder instead. "I knew it, I knew it." He rocked back and forth on his boat shoes, shaking his head. "We worked at the Nantucket Beach Club together years ago. I saw you standing across the room and I felt like it was twenty-five years ago. You look just like her."

"Are you staying here?" I asked.

"No, I just stopped by for one of Gavin's muffins."

"Hate to interrupt, but I need these," Liz said, taking the coffees from my hands and glaring at me. "We're very busy, in case you didn't notice."

Liz was invisible to Paul Morgan. He kept talking. "Is she still a firecracker? She is, isn't she?"

"She's a teacher." I didn't want to lie, and I also didn't

want to tell him that she more closely resembled a wet sock.

"I bet she's a great one," he said. "She was the prettiest, most vivacious girl on the island that summer. Now, don't look so shocked; us old people were young once, too." I studied his face. I was having a crazy urge to go check the diary and look at that picture again.

"Cricket," Liz called. I turned to see her gesturing at a table full of dirty plates and a family hovering nearby, wanting to sit down.

"It was nice to meet you," I said. "I've got to get back to work."

"Give your mother my best, won't you?" He reached into his pocket, pulled out his wallet, wrote something on a business card and handed it to me: *Paul T. Morgan, Esquire.* "That's my cell phone number. If you need anything while you're on Nantucket, let me know."

"Thanks." I slipped his card into the back pocket of my shorts and walked outside, where I made an absentminded, totally unhelpful loop around the yard, imagining my mother's firecracker self captured and held hostage somewhere on Nantucket, waiting to be shot into the sky.

As soon as we were done cleaning, I flopped on my bed and opened the Emily Dickinson diary. I studied the picture, but it was pointless. You couldn't see the guy's face.

I read the next entry, written around a poem about the

"majesty of death." Obviously, Mom wasn't too influenced by Emily Dickinson.

> Dear Emily,
> Alarm! Alarm! Call 9-1-1. It's a LOVE EMERGENCY! On second thought, call the fire department because I am hot to trot! Lover Boy and I talked for almost a half hour today. He stopped to chat with me at the reception desk for his whole break.

Hot to trot? Love emergency? Who was this person?

> Emily, from his ice-blue eyes to his cute butt, he's a head-to-tail fox. If you lived now and you saw him strolling under your window, you might even come out of your house. The attraction is undeniable. Right before a guest arrived and asked him to help with his bags, he leaned over the desk and told me I was making it hard for him to concentrate! I nearly had to wring out my underwear.

Oh, Mom. Disgusting!

> He has this smile that made talking to him so easy, like the most natural thing in the world. Oh, I found out that he's twenty-two and just

graduated from college. He was a little shocked when he found out I was seventeen, but I have a feeling it's not going to stop our love OR our lust.

Love, K. No longer the owner of a lonely heart.

I tried to visualize Paul T. Morgan, Esquire. I could see his big smile with the deep lines on either side of his mouth, the perfect top teeth and crooked bottom ones, the distinguished nose and thick head of graying hair. I don't know if it was just my imagination fueled by hope, but when I closed my eyes and let the image of his face fill my mind, his eyes were glacial blue. Maybe it was time to close Mom's Second Glances account after all.

Twenty-five

"DON'T TOUCH ANYTHING," GEORGE SAID WHEN I WALKED
into the annex later that week with his cheddar and chutney
sandwich in one hand and a cold lemonade for myself in
the other. The sandwich was his reward for finishing three
chapters in one week. One look at his dishevelment and
you'd have hoped he'd done something significant. There
were big circles under his eyes, his T-shirt was rumpled
like it'd been slept in, and I could see the plaque on his
teeth. He needed a hot shower with some powerful deodorant soap and a vegetable brush. And I'm no neat freak, but
it was gamey in the annex. Liz and I had been instructed
not to clean in there, for fear we'd mess something up, but
now the smell was a little too human. I took a step toward
the window. George put a hand up to stop me. "Seriously,

don't touch. I have a system. Each pile is a zone. The zones cannot be messed with."

"George, it's a toxic zone," I said, and opened the window.

It was true that while there wasn't one patch of clear space in the whole annex, there did appear to be a strange order to the room. The index cards I'd brought him yesterday covered the floor in a rainbow. The bed was blanketed with documents on which I could see George's now-familiar chicken scrawl. His dresser was stacked with papers, and by the bathroom door was a pile of magazines that were marked with Post-it notes. The one on top was a *Vanity Fair* opened to a picture of Boaty and his wife, Lilly, sitting in what I now recognized as a classic Nantucket garden, with a weathered wooden bench and a trellis climbing with roses.

"And where should I put this?" I held up the sandwich.

"Oh yeah. Um"—he put a finger to his lips and scanned the room—"there." He pointed to a chair covered with clothes.

"Really? Like *on* the clothes?" George nodded as if this were perfectly normal. "Ooookay." I cleared a little spot on the chair for the sandwich. He spun around in his chair and focused on the computer like it was about to tell him the secret of life.

"Come on, Bernie, you said four o'clock; it's four eighteen. I love you, buddy, but don't make promises that you can't keep." George tugged at his hair with one hand and refreshed his e-mail with the other. He studied the screen with intense concentration, refreshed again, and then hooted with glee. "Yes," he said, pointing to the computer screen. "You the MAN!"

"Who's Bernie?" I asked.

"The guy who does my transcribing." He hit a button and the printer sprung to life, spitting out pages. "And I need these interviews now, because I've got some momentum, Cricket, and I'll be goddamned if I lose it. I'm actually on schedule."

"Who are those interviews with?" I asked as he collected the papers from the printer and scanned them quickly with his eyes.

"Lilly Carmichael," he said, stacking the papers on his desk. "We talked about their courtship and his proposal. Gotta have romance. The ladies will love it, and let's face it, they're going to be the ones buying my book."

"She looks kind of . . ."

"Uptight?" George asked.

"Yes," I said, picking up the *Vanity Fair* with the picture of Boaty and Lilly. She was pretty, but in an overly delicate way. Boaty was leaning forward, animated, like he was in the middle of a story, and she was sitting back, looking to the side. I couldn't help but think that the photographer was making a statement with this picture.

"Yeah, well. She's not exactly the life of the party," George said, tilting his head and raising his eyebrows

"That's kind of weird. You would've thought he could get any girl he wanted."

"What can I tell you? Love is strange."

"Where did he propose?"

"Nantucket, of course. Her family's been coming here forever. He washed ashore for a summer job and they fell in love. It was a quick engagement. People thought she was knocked up, but she wasn't. Not for another ten years." He slapped a Post-it note on the transcription, scribbled something on it, and then looked up with big happy eyes. "Oh, guess what? I got an interview with Robert next week."

"Awesome." We high-fived. I knew he'd wanted to interview Robert Carmichael, Boaty's brother and Parker's father, for a long time, and that Robert had been hard to nail down. He was going to run for Boaty's seat in the Senate in the special election next month and was crazy busy.

"I'm going to need you to drive me to their home and pick me up. I'm finally going to use that damn car." Before he'd broken his ankle, George had arranged to rent a car, but of course he couldn't drive it and he couldn't get a refund. So it sat in the inn's driveway, swallowing money. George claimed he could hear it make a *ka-ching!* cash register sound effect each evening. "You might have to hang out there and wait for me. We'll get a sense for what the scene is."

"Right," I said. Where would I "hang out"? I was picturing some sort of maids' quarters. Possibly a pantry area stocked with gourmet canned goods. Would Parker be there? Would Jules? I'd stay in the car, I told myself. I'd park in the shade, bring a book.

"And please, please, please remind me to use both my phone and digital voice recorder," he said, his hands pressed together in a prayer. "If I lost that file, I'd be screwed. In the next few weeks I may need your help a little more than usual. We're in the thick of it, Cricket. We're right in the thick of it."

Twenty-six

HURRICANE KAYLA HAD A DATE WITH NANTUCKET ON Friday. Everyone awaited her arrival like she was a gorgeous, petulant diva. Whether I was serving coffee at the inn, buying sunscreen at the pharmacy, or picking up a ham-and-cheese croissant for George at the Even Keel Café, Kayla's name was uttered again and again under the gray restless sky.

The shops on the harbor boarded up their windows in preparation for the destructive winds. Surfers, who I could pick out by their wet-suit tans and *I'm not a preppy or tourist* snarls, looked more purposeful and had a gleeful spark in their eyes. Many guests canceled their trips or went home early, hurrying to get tickets on the last ferries and planes, leaving the inn less than half full in the height of the season. Those who stayed played the board games that'd been around for decades and read books by the fire in the library. They ate slices of Gavin's blueberry and peach pie and sipped tea or red wine, feet curled under them, peeking out the windows, analyzing clouds, reveling in coziness and anticipation. They wanted a hurricane story. I did too.

But Kayla stood us up, swirled her windy skirts, moved out to sea, and cooled her temper over the deep impartial ocean, leaving us with three days of rain. Fat, ceaseless drops filled the sidewalk cracks, overflowed puddles, and sent little streams twisting down Main Street. The grass in the back-yard was rain drunk, so green it was practically humming.

The deluge gave George new drive and power. He was like the water wheel in the Industrial Revolution–era mill we'd toured for social studies in the seventh grade, cranking out chapters ahead of schedule, appearing in the kitchen for pie and dances of glee, and then disappearing back into the annex for another round of Coke Zero–fueled productivity.

With so few guests and such a light cleaning schedule, Liz and I finished early and went to the one movie the-ater on Nantucket. It doesn't look like a theater from the outside. It's just a regular-sized gray-shingled Nantucket building that's also a restaurant and bar. I'm not sure if it's because people were in a hurricane mindset where normal rules didn't apply, but the ticket taker didn't card us and he let us bring drinks into the theater.

We drank Irish coffees with whipped cream as we watched a romantic comedy. It was about this girl who works in a New York City flower shop and falls in love with a corporate lawyer who wants to build a megamall next door. It was dumb, but I still loved it, because in the dark, in the glow of someone else's story, I was free to think about Zack—how he tasted like mint and salt, how his hands left little swirls of energy where he'd touched me.

It had been over a week, and Zack and I hadn't texted, talked, or seen each other. My guilt had started to subside, heading out to sea with Kayla. I watched the lawyer kiss the florist girl, the city sparkling behind them. As a spare, sweet folk song filled the theater and the girl on screen gave in to the lawyer's lips, loosened his tie, and staggered to pull off her funky cowboy boots, my cell vibrated with a text. It was Zack:

I'm breaking our rule. Join me?

Twenty-seven

THAT NIGHT, I PICKED UP MOM'S DIARY AGAIN, SKIPPING over her make-out sessions with "Lover Boy," which she described in way too much detail for me to handle. There are certain words one just doesn't ever want to associate with one's mom and her activities. Words like "hard-on." It was especially gross now that I had a picture of Paul Morgan, Esquire, in my head. Instead, I started looking for romantic clues, places, and things I could mention that might dust off some shiny magnetic piece of her and pull her back out to this island. Once she was here, I'd arrange a meeting with Paul in one of their favorite places, and their old love would bring Mom fully back to life. I'd have to be subtle. I'd have to make it seem like it was her idea. I found an entry that looked relatively innocent and, pencil in hand, searched for key words.

Dear Emily D.,

Lover Boy and I dared to meet in public today. It was hard to get away. Aunt Betty took me to the yacht club for tennis (Aunt Betty's athletic, for a seventy-three-year-old biddy) and she insisted on us having lunch with her friends afterward. But finally (after Aunt Betty's second martini), I was able to sneak off. I met Lover Boy at Cisco and we spent the whole afternoon kissing in the surf like the cover of the Against All Odds album. Then we went back to his place, where we ate lobsters and drank beer and made out some more. Aunt Betty would kill me if she knew, but this is what being seventeen is all about. What is life, if not for living?

Cisco Beach, I wrote in my notebook. *Lobsters and beer.*

I know I write a lot about how hot he gets me, but the truth is that I could spend all day with him every day. He's a cocky bastard, but he makes me laugh. There's this weird part of me that's like, <u>Be careful</u>. I can practically see the red flag warnings each time I close my eyes and we kiss. But I honestly don't give a shit. He's like a drug! And I'm addicted! Sometimes, I feel like we're that

Air Supply song, and that we're making love out of nothing at all.

I had to laugh. Oh my god! That song is so cheesy!

There was a tap on my window, and I sat up quickly, my body contracting in a flash of tension. But I smiled when I saw it was Zack. He laughed at my scared reaction, and my heart raced for a different reason. I opened the window. It had finally stopped raining, but the air was misty, full of secrets.

"I couldn't wait anymore," he said.

"Shh," I said, putting the book and notebook on the dresser and gesturing for him to come inside. Zack crawled in the window. He looked around.

"Nice room." He reached up and touched the slanted ceiling. "I like these old places."

"This one is haunted," I said, gathering the sheet around me. I was only wearing a T-shirt and underwear. "By a sea captain."

"Doesn't surprise me. Oh, hey. Fitzy saw that ghost again. The seventies girl."

"How does he know she's from the seventies?" I asked.

"Her clothes."

"Is she wearing bell-bottoms?"

"I don't know. But ghosts wear clothes. I mean, when people see ghosts they're always dressed, which is really weird when you think about it. Whatever you die in is the outfit you're stuck with for eternity."

"I guess it'd be creepy if they were all naked," I said.

"Good point. You love poetry, huh?" Zack asked.

"Not really," I said.

"I saw you. Your eyes were glued to that book." He sat on the edge of the bed.

"You were watching me?"

"For like a second." He reached for the book on my dresser.

"Don't touch that!"

"Whoa," he said, searching my eyes. "What's in that book?"

"Nothing," I said.

"I want to see," he said, picking it up.

"It's private." I leaped up, letting the sheet fall in order to grab the book from him. He smiled, staring at me, as I shoved it under the bed.

"Underwear is just like a bathing suit," I said as I climbed back under the sheet, blushing like a fever.

"No," he said. "It's different. We've been through this before. Remember?"

"Oh, yeah," I said, recalling the conversation we'd had at the Claytons' house when he'd seen Jules in her bra.

"What's wrong?"

"Nothing," I said. I was thinking about that night. It was the night Nina died, but Zack hadn't put it together, and I didn't want to remind him.

"Jules misses you, you know. I saw her looking at one of

those books you guys make, with all the letters and magazine clippings. What do you guys do with those things anyway? Are they like scrapbooks?"

"No. They're collage books. Jules brought one of our books with her?" Zack nodded. Jules and I bought hardcover sketch pads from the RISD art store and made collages in them. We saved all the notes we passed to each other in class and used rubber cement to glue them into the book. Then we made collages based on the notes. The collages and notes could be on any subject, from Jay Logan, to a book, to a certain style of jeans, to the way a movie made us feel. The fact that she even brought one to Nantucket was a good sign. We traded it back and forth every week, each of us adding a new entry. That was *our* book, *our* thing. She couldn't just add to it without thinking of me. "Maybe I should call her."

"I don't know," Zack said as he leaned against the wall. We held each other's gaze. Part of the reason he was climbing in my window was because Jules and I weren't talking. "It's like there's this wall around her right now. And no one is allowed in. No one."

"Parker is," I said.

"Parker can't even see the wall. That's the whole point."

"Oooh," I said. I hadn't thought about it like that before. It made me feel stupid and better at the same time. Zack put his hand on my sheet-covered foot and started to massage it.

I inhaled sharply. "Zack, we promised. No touching."

"It's just a foot," he said. "A foot under a sheet."

"Have you done this before?" His hands were strong, seemed to know what they were doing.

"Rubbed a girl's feet? No," he said. He looked older than sixteen. It was something about the way his jaw flexed. "This is pure instinct."

"You might have a future in it." I wiggled my other foot out from under the sheet. He covered it with his hands, went to work, barely touching my toes.

"Stop," I said, laughing. But he was grazing my toes even more lightly now, and I tried to kick my feet free. "Stop." I twisted free, sat up, and grabbed his hands. "Stop." Our eyes locked, and we sat there staring at each other. He slid the sheet up to my knees, drew little circles on my kneecaps, maintaining eye contact. I watched him register the smile I was fighting. He leaned in and kissed me.

"Zack," I said, trying to be calm. "We can't do this. We promised."

"Just one more time," he said, smiling. "We won't tell anyone."

"But this is it," I said.

"This is it," he said, his hand sliding up my thigh.

"And no one can know. Ever."

"Would you be embarrassed to go out with me?" he asked.

"No," I said. "Of course not." But I knew a part of me was lying. I was going to be a senior, and Zack was only going to be a sophomore. "It's just Jules. She'd be mad."

"Okay, no one will know," he said, lying back on the bed.

"We'll be secret lovers," I said. I wasn't thinking.

He grinned. "I didn't know we were going that far."

I shook my head, realizing that lovers meant sex. "We're not. That's not what I meant."

"Are you sure?" he asked as he pulled me down next to him.

"I'm sure," I said as he took off his glasses and his lips found mine. I closed my eyes and saw flecks of red.

Were they the little warning flags Mom had written about?

Twenty-eight

"BEEP-BEEP," I CALLED OUT THE WINDOW OF GEORGE'S rented Jeep. I didn't think Gavin or the old lady in the muumuu who was snoozing in the hammock would appreciate it if I leaned on the car horn. Today was the big interview with Robert Carmichael. I drummed my fingers on the steering wheel, which was hot from the sun. "Beep-beep," I said again. George told me that we needed to be ready at three o'clock, and it was already 3:10. What was he doing, curling his hair? He waved from his window, giving me the one-minute signal.

I tilted the rearview mirror in my direction. Even though George had assured me I wouldn't have to hang out at the house, that this was purely a drop-off/pick-up situation, I was still nervous about running into Parker. I wanted to look good. Composed. Liz trimmed my bangs last night, and I had on just a teeny bit of lip gloss and blush. I was already sweating a little through my white blouse with the tiny blue flowers on it. I fiddled with the air conditioner and smoothed my linen skirt over my knees.

I wondered if part of my desire to look so wholesome and put together was to cover up for what I was doing at night. Zack had been sneaking into my room for make-out sessions that were becoming more and more intense. I had two rules: One, underwear stayed on. This prevented sex and other irrevocable acts. Two, no sleeping over. If he didn't spend the night at home, Jules or Mr. Clayton would definitely start to notice. Each night we said was "the last time," but the phrase had become a joke. Night after night he appeared at my window with a big grin, even though I'd told him the front door worked just fine.

"I like the window," he'd said. "I mean, since we're 'secret lovers,'" he added in a breathy voice.

"Shut up," I'd said, and helped him tumble inside.

Last night had felt a little dangerous. We'd fallen asleep for a few hours, our limbs entangled. Luckily, I'd awakened before the sun came up, and he'd climbed on top of me, stealing one more hip-to-hip kiss before he slipped back out the window, into the dark pre-dawn air. I heated up like an August afternoon at the thought of it, and dabbed some cool foundation under my eyes. At least I knew he wouldn't be there. He works on Tuesdays.

"George?" I called out the window.

"Give me five minutes," he called back.

I opened the diary. Maybe I could find a clue as to how Mom and Paul broke up.

> Dear Emily,
> This girl from Miss Driscoll's, that boarding school where I spent one miserable semester, was at Cisco today.

Oh, yeah. I'd forgotten that Mom had spent a semester at a boarding school. She told me that she hated it. She described living in a dorm called Tittsworth Hall, where at least half the girls were anorexic. At night, they would ball up slices of Wonder Bread and eat "bread balls" and red-hot candies and play truth or truth because no one wanted to dare. It sounded creepy.

> She always acted so much cooler and better than me. Her dad is some kind of megamillionaire. She started talking to us and she was ALL OVER Lover Boy, batting her eyelashes and smooshing her boobs together. She invited me to some party, but I could tell it was just to get to Lover Boy. In front of my face! Gag me with a spoon. Get your own boyfriend. After she left, Lover Boy called her pig nose. Ha, ha, ha.
> Anyway, his parents are visiting this weekend. I wanted to meet them. I know they would like me

if they met me, but he says he wants to wait. He
says they won't understand him dating a girl who's
in high school.

I wrote in my notebook: *Possible reason for breakup* = *age
difference*. This made me feel better. They were so old now.
No one cared if a forty-nine-year-old and a forty-four-year-
old got together.

Anyway, last night we did it in the dunes under
a full moon.

Dunes, I wrote in my notebook and underlined it, and
did my best to block out the "doing it" part.

And after, he told me that he loved me! I
guess I knew this all along, but to hear him
actually say it, Emily, I swear there's nothing better
in this whole world. If you only knew, you wouldn't
have stayed inside your house in Amherst. Although,
I have to say . . . some of these poems make me
think maybe you had a lover. "Wild Nights" isn't
about the weather!

I flipped to the index, found the poem, and read it.
Mom was right. This poem was definitely about sex. I ear-
marked the page, certain it was going to be one of the ones
Mrs. Hart would focus on. I learned from our ninth-grade

discussions of *The Canterbury Tales* that Mrs. Hart might be ancient but she was also raunchy. It was no wonder she and Mrs. Levander were such good friends. They probably got together on the weekends for wine and Bonnie Raitt and sex talk.

"Let's blow this pop stand," George said, startling me as he shoved his crutches in the backseat and hopped into the Jeep. I shut the diary and my notebook and buried them in my bag. George was all cleaned up for the interview. He'd shaved, showered, and was wearing clothes that were either brand new or that had actually been ironed. Somehow, it seemed more likely to me he'd bought them. He had a leather satchel in one hand and a Coke Zero in the other.

"I see you have your man-soda," I said.

"You know it," he said as I started the engine and backed out of the inn's driveway. Sometimes I wondered if George had Coke Zero pulsing through his veins instead of blood. "And I see you're wearing your business casuals. Very nice." Noticing my confusion, he added, "You're dressed for work in an office. It's a good thing. Very appropriate, very professional."

"Well, I'm going to a future senator's house. So, how long are interviews?" I asked.

"Well," he said, "that's kind of like asking how long a conversation is. It all depends."

"How long should I hang around 'Sconset?" I asked.

"Shouldn't be more than an hour. I'll text you when I need to be picked up. Just don't go too far. I don't want to be hanging around on their front lawn, waiting to get picked up. That could get awkward."

"Got it."

He glanced at the Emily Dickinson book in my bag. "I see you brought a little light reading."

"For school," I said, slowing as I passed a helmeted family on bikes. "So how do you get these people to tell you anything good?"

"Here's the thing. Everyone has a story to tell." Out of the corner of my eye I saw George fan out his fingers, the way he does when he's explaining something he's passionate about. "Everyone's life has love and death and drama and hope and fear. And if you make them comfortable, if they feel they can trust you, they'll tell you. They actually *want* to tell someone." I always know when George is done making a point because he folds his hands together and rests them on his big belly.

"What are you looking for from Boaty's brother?" I asked. "What do you want him to tell you?"

"Family stories. The humanizing details. Anecdotes that reveal character. Boaty wasn't born into this world. He scrambled to get to where he was. I want stories that show that incredible determination, drive, and intelligence. I also wonder when he started stepping on people. Who was that first rung on his ladder to the top? People think his career started at the state house, but I think it also started when he figured out how to charm the right people into leaning over so he could step on their backs."

"You think his brother's going to tell you *that*?"

"He might tell me without telling me, if you know what I mean."

George shifted in his seat. I slowed down to take a look at the cross that Zack had pointed out to me, the one where the ghost likes to hang out. As I looked out the window, I noticed that George shuddered. I screamed, which made George scream and grab at his chest.

"You just got the chills! You just got the chills!" I said, slapping the steering wheel and accidentally slamming the horn.

"You scared the living shit out of me!"

"Holy, holy shit, you just got the chills."

"Eyes on the road, Thompson," George said, putting his hand on the wheel and steering us more solidly to the right side of the road. "Eyes. On. The. Road. Jesus, how long have you been driving?"

"Almost two years, but holy, holy shit." I shook my head and pointed at him. "I can't believe it, you got the chills."

"Yes, I've been coming down with something since, like, May."

"The ghost," I said. "There's a ghost girl at that cross back there. And they say that's why people get chills when they pass it. And that's why I was watching you, and oh my god. Oooh, should we drive by and see if it happens again?" I couldn't wait to tell Zack. How come it never happened to me? Was I not spiritual enough for ghosts to contact?

"No, no, no. Let's just focus on getting there alive."

"All the kids are talking about it," I said, knowing George liked to know what "the kids were talking about." As a journalist, he felt it was his duty, but he was too focused today and he didn't bite.

"Oh, okay, slow down. It's up here." I braked, looking for the correct address. "And turn left," George said as we turned into a wide driveway. "Secret service," he said to me, and rolled down the window to talk to two guys in dark suits wearing wires. I felt bad for them. They looked so hot. One guy said something into a walkie-talkie-type thing and waved us in so that I could drop off George by the front door.

"You okay?" George asked as he reached for his crutches in the back. "You look like you just saw that ghost."

"Yeah." The house was huge; it looked like it could hold at least four of my mom's house. But that's not what was making me sweat through my white blouse. Next to a Mercedes, a silver Porsche Cayenne, and a red Volvo with a Hotchkiss sticker (Parker's boarding school) was the Claytons' land yacht. Jules was here. My heart pounded.

"Hey, this is just money," George said. "Don't let it intimidate you, okay?" Then he opened the door and stepped out, balancing as he gathered his satchel and notebook. I could hear kids' voices coming from the backyard. There was obviously a pool, because I heard cannonball splashes and girls laughing. It sounded like fun, like what I'd had in mind for myself when I came here. Shit, shit, shit.

George closed the car door with the butt of his crutch

and headed up the front steps. He had just reached the front door and was about to knock when I noticed his phone on the seat.

"George, wait," I said, hopping out of the car and jogging to him with the phone.

"You're the best," he said as I pressed it into his hand.

"I'll be waiting for your text," I said, and walked quickly back to the car I'd left running.

I heard Jules's unmistakable laugh: the confident, contagious one that always made me feel we were at the center of the world. I felt sad in a bottomless way—like a plane dropping in turbulence, an elevator plummeting to the basement. I hurried into the car and drove away, my palms sticky and my breath sharp and shallow.

Twenty-nine

WHEN I PULLED INTO THE CARMICHAELS' DRIVEWAY AFTER
an hour of driving around Nantucket with the radio blar-
ing as I tried to get my head together, I saw Jules following
Parker into the house. She was barefoot, wearing a yellow
bikini, with a short white towel fastened around her hips.
She was hopping on one foot and pounding the side of her
head as she tried to get water out of her ear. I winced as
I drove up. She looked up, squinting. Our eyes met. We
both froze. I was going to have to get out of the car now.
I couldn't just sit there. I parked, trembling. I took a deep
breath and stepped out of the car.

"What are you doing here?" she asked as I approached
her. I saw her eyes darting over my body, taking in my business casuals.

"I have an internship," I said. "With a journalist. And he's here."

"The guy who's interviewing my dad?" Parker asked. She was dripping with pool water. She dabbed her face and stuck a towel-covered finger into her ear, grimacing as she screwed it in. Parker was so confident about her place in the world she could do that kind of thing in public. I looked at those rock-hard thighs. Parker looked like she could kick her Volvo over to Martha's Vineyard.

"How'd you get an internship?" Jules asked.

"It's a long story," I said.

"The book is about the whole American royalty thing, right?" Parker asked. I nodded, smiling. "What do you do for him?"

"Basically, I just help keep him organized; I get him whatever he needs. Sometimes I give him feedback," I said. "You know, on the writing." I figured on some level this was true. Just the other day he'd asked my opinion about an interview.

Jules was staring at a rock. With one pointed foot she traced an arc in the Carmichaels' spongy green grass. It was bright, uniform grass, the kind that's bought and then unfurled on the ground like bolts of fabric. "It's your birthday in a few weeks," she said, shielding the sun from her eyes, squinting at me.

I nodded. "My eighteenth."

"Whoa, you're old," Parker said. "No wonder you have an internship. I feel better." She snorted. "For a second there

I was like, should I have an internship?" She picked at a bud on the branch of a tree and decimated it with her short fingernails. "But I'm only sixteen."

"You'll be seventeen in September," Jules said, not even looking at her. Was she standing up for me?

"Bitch," Parker said, like this was her little pet name for Jules. "C'mon, let's get ready. I don't want to be late meeting Jay."

Jules and I had eighteen conversations with our eyes.

"There you guys are," said Zack, who emerged from the backyard in his bathing suit. He must've seen me before I saw him, because he didn't look surprised. He smiled as he jogged over. Now it was my turn to study rocks. Ever since Zack and I had started making out, my body had taken on a life of its own. My breath was unpredictable, my skin capable of burning up in an instant and searing my hairline, and there was this lightness that occasionally took me over, making me feel like I was made of balloons. He shook out his hair, spraying us all with little beads of water. Jules pushed him absentmindedly and he pushed her back. Why did he have to be her brother?

"Hello, Cricket. How are you?" he asked. He sounded stiff and formal.

"I'm fine," I said. *I thought you worked on Tuesdays.* I could feel myself making a weird expression. He looked good in his trunks. God, did he look good. He was pale but strong. The sun was glistening off of his wet skin. I knew that body now. My heart was like a dog, hopping and pulling on the leash, like it wanted to jump up and lick his face.

"Is that your journalist?" Jules asked. I turned, relieved to see George come out of the front door, his satchel swinging awkwardly at his side.

"I gotta go," I said, turning on my heels and jogging to meet George.

"Do you know those kids?" George asked as we climbed into the Jeep and I started the engine.

"Yeah," I said. "Kinda." I looked in the rearview mirror, expecting Zack to be the one watching us go. But he and Parker were gone. It was Jules who was watching me drive away. She looked frozen, standing on the edge of that perfect lawn in front of that perfect house. Her eyes were wide, mouth half open, like she was stopping herself from running after me.

Thirty

"THAT WAS SO WEIRD TODAY," ZACK SAID THAT NIGHT when he crawled in my window. "You were so nervous. You were sweating."

"But you don't think she caught on, do you?" I asked. I was sitting on my bed in a tank top and the girlie boxers I wore as pajamas.

"No way," he said. "She has no idea." I sighed and closed my eyes. Inside I tuned to the relief channel, but quickly switched to the guilt channel and back to relief and then guilt again. I hadn't been able to get Jules out of my head. The worst part was how badly I wanted to share with her what was happening to me. I wanted to tell her how I wasn't doing that thing that I do with guys, making mental notes of who had called or texted whom last, always keeping score and trying to stay on top. I wasn't planning out what I would say to Zack in advance or practicing lines that I thought might make him like me more. I was just being me. I wanted to tell her how I was actually enjoying making out, not just because it reassured me that a guy liked and wanted me, but because it felt good. And I wanted to know how she was. I wanted to hear her stories. The guilt channel was on full blast now, hissing its fuzzy reception. How to make it stop? I promised her, silently, to stop this with Zack.

"I'm too old for you," I said, sliding down the bed, away from him.

"I know. A whole eighteen months or something. You're corrupting me." He slid closer. "Have you ever had sex?"

"No." I pulled back, examining his face. "You have?" He nodded, laughing at my shocked expression. "Valerie?"

"She *is* French," he said.

"Were you in eighth grade?" He nodded. *"Eighth grade?"*

He snaked his hand around my waist, but I pushed it away.

"Does Jules know?"

"No."

"Did your mom know?"

"No." He put a hand on my knee.

"We shouldn't be doing this. We really shouldn't." I stood up and walked to the other side of the tiny room.

"Don't say that," he said, following me. He kissed me. I pulled away.

"But we can't keep doing this. I was thinking about what

you said about the wall around Jules. And I feel like I looked over the wall today for like a second, and I saw how sad she really is. And if we keep doing what we're doing, I'm just going to be heaping more sadness on her."

"Okay, well . . ." He let go of my hand. "Let's get away from the bed. Let's go somewhere," he said. "Let's get out of here."

"Where?"

"I don't know," he said. "But I need you to put on as many clothes as possible."

"Oh, I know," I said, remembering George and the shiver. I grabbed a sweatshirt. "Let's go see the ghost."

I told him about George getting the chills, as we headed out to the white cross in the land yacht. We drove by a few times, seeing if one of us would get the chills, but nothing happened. So we just parked in front of it. We sat and waited for something to happen, for the temperature to drop or a ghostly pair of bell-bottoms to strut past the headlights.

"Where does Jules think you go at night?" I asked as we waited. The air was soft and still and full of summer. The crickets were loud.

"She doesn't know I'm gone. No one knows I'm gone." He slapped a mosquito on his arm.

"What about your dad?"

"Jules is so out of it right now, and with my dad, it's like an actor is playing him. A bad actor. They won't even say her name. It's like living with people who are only half here."

"I know what that's like," I said, thinking of Mom and the way I could look into her eyes and see she was somewhere else, somewhere very far away that I didn't know about. It made me want to scream at her. Life was happening here in front of her, not in that faraway world. "I know exactly what that's like."

I pushed the seat back and dangled my feet out the window. We sat there in silence for a bit, each of us in our own world. The image of Jay's face came to my mind. I could hear him telling me off. I could hear myself telling Jules I thought his brother was a loser. My whole body tensed as I remembered it. I wish I'd never told Jules anything. What about my other secrets, the other things I shouldn't have said but did because I'd trusted her? Forget girls who died decades ago; words were ghosts. They were what haunted me.

"I don't think the ghost girl is going to show," I said.

"Yeah," he said. "Ghost girl's not into us. Let's go someplace better."

We went to Steps. The moon was three-quarters full— bright, glowing, shining on the black ocean. The waves were low and calm. We rolled up our jeans and walked in up to our ankles. The water was warm, holding the memory of the sun.

"That's it, I'm going in. I have to," Zack said. I watched as he lifted his sweatshirt and T-shirt off his head in one move. He was so lean and strong.

"In your underwear?" I asked.

"Hell, no," Zack said, and unbuttoned his jeans. I covered my mouth with my hands. He met my gaze and pulled them down, with his boxers, over his hips. There it was! I'd felt it, but I hadn't seen it. "Oh my god," I said, not realizing I was thinking aloud.

"Feast your eyes." He laughed. Then he beat his chest and let out a war cry.

"Zack!" I laughed, intoxicated.

He turned around, faced the ocean. Boy butts are so different, so compact. "Woo-hoo!" He whooped, ran into the waves, and dove under. "It's perfect," he said when his head popped up. "You have to come in. It's beautiful."

"I can't," I said, remembering my promise to myself about Jules.

"Your loss," Zack said. "It's amazing in here." It looked amazing. He looked amazing bobbing up and down in the silvery black water. I thought of Mom's words to Emily Dickinson: *What is life, if not for living?* I took a deep breath, then stripped off my clothes and ran in, covering myself with my hands until I was in the water. I slipped under a gentle wave, and when I came up, Zack was in front of me. He was smiling but serious, and I felt my cheeks brighten. He took my hands and pulled me close to him.

"Come to me, mermaid," he said.

"La le loo-loo la lee loo." I floated my legs up, dipped my head back, and sang an off-key mermaid song. I felt like the moon itself, all lit up. Then I noticed little lights around us in the water.

"Oh my god, what is this?" I asked. The water was sparking, glowing, like there were fireflies underwater.

"Phosphorescence," he said, splashing the water to make it glow.

"It's crazy." I ran my hands through the water, trying to catch it, then kicked my legs up and floated around on my back. I wasn't made of bones anymore. I was made of starfish and moonlight and phosphorescence. I started laughing for no reason at all.

"What?" Zack asked, treading water, his hands leaving trails of light.

I put my feet back on the bottom and laughed again. I'd never felt so full, so bright, so completely alive. "I think," I started, but then ducked back under, finishing the thought underwater so that I'd get to say it, but he wouldn't hear. *I think I'm in love.*

Thirty-one

"HONEY, I DON'T SEE THE NEED FOR ME TO COME TO Nantucket. You're doing just fine, and it's only a few more weeks until the summer's over." Even through the phone, I could tell Mom was distracted. She was probably playing computer hearts. I sat on the back steps of the porch, sipping lemonade from a fresh batch Gavin had just made. I used Mom's distraction as an opportunity to skim my notebook for key words and phrases I'd copied from the diary.

"But, Mom?" I said into the phone.

"Yeah?"

"*What is life, if not for living?*" I was hoping she would recognize her own quote.

"Is that from that Weight Watchers commercial?"

"No. It's from something else."

"Well, I don't see what it has to do with me coming to Nantucket, especially since I get seasick on boats." Yeah right, I thought. In the diary, she and Lover Boy had been on numerous boat trips. There was a ferry ride to Cape Cod for a stolen night in a motel, into which they checked in as "Mr. and Mrs. Donald Duck." There was also a zippy cruise in a Boston Whaler out to Tuckernuck Island, not to mention a secret sunrise sail. Mom's computer zinged with a hearts victory.

"Mom, are you sure you have seasickness? Are you sure that you're not inventing that?"

"Excuse me, but I think I know whether or not I get sick on boats."

"Then take a pill!" I said.

"Watch your tone, please," she said.

Gavin knocked on the sliding glass door and made a "keep it down" gesture. I gave him the okay signal. I hadn't realized I'd yelled.

"Sorry, Mom. I just want you to picture this." I glanced at the notebook, skipping over any boat-related notes. "Dunes. Sunsets. Lobster. Cisco Beach. Beer."

"Beer? I don't drink beer," she said. "What's this about? Oh no. Have you signed me up for some singles' thing? I told you—"

"No, Mom. I just want you to come out here for my birthday," I said. "It's only a week away."

"You were nine the last time you wanted me around on your birthday."

"Yeah, well, I'm going to college next year so maybe I'm feeling sentimental."

"Well, that's very sweet. But I'm afraid I'd come all the way out there and you'd just want to be with your friends, not boring old Mom." Boring old Mom? I was staring at the words "nude beach" in her diary. "How about when you get back, we go out to Sue's Clam Shack? Are you sure there's no one that you want to see out here?"

"The only person on Nantucket I want to see is you, and I'm going to see you in just a few short weeks." *Zing!* A hearts success.

"I just want you to think about it. Promise me you'll think about it."

I hung up and opened the book, wishing I could find the right words, the ones that would lure her back out to this island, this unlikely rock of love. The problem was that in the diary she was more specific about what she and Lover Boy had done to each other's bodies than where exactly they'd been. I wasn't about to recite those passages to her. I could barely read them without wanting to barf. A page caught my attention—she'd written in a circle around a poem.

Dear Emily,
Right now I'm sitting in front of the library, where I've come to escape Aunt Betty, who was lecturing me on the importance of knowing how to

properly set a table. She thinks my parents haven't taught me any feminine charms. All I want to do is think about last night with Lover Boy. On one hand, I'm confused because he canceled our last date. He said he needed to work on law school applications and it gave me a weird feeling. It's still only summer and he's barely mentioned law school this whole time! On the other hand, I wonder if I'm being paranoid. He cares so much about his future. He has big dreams. I want him to follow his dreams! And it was just last week when he told me that he loves me, and I knew it was true when he said it, the way you just know. He loves me!

I'm listening to the crickets as I write this. And I just realized that I'm writing here on your poem about the cricket. I love that crickets are here in this magical time, when it's not night or day but some in-between time. I'm deciding right now that when I want to think of a day with magic in it, I'll think of this day. I will say to myself: Cricket. It will be my secret code word for magic or love or both.

Love, K

My name. Mom had always said that I got my name because I used to chirp in my crib. But that wasn't the whole truth. I read the poem.

The cricket sang
And set the sun,
And workmen finished, one by one,
Their seam the day upon.

The low grass loaded with the dew,
The twilight stood as strangers do
With hat in hand, polite and new,
To stay as if, or go.

A vastness, as a neighbor, came,—
A wisdom without face or name,
A peace, as hemispheres at home,—
And so the night became.

I wasn't just Mom's daughter. I was her word for magic.

"What's up with you?" I looked up. It was George, taking a fresh-air break, something I'd encouraged him to do. I'd told him it didn't matter that he was on crutches, he needed to hobble around the block every six hours or so. His skin had started to look yellow.

"I think I finally get Emily Dickinson," I said.

"That makes one of us," he said. "Hey, will you come listen to this? I need your young ears to decipher part of Lilly Carmichael's interview. I've been to too many White Stripes concerts or something."

"Sure." I closed the diary and followed George into the

annex, which was officially on the verge of spontaneous combustion.

He played the digital recording on the computer. Mrs. Carmichael's voice was smooth, like one of Mom's books on tape: *"Boaty's proposal was very romantic. It came as a great surprise. I'd had a mad crush on him all summer. But that hardly made me unique; so did all the girls."*

"Yada yada yada," George said, skipping ahead. "She goes on about this for a while. Tell me something I don't know." He pressed PLAY. "Okay, now listen."

"Boaty and I went for a sunset sail. I didn't even want to go! Can you imagine? I kept telling him that there was a big clam-bake I'd been looking forward to and we could always go sailing tomorrow night, but he insisted that the sunset that evening was going to be the best of the summer. And it was. It was glorious. As I was admiring it, he pulled from his pocket a ring made out of seaweed. He had no money then." Lilly's voice softened. I could hear her smiling. *"It was such a surprise! The only thing on my mind the whole day was getting to Paul Morgan's clambake, always the party of the season."* On the recording, George asked who Paul Morgan was. Lilly answered. *"Paul was the boy my parents wanted me to marry. He was from an old Nantucket family, had all the money in the world, all the right credentials. My mother always thought he was the one for me because—"* Here the voice became indecipherable.

"Oh, Paul Morgan!" I said as the familiarity of the name landed.

"You know him?" George asked, pausing the interview.

"Yeah, I do." This wasn't true; I just felt like I did. "Well, not really. I've just met him and I've heard a lot about him."

"From whom?"

"My mom. They dated at one time."

"Oh." George tilted his head. "Interesting. Okay, so listen hard; this is the part I can't understand. It sounds like she's saying her mother always thought Boaty was interested in Lilly's 'local vision.' But that makes no sense," George said. What the hell is 'local vision'? And why would that be a bad thing for him to be interested in?"

"Play it again." I said. He did. "One more time." He watched me as if I were a medium. I clapped my hand on his shoulder. "Social position. She's saying social position." My eyes widened. "Her mom thought that Boaty was a social climber!"

"I think you're right." George played it again, his face frozen in concentration. He sighed with relief. "That's it." He scratched his neck. "No wonder she mumbled."

He was waiting for me to respond, but my mind wasn't on the recording. It was on Paul Morgan.

I hadn't realized that Paul Morgan was such a prominent, wealthy man. I wondered if that would scare Mom away. She said she didn't trust rich people. I'd have to make sure they met someplace low-key. How was I ever going to make it seem like this was all her idea?

Thirty-two

"WHAT'S THIS?" I ASKED, THE NEXT AFTERNOON. LIZ AND I were in the kitchen. I was staring at a neat little package wrapped up sweetly in pink tissue paper. It was tied with a strand of lace. Liz and I were relaxing after a long morning. All the beds were made, all the toilets had been wiped clean, and all the wicker wastebaskets emptied.

"Early birthday present," Liz said. "Go on, now. Open it."

"Liz, you didn't have to," I said. "My birthday isn't until Tuesday."

"Open the damn present," she said, a mischievous grin plastered on her face. Gavin wandered into the kitchen with a stack of mail.

"Something came for you, Cricket," he said, handing me

a fat manila envelope with my name and the inn's address written in my father's familiar chicken scrawl.

"Thanks," I said.

"Gavin, did you know that it's Cricket's birthday next week?" Liz said. "She's going to be eighteen years old."

"Is that so?" Gavin said. "I'll have to make a cake. Chocolate with a raspberry filling okay?"

"Yum. Thanks, Gavin," I said as I worked at the knot of lace that was binding my gift. Gavin turned on the teakettle and sorted through his bills, not knowing how relieved I was that I was going to have a birthday cake—a chocolate one, with raspberry filling! I needed something to replace the tradition Jules and I had started five years ago.

Ever since Jules came to Rosewood, we did pajama birthdays. On our birthdays, Jules and I always brought each other waffles with strawberries and whipped cream in bed. And the breakfast tray was always adorned with Lulu, a stuffed pig we'd bought when Nina took us to FAO Schwarz in New York.

We were way past the age of stuffed animals, and neither of us was a stuffed animal kind of girl, but we both loved this pig. There was only one left in the store, and we'd fought over who would get to buy her, or "adopt" her, as Jules insisted. Nina suggested we split the cost and have joint custody. So every birthday we traded her back and forth. Whoever had Lulu in her possession had to take care of her and give the other "mother" monthly reports on her well-being. *Lulu has thrived this spring,* Jules had written in one note. *She continues to be fuzzy and friendly and has developed a passion for Bruce Springsteen.*

Lulu has experienced her first crush, I wrote to Jules the next year. *On a stuffed giraffe in our attic. He's a little old for her, I think, but these sorts of urges are natural in a young pig.*

The teakettle whistled. Gavin poured the water and dunked the teabag.

"Oh, for Christ's sake," Liz said, using kitchen sheers to cut the ribbon.

"I love watching people receive gifts," Gavin said as he blew on his tea. It was some weird medicinal tea, and its bitter aroma filled the room. "Go on, open it."

Very slowly, I unwrapped the tissue paper, which smelled faintly like perfume, and lifted up a delicate, minuscule black lace thong.

I crumpled it in my hand, hiding it from Gavin. Liz squealed with glee.

"You set me up, Liz," Gavin said, shielding his eyes and walking back into the living room. "That's not nice."

"Didn't want to rob an old man of a thrill," she said, wiping tears of laughter from her eyes.

"Liz!" My face was burning up. "What am I supposed to do with this?"

"Do I have to explain?" she asked, cackling. "Don't act like such an innocent. We share a wall. A very thin wall. I know what you're up to at night, and I can't stand the thought of you shagging in your cotton knickers."

"How do you know I wear cotton underwear?"

"Oh, I'm sorry, what do you wear, then?" Liz asked. I stared at the table. The only underwear I owned were cotton. Mrs. Levander told us other materials led to yeast infections. "Just as I thought. Well, not anymore. Cotton knickers are for little girls, and you, my dear, are about to become a woman."

Thirty-three

ZACK AND I WERE AT THE BEACH WHEN I FINALLY OPENED the manila envelope from Dad. I couldn't wait until next week, but there was something about opening a birthday present alone that was just sad. Half the fun is someone watching.

"Let's see what you got," Zack said. Inside was a birthday card with a sparkly fairy on it, something more appropriate for an eight-year-old. But I didn't mind that. Dad still thought I loved girlie-girl stuff, and I smiled thinking of him searching the card aisle in CVS for something he thought was glittery enough for me. It was signed Dad and Polly, each in their own handwriting. There was also a note that said Alexi was having a sixth birthday party at their house, and if I wanted to come home for the party, they'd pay my way.

"'Alexi wants to spend more time with his new big sister,'" I read aloud to Zack. "Yeah right. That kid doesn't like me." It was true. Whenever I sat at the kitchen table for dinner, he turned his chair to face the other way.

"What's the gift?" Zack asked.

I unwrapped the present: a pair of jeans. Not just any pair. Clover, the new brand I'd seen in *InStyle* magazine that all the celebrities were wearing. I squealed with happiness. "Check it out," I said, and held them up. "Oh my god, they're awesome. I actually like them."

"You sound so surprised," Zack said as I slipped them over my bathing suit and spun around. They fit perfectly.

"This is a first," I said. "My Dad met the Great Birthday Challenge."

"What's that?" Zack asked.

"Every year since I was twelve, Dad has bought me an outfit that he picked out himself," I explained as I pulled the jeans off and folded them back up into the envelope. It was way too hot for jeans. "He said it was one of the great challenges of a father's life to buy his teenage daughter clothes that she actually liked and wore. The true test would be if I didn't exchange it."

"What was the worst gift?" Zack asked.

"My fourteenth," I said, and lay back in the sand. "It was a sparkly pink jean jacket." I looked up at the clouds, remembering some of the other "fashions." "And another time, he bought me one of those knitted dresses, but it looked like it'd been made by someone's drunk grandma." Zack laughed and started pouring sand over my legs in loose fistfuls. Zack was definitely a guy who thought girls were funny.

"But last year he actually came really close with this T-shirt dress thing." I shut my eyes and pictured it. It was the absolute best version of the scoop neck, cap-sleeve, empire waist style that everyone was wearing last summer. It looked so good but also had that "I'm not even trying" look.

"So what was wrong with that one?" Zack asked, patting sand around my legs.

"It was the color of mustard."

"Dijon or French's?"

"Grey Poupon." I ran the warm sand through my fingers. "I told him I loved it when I unwrapped it."

"Why?" Zack asked. He was covering my knees now.

"It was my first birthday since the divorce, and we were eating lobster at a nice restaurant and he was looking happy again. I didn't want to ruin it." I realized now that Dad had probably just started dating Polly around that time. I remembered noticing how cheerful Dad had been, that the color had returned to his face. Zack scooped sand around my thighs. I continued the story. "Dad was like, 'You really love it? You're not going to take it back?' and I was like, 'Yup, I love it.' But he didn't believe me." I could picture him narrowing his eyes and studying my face. The more I tried to convince him, the more obvious it was I didn't actually love it. "I finally fessed up after the chocolate mousse."

"Was he sad?" Zack asked, patting the sand over my legs.

"No," I said. I remembered Dad laughing and slapping the table with his hand. "God, I came so close!" he'd said. "So close and yet so far. I've failed the Great Birthday Challenge again, and I don't have that many more years left. I have to get it right while you're a teenager."

"It just made him more determined," I told Zack. "He said, 'Next year, on your eighteenth, I'm going to nail it. Mark my words. Next year I'll have a victory, even if I have to get a subscription to *Vogue*.'"

"He did it," Zack said. He was now carving a design into the sand that covered my legs. "He met the Great Birthday Challenge."

"Yup," I said.

"Why do you sound disappointed?" Zack asked.

"I don't know." Even though I loved the jeans and I wouldn't have traded them for anything, I kind of missed the sparkly jean jacket, the floral overalls, the purple jumper. I was too old for them now. For the first time on a birthday, I actually did feel older. Zack pulled my arms so that I was sitting upright. He'd transformed my legs into a fishtail, with scales and fins.

"I'm a mermaid," I said.

"A mer-chamber-maid," Zack said. "A very rare species. One hasn't washed up on these shores in a hundred years, and you need to get back in the water before the evil scientists spot you and take you to their lab for experiments."

"Oh," I said as he stood and opened his arms. I looked up at his eyes crinkling at the corners with a smile that was meant just for me. Warmth flooded my chest. I broke out of my sand encasement, put my arms around his neck, and hopped up. He caught my legs. "Hurry," I said. "Get me to the sea! We don't have much time!"

As we charged toward the water, a family of shorebirds scattered. I screamed as he dropped me in the cold salty water.

Thirty-four

THE NEXT DAY, I WAS CLEANING OFF THE TABLES ON THE patio after the breakfast rush when my phone buzzed in my back pocket. A text. I thought it was going to be Zack, who'd sometimes send me a quick message when he woke up; or maybe Liz, who sent me ridiculous sex tips throughout the day with suggestions for various positions. But it was Jules.

Meet me for lunch at the Even Keel?

I texted back immediately. My hand was shaking.

Yes! When?

Noon.

I work until 3 ☹.

We usually finished by two thirty, but I'd need some time to get my head together.

3:30?

OK C U then.

"Put that phone down," Bernadette said as she wiped down the tables, piling dirty cloth napkins in the laundry basket. "This isn't break time." I was too stunned to let Bernadette's tone bother me. I slipped my phone back in my pocket and carried an armload of dirty dishes into the kitchen, where Gavin was mixing something up in a ceramic bowl.

"Try this," he said, handing the batter-covered rubber spatula for me to sample. He was expanding his afternoon cookie repertoire lately, experimenting with new flavors. I ran my finger along the spatula's edge and tasted the sweet batter.

"Lime?" I asked.

"New recipe," Gavin said. "What do you think?"

"It's sweet and tart. It's kinda . . . complicated," I said.

"Complicated, huh? That's not exactly what I'm going for with my cookies."

"I mean complex," I said. I was mixing up my own recipe inside as I thought about seeing Jules. There was a half a cup of guilt over the fact that I was secretly dating her brother, a tablespoon of ice-cold fear that she'd found out about Zack and me, two pinches of boiling anger when I remembered how she'd acted at that party, a teaspoon of whipped hope that she missed me as much as I missed her, and a sprinkling of giddiness that I might get my best friend back.

Gavin sighed. "Well, I guess 'complex' could be good."

He used a tablespoon to drop the batter on a cookie sheet.

"Lime cookies will taste so good with your sweet peach sun tea."

"Now, that's a good idea, Cricket." Gavin's face brightened, his big smile deepening the lines around his mouth and revealing his slightly tea-stained teeth. "I knew I hired you for a reason." If I thought sweet peach sun tea would make this conversation with Jules easier, I'd have downed a gallon.

I was shaking when I entered the busy café. It was noisy with fifty conversations. It was 3:28 and the place was still slamming. I scanned the room for Jules, hoping that I'd arrived first. She wasn't inside, so I walked to the back patio. Jules was sitting at a shady table, a cup of coffee in hand. My ears started to hum. She looked up and waved, a half smile on her face.

"Hey. How's it going?" she asked.

"Fine," I said. I was so relieved when the waitress approached almost immediately. I ordered a chicken Caesar salad and an iced tea.

"I'm all set with coffee," Jules said to the waitress.

"Oh," I said, feeling dumb that I was going to be the only one eating. She had said lunch in her text, right? Shit. I wasn't even hungry.

"I already ate," she said with a shrug. "So, what's going on with you?"

I'm wearing a thong! I want to tell her. *I went swimming with a boy! Buck-ass naked! I think I'm in love. With your brother!*

"Not much," I said, folding my hands in front of me on the table. We were like those people we would see at The Coffee Exchange in Providence on Internet dates. While we were doing homework we listened to people on coffee dates have the world's most awkward conversations. We'd pass notes back and forth with our commentary. *He just wants to squeeze her big boobs,* Jules once wrote on my social studies folder as a girl went on and on about feminist theory and her bearded date made noises of pretend interest. *She's refusing to mention his vampire fangs!* I scribbled to Jules on the corner of her math homework another time when a guy at the next table polished his fake fangs with his index finger while his date talked about her dance class. *And he's dying to discuss!*

We sat there for another thirty seconds in awkward silence, each of us taking in the café surroundings as if we were foreigners observing American island culture. Finally, I just came out with it. "Let me just start by saying that I'm really glad you texted me. I've been so, so worried about you."

"You don't have to worry about me, Cricket."

"But, Jules. I care about you. I'm your . . . friend." I'd stopped myself from saying best friend.

"My mom died," she said. "You can't expect me to act normal."

"No," I said. "I know."

"You have to let me act how I want to," she said. The tips of her ears reddened.

"But even if you want to act mean? Like telling Jay what I said about his brother. Do you like him?"

"No," she said, shaking her head.

"Why did you do that?" The waitress dropped off my iced tea. I looked her in the eye and smiled. "Thank you so much," I said. If she overheard any of this, I wanted her to be on my side. I pounded the straw out of its paper case and took a long drink.

"I was drunk, and it just came out."

"Yeah, well, thanks. He'll never go out with me now. And that night, at the party, you were acting like a different person."

"I am different," she said, as if I were proving her point.

"But you're still you," I said. "You're still Jules Clayton."

"I'm not," she said.

"But *I* didn't do anything wrong."

"My family is mine. You've been acting like it's yours."

"We were all acting like that," I said, my voice trembling with hurt. I crossed my arms. "You invited me to spend the night all the time. Nina always set a place for me at the table. Even on school nights. I didn't do anything wrong." Jules raised her eyebrows at me. "What? What did I do?"

"The memorial service?" She said this like it was the most obvious thing in the world. I looked at her blankly. The Caesar salad landed in front of me.

"Fresh pepper?" the waitress asked.

"No, thank you." I turned back to Jules. "What did I do?"

"You weren't supposed to talk," Jules said. She sat back and folded her arms.

"But I asked you afterward, remember? And you said it was fine. You said it was great."

"Mom had just died," she whispered. "I didn't know what I was saying."

I stared at the salad I knew I wasn't going to be able to eat. "I thought . . . I mean, when you were up there you looked like you were about to laugh or die. You even said yourself that you were freaking out."

"It wasn't your place. She wasn't your mom. She was mine."

"I thought I was helping," I said.

"Well, you were wrong."

"Your dad didn't mind. Zack didn't mind."

"I did," Jules said. I sat back, inhaling the coffee-scented café air. I didn't want to be wrong and I didn't want her to be right, but as I watched her shoulders rising and falling with deep, shaky breaths, it was so clear.

"I'm sorry," I said. "I'm really, really sorry." I wanted to fling myself over the table and hug her. I wanted to reach out and touch her hands. She put her hands in her lap in such a way that made me feel like I might never be able to touch her again. I balled up my hands. My eyes filled.

"Sometimes I think I smell her perfume," I said, wiping the tears away with a stiff napkin. "It happened once when I got off the ferry, and again when I was walking past The

White Elephant. Does that ever happen to you? Do you ever smell her perfume?"

"Marc Jacobs perfume is really popular." Jules shook her head and stirred her coffee. I sensed I was annoying her. I willed my tears to stop. "Look, I can't explain how I'm feeling, but that's the thing. I don't want to explain how I'm feeling, and I shouldn't have to. No one else is asking me to."

"Okay," I said. "I understand." I pushed the salad around on my plate. "What made you text me?"

"Zack," she said. "Freak boy."

"Oh." My shoulders caved as guilt flooded my chest.

"He said I owed it to you to at least tell you why I was mad. He believes in discussing feelings." She rolled her eyes.

"Oh," I said, and slid the pepper toward her, wondering if she'd build a leaning pepper tower like she always did at school.

"So what are you doing for your birthday? It's on Tuesday, right?" she asked, ignoring the pepper.

"Yeah. I think the people at the inn are going to have a little party maybe."

"That sounds nice," she said. I met her eyes. "I better go. I'm working tonight." She picked up her bag like it weighed a hundred pounds. "Look, I feel bad, okay? I know you didn't mean it."

"It's okay."

"And I know I've been a total bitch." She closed her

eyes, defeated, and then swung her bag over her shoulder and sighed.

"It's okay."

"Happy birthday, Cricket." She smiled. It wasn't a real smile. But it was close.

Thirty-five

"I'D KILL FOR YOUR FLAXEN TRESSES," LIZ SAID OVER THE noise of the hair dryer. I was sitting in front of the vanity in her room in my bathrobe. She had put hot curlers in my hair a half hour ago, and now she was taking them out, revealing wavy perfection. My hair had never looked so good. I'd thought curlers were for grandmas, but now I was thinking I needed to ask for a set of these for Christmas.

"You're giving me magazine hair!" I clapped.

"Tonight is the night," Liz said.

"I don't know about that," I said.

"Oh, who are you kidding?" Liz said, laughing.

"Seriously, I can't do it with this guy, but I still want to look hot."

"You're going to torture this poor bloke," Liz said.

Zack was taking me out on a real date for my birthday, which was technically at 12:31 a.m. He wanted to be with me the moment I turned eighteen, so we were celebrating Monday night. We were going out to dinner at Gigi's, the place where he worked as a busboy and one of the nicest, most expensive restaurants on Nantucket. It was not a place for children. It was a place for women in high heels and expensive dresses and men in ties and loafers. I'd peeked in the windows once and seen a grown couple making out.

"Are you sure you want to take me there?" I'd asked Zack when he told me the plan. The cheapest thing on the menu was the bleu cheese hamburger, and it was thirty-three dollars. But he'd said yes. He and the chef, Anne-Marie, had become friends this summer.

"Anne-Marie promised me an unforgettable meal, on the house. And Jeff, the manager, said he'd turn a blind eye if I happened to bring in a bottle of champagne, which you know I have."

"Are you sure your dad won't miss that champagne?"

"Uh, yeah," Zack said. "I'm sure."

"Okay, then," I said. "I'll meet you there."

"Eight o'clock?"

"Eight o'clock."

I was a little worried about people seeing us together. Every day felt like an extension on a paper, one more day of putting off something we had to do—break it off. But every day also tasted like ice cream. And I always wanted another bite.

I'd been thinking about this date all day while I cleaned. After Liz and I finished the rooms, I checked in with George, who was now communicating only with hand signals. The particular one he was giving me meant go away.

So I took a long shower, using the Bumble and bumble shampoo a guest had left behind. I'd waited a week for the guest to call and reclaim it, but there hadn't been a word. The shampoo was mine. I sat down in the shower to shave my legs. I toweled off, put on some nice lotion, and once I was completely dry, I slipped the green dress over my head. I looked in the mirror. Perfection. Liz insisted I put a robe over my dress as she did my hair and makeup.

"Ouch," I said, when one of her curlers snagged, pulling my hair.

"Well, do you want to be beautiful or do you want to be comfortable?" Liz asked as she untangled it.

"Can't I be both?" I asked.

"No," she said, slapping some product on her hands and twisting the ends of my hair. "You must choose. Beauty or comfort."

"Fine," I said. "Beauty."

"Good girl."

Thirty-six

WHEN I HEARD THE WHISTLE ACROSS THE STREET, I KNEW it was meant for me. Since I'd stepped out of the inn, I'd felt eyes on me. Liz had worked wonders with my hair, making it appear thicker and bouncier than ever before, and she'd applied little fake eyelashes one by one with a pair of tweezers to "open up" my eyes. At first I told her there was no way I was going to let her put fake eyelashes on me, but she assured me they'd look great. She was right.

But it was the dress that was turning heads. This dress was a beautiful-girl costume. Another whistle. I thought maybe it was Zack, but when I turned my head, it was Jay. He was across the street, flanked by Fitzy and Oliver. They had fishing poles over their shoulders. Jay was holding a tackle box, and Fitzy was barefoot, smoking a cigar.

"C.T.," Jay said.

"Hi," I said, and waved.

They watched me cross the street. Fitzy narrowed his eyes and puffed on his cigar. Before I'd arrived, I had this idea that Nantucket was so small that it would be impossible not to run into the people you knew. But it wasn't like that. I hadn't seen these guys since that night at the party in 'Sconset. A few times, I'd actually tried to will Jay to appear so I could explain to him, in my own words, how sorry I was about what I said about his brother. Maybe there'd been a delayed reaction to my prayers, because there he was, looking happy to see me. I wondered for a second if I should be nervous, if this was a trick, if Jay was going to make me think everything was cool and then tell me off, but I didn't think so. He was drinking me in like a cold glass of lemonade.

"I don't believe we've met," Fitzy said.

"Yes, we have," I said.

"I think I'd remember," he said. "What's your name?"

"Cricket," I said. I watched him listen. This was the power of looking good. It made boys pay attention. It popped their little independence bubble.

"I'm Andrew Fitzpatrick," he said, and planted a cool kiss on my hand.

"Cricket Thompson"—Jay glared at him—"is a friend of mine from Providence." A friend? I met his gaze. Jay's bright blue eyes shone against his tanned caramel skin. There was no doubt about it: Jay was probably one of the best-looking guys in the world, and summer had given him a glowing confidence. He's going to be important someday, I thought.

"Where are you off to looking so beautiful?" he asked.

"Dinner," I said, feeling myself flush.

"What I wouldn't do to be dinner," Fitzy said, shaking his head and biting his cigar.

"You sound like someone's gross uncle," Oliver said, laughing.

"How about you guys go ahead," Jay said, nodding his head at Fitzy and Oliver. "I'll catch up with you later."

"How come you get a private audience with this gorgeous woman?" Fitzy asked him.

"Because she's my friend," Jay said. There was that word again. *Friend.*

"We'll just pop into the pharmacy for a hot dog," Oliver said, slapping Fitzy on the back. "Would you like a dog, Jay?"

"I could eat a dog," said Jay. Fitzy snuffed his cigar, and the two of them went inside the pharmacy.

"Listen," I said, "I need to apologize. I'm so sorry for what I said. It was horrible and judgmental and I'm just so sorry."

"Apology accepted," he said.

"Really?" This seemed too easy.

"Jules told me she'd taken the comment out of context."

"She did? Really?" He nodded. "Oh my god, that's great." I breathed in deeply. Air filled a spot in my lungs that had been puckering since the fight. Jules had made things right. She had forgiven me.

"She also showed me this." Jay pulled out of his pocket the list I'd made the morning after the party at Nora's, my top five reasons for liking Jay Logan.

There was tape along the edges, and I could tell that Jules had saved it in our notebook and removed it to give to Jay. "I especially liked number five," he said, and I reread it. *Jay always sticks up for his brother so I know he's a good guy with a real heart.* "I guess I also like number one." *He has big, dreamy eyes and the best boy butt I've ever seen.*

"I'm so embarrassed," I said.

"Don't be," he said. "It's nice."

"Oh," I said. "Well, I'm just so glad this is cleared up. . . ." I trailed off. He was gazing at me the way I'd wanted him to since the eighth grade. His smile was so bright and winning, I was in a spotlight. The people passing by all seemed to notice us. They were looking at us the way I'd looked at the glossy, dressed-up Nantucketers when I'd stepped off the ferry. My throat was dry.

"Me too. 'Cause I was hoping you'd be my girl next year." His girl? So old-fashioned. And yet . . . like something Jay-Z might say to Beyoncé. It was the invitation I'd been waiting for for three years. Was he asking me out? He was, right? Being Jay Logan's girlfriend would be like winning a prize. I'd be untouchable. Golden. Chosen for a better life. It would be like getting into Princeton, early admission, with a full ride for specialness. I smiled.

"Is that a yes?" Jay asked, and stepped closer to me.

He was standing so close, glimmering like some kind of

American hero in his faded Whale's Tale beer T-shirt. We would be the couple of the year. I drank in the possibility. There had been times when I'd imagined this moment at lacrosse practice, and it always made me run faster.

"I've thought about that night at Nora's," he said. "I really wanted to kiss you."

"Me too," I said. It was true. I'd obsessed about that moment at the beginning of the summer. But not recently. Now that I thought about it, I hadn't fantasized about kissing him, or played the Jay playlist for weeks. It struck me that I didn't want to go any further with him than this. Right here. This was enough. This was the fantasy. Maybe this whole time, the possibility of Jay was all I'd wanted. But before I could tease this thought apart from all the others that were going through my mind, he placed a gentle hand on my back, leaned in, and pressed his lips to mine. Jay Logan was actually kissing me!

I pressed back. I did. I kissed him back because I had to know if it was the idea of Jay or Jay himself that I liked so much. I tingled with a feeling that I was doing something wrong, which was confusing because tingling is tingling.

"Nice move, Logan," said Fitzy. "Way to break your buddy's heart." We pulled apart. There were Fitzy and Oliver, hands full of hot dogs. The church bells chimed eight o'clock.

"I'm having a party on Friday," Fitzy said. "Eighty-two Cliff Road. Bring your sister."

"I don't have a sister," I said.

"Damn," he said.

"I have to go," I said.

I spotted Zack as soon as I pushed open the bright red door of Gigi's. He was sitting at a table by a window with a bouquet of wildflowers and a bottle of champagne, looking at his watch. He was wearing a button-down shirt and his Nantucket Reds.

"Hi," I said. He looked at me and stood up. He was only six feet away, but I couldn't get to him fast enough. Any confusion I'd experienced on the walk over vanished like a drop of water in direct sunlight. He put his arms around me and I kissed him. And when I did: phosphorescence.

"I'm in love with you, Zack Clayton," I said.

"I'm in love with you, too," he said, and kissed me again. "I'm in love with my secret lover."

Thirty-seven

IT HAPPENED IN MY LITTLE ROOM WITH THE SLANTED ceiling right before the sun came up and all the champagne was gone. It wasn't what I thought it would be at all. It wasn't as easy as they make it look in the movies. It took kind of a while to get everything all lined up and protected and ready to go. The actual sex part was pretty short, and I was relieved it was short. I know I'm supposed to want it to last, but I didn't. I've heard that's kind of normal for a first time. I kept my eyes open, when I always thought I'd be the type to keep them shut. Oh, and the kissing was still my favorite part, which isn't what I thought, that the first thing you do with a boy could be the best. And I did feel different afterward; I felt all shaky and energized. Maybe that's because it's good exercise. I think that's what they say, anyway. And my face was really hot, and that made me feel pretty. I didn't think I would feel pretty. Or if I did, I thought it would be in a flowing-white-nightgown kind of way, not a cheeks-full-of-embers way.

I wanted to call someone. And not because I wanted to spill every little detail, but because I wanted it to be known that something had happened to me. I wanted to stay awake, even as Zack seemed to be drifting off. I touched his muscular back. He was the most beautiful thing I had ever seen. I picked his button-down shirt off the floor and put it on to sleep in. It smelled like him. I promised myself I would always remember the moment of putting on his shirt.

"Are you sure you wouldn't be embarrassed to go out with me?" he asked, his arm around me as we spooned.

"Yes," I said. "I'm sure." This time, I meant it.

He kissed my hair and I heard his breath deepen as he fell asleep.

I thought I was awake all night, because I remember the sky whitening and the birdsong and smiling at the ceiling. But I must've drifted off, because when I heard the knock at the door, I was dreaming I was back in Providence, sitting in front of a roaring fire on the big sofa in the living room. In my dream it was winter. Outside, a snowstorm howled. The sky was purple-gray, snow was flying sideways, and the wind was knocking against the windows, but I was under the cream-colored blanket. I was warm, warm, warm.

But the knocking was too persistent for a dream. It was real.

"Cricket?" a voice said. I knew that voice. I missed that voice. I loved that voice. The sound of it lured me out of the warm bath of sleep. My eyes fluttered open. There was Jules with Lulu the pig in one hand and a waffle topped with whipped cream in the other. For a second, I smiled. She'd brought Lulu to Nantucket! She'd found my room! She'd remembered my birthday! She'd made a waffle and carried it all the way from Darling Street! And oh, there was something I needed to tell her. As I held my breath trying to remember what it was that was so important, so wonderfully important, I watched her face register disgust.

"Zack?" she asked.

Thirty-eight

I SAT ON THE PATIO, WEARING THE CONSTRUCTION PAPER birthday crown Liz had made me, taking deep breaths, trying to focus on the bouquet of yellow and white flowers in a vase in front of me, which had arrived just an hour ago. I'd read somewhere that flowers absorb negative energy, making the space around them more positive; this was why flowers made sick or angry people feel better. I was hoping it worked for worried people, too. It was almost four o'clock and I hadn't heard from Jules or Zack since they'd left this morning at seven, even though I'd been calling both of them obsessively. As soon as Jules saw Zack sleeping shirtless beside me, she'd put Lulu and the waffle on the floor and left without another word. She slammed the door on her way out, which woke up Zack. When I told him what had just happened, he kissed me once and left to find her.

When the delivery boy dropped the flowers at the front desk and Gavin called out, "Flowers for the birthday girl!" I thought they were from Zack, and my heart pushed against my ribs as I stripped off my pink latex gloves and dove for the card. For a second I thought that maybe he hadn't been able to return my four phone calls and six texts because Jules had been nearby, but somehow he'd found time to send me flowers. Or maybe, I thought, he felt that because we'd had sex for the first time last night, some higher form of communication was necessary—communication by flowers. But I opened the little white envelope and my eyes landed on the word *Mom* with a thud.

"They're from my mom," I said to Gavin.

"That was lovely of her!" Gavin admonished me gently. "Don't sound so disappointed."

It had been Liz's day off. (I was surprised when she didn't switch with me for my birthday, but she and Shane had both orchestrated Tuesdays as their day off and they were sacred to her. They refused to spend a single Tuesday apart. She was bringing him to my little birthday party.) She'd spent the night at Shane's, so I hadn't even been able to tell her what happened. I wondered if Bernadette had been able to sense my anxiety, because she'd been nicer to me than usual, meaning that she left me alone and didn't make me crawl under beds to hunt the dust bunnies.

The first time I'd seen Liz today was fifteen minutes ago when she placed the crown on my head and disappeared into the kitchen, leaving Shane and me to make awkward conversation on the patio. Thankfully, he'd gone inside after a minute, leaving me alone with my thoughts. My head was too busy and too tangled to make small talk. On the one hand, I was thrilled. I'd had sex! I was in love! I was different and my cheeks had been blushing for eight hours straight to prove it. I'd catch glimpses of myself in mirrors and place a hand on my new face. I was warm and glowing. At the same time, guilt and shame washed over me in waves, sending acid to my stomach. All I wanted to do was steal Liz away so that I could tell her everything, and she could both celebrate with me and reassure me that I wasn't a terrible person, that what I'd done was understandable and okay, that Jules would come around and be happy for me.

I could feel the late afternoon sun burning my arms as I listened to Gavin and Liz gather plates, forks, and glasses for the iced tea for my mini birthday party.

"You look like one conflicted birthday girl," George said as he walked up the porch steps. He was finally off of his crutches and was carrying something in his hand. It was wrapped in newspaper.

"I have a lot on my mind," I said, forcing a smile.

"I can see that." He put the newspaper-wrapped item in front of me. "Here. This is for you. Open it."

"Wow, thanks, George." I hadn't expected a gift from him. I smiled when I saw the Apple logo on the box. "Oh my god, George, is this the new iPad?" It was the one that just came out. "Wow! Are you sure?"

"Yes." George put his elbow on the table and rested his hand in his palm. He smiled. "Do you like it?"

"I love it! This is so nice."

"You've been a great intern. I couldn't have done it without you. It's the least I can do." He tapped out a beat on the table.

"It's so cool." I took it out of its box. "Thank you so much."

"And check this out," he said, motioning for me to hand it to him. He showed me a voice-recording app. "I don't know if working with me this summer will have any influence on you, but just in case, I figure you should be prepared. You never know when you might find yourself in the middle of a great story. They're happening all the time, and now you can record them." He nodded at someone inside and put an arm on my shoulder. "Now, cover your ears, Thompson, I don't want to hurt you with my singing voice."

"Happy birthday to you. . . ." George started as Gavin carried a dark chocolate cake decorated with a wreath of sugary violets and topped with eighteen sparkling candles out to the patio. Liz followed with a pitcher of iced tea topped with lemon slices, and Shane carried a tray of glasses, forks, and the nice, gold-rimmed china plates.

"Happy birthday to Cricket," they all sang. "Happy birthday to you!"

As I was blowing out the candles, I wished for two things at once.

Liz shrieked. She was looking at the newspaper the iPad

was wrapped in that I'd left on the table. It was *The Inquirer and Mirror*, the local Nantucket paper. "Cricket, it's you!" she said, pointing at the cover photograph. "It's you in your green dress with your secret boyfriend." It was a big picture of Jay and me, kissing on Main Street. The headline read: "Young Love Blooms in the Perfect Summer Weather." She laughed. "I guess he's not your secret boyfriend anymore!"

Thirty-nine

ZACK HAD TO HAVE SEEN THE PAPER. IT WAS EVERYWHERE on this island. *The Inquirer and Mirror*, with Jay's and my picture on the front page, would not go unnoticed, not in a million years.

After the birthday party, after I'd forced myself to eat a piece of cake and smile and thank everybody for celebrating with me, I decided to go for a run. Liz had made pointed eye contact with me throughout the party. She kept pinching my thigh and asking me if I felt different. I'd managed to nod and give her a thumbs-up and even laugh a little, but it had taken all of my strength.

I didn't want to talk to her about what had happened anymore. I didn't even want to try to get her on my side. I wasn't even on my side. Why would she be? What I had done to Jules, losing my virginity to her little brother only a few months after her mom died, was terrible. And kissing Jay, while it had seemed innocent at the time, even *productive* in some way, had been a huge betrayal of Zack's trust. How would I have felt if I saw a picture of Zack kissing another girl on the very same night we'd had sex? Horrible. Miserable. Pissed. I clutched my stomach as though I were swallowing poison, not buttercream frosting. Thankfully, Shane wanted to take Liz surfing, and she never said no to surfing with Shane. So when the party ended, I could just drop the charade and remove the happy mask.

I was too anxious to stay inside. I was too anxious to merely walk. I needed to run. I needed to sprint. I needed to work up a salty sweat and hear my feet pound the pavement and feel the sun searing the back of my neck. I needed to feel my heart pump blood and my breath get ragged and scratchy in my lungs. I needed to jump into the depths of the cold Atlantic Ocean. I needed to plunge my head under the water, open my mouth, and scream so loud the ferries rocked.

I put on my sports bra and bikini bottoms under shorts and a T-shirt and laced up my sneakers tight. I slipped my ponytail through a Red Sox hat that had been lingering in the lost and found for three weeks, and pulled the brim low over my eyebrows. I jogged out of town on Centre Street to Cliff Road.

I was halfway to the beach when I saw the red Volvo coming toward me. That was Parker's car! Quills of panic pierced my stomach. I bet Parker knew everything. I bet Jules had told her. Parker was confident, fearless, and mean. And she was driving fast. I stopped and turned away from the road, wishing I had a shell to hide under. Was Jules in the car? Was Zack? I tried to make it look like I was tying my shoe. I was shaking, practically hyperventilating.

What had happened back in Providence was an accident. I thought I was doing the right thing by speaking at Nina's memorial service. I had stood up and spoken with the best of intentions. And no matter what Jules thought, I'd followed her out to Nantucket out of love for her. But what had happened last night was no accident. And kissing Jay wasn't a mistake, either. I'd kissed him back.

I heard the Volvo slow and I squeezed my eyes shut, covering my face in some primal pose of protection. I heard a window roll down. My heart was knocking desperately against my ribs. "Are you okay?" someone asked. It wasn't Parker and Jules in the Volvo, but a grandma and grandpa. "Do you need some help, sweetheart?"

"Just a runner's cramp," I said, catching my breath. "I'm okay." I stood up.

"You're positively crimson. And probably dehydrated." The woman handed me an Evian. "It's too hot for running. Do you want a ride somewhere?"

"No. No, thank you," I said, taking the chilled bottle. They drove off.

It wasn't Parker, but I couldn't seem to transmit this

message from my brain to the rest of my body. I was shaking. My legs felt like jelly. I couldn't seem to fill my lungs with the air they needed. I wanted to get back to the inn, turn off the lights, and hide under the covers in my little room with the rose wallpaper and the slanted ceiling. How was I going to get there if I couldn't walk, if I couldn't even breathe?

"I'm taking a few days off," I said to Gavin the next morning. He was sitting at the reception desk, penciling something into the giant reservation book. "I think Bernadette can cover for me."

"What?" he said with a furrowed brow. He sounded annoyed for the first time since I'd met him. "You know, usually you try to arrange someone to cover for you *before* you announce that you're taking time off."

"I'm really sorry, but it's a family emergency." This wasn't a lie. This did feel like an emergency. Hot tears pricked my eyes.

"Is everything okay?" he asked. I nodded, unable to speak. "When are you leaving?"

"Tomorrow," I said. I'd called Dad last night and he was still willing to fly me back to Providence for Alexi's birthday party. He booked me on a flight that would land in Providence at three thirty. I'd be at his house by four o'clock. I wanted to get off this island as soon as possible. They call Nantucket the faraway island. It's so self-contained that it really can make you feel like you're in an enchanted, distant world, that some magical mist separates you from reality. But it can also make you feel trapped and isolated. I wanted to get out of there.

"Cricket," Gavin called as I walked down the hall. "You are coming back, aren't you?"

"Yes," I said, without looking at him. "I'll only be gone for two days." I'd already hurt and pissed off so many people, what was one more lie?

"You look like hell," George said when I went to tell him that I'd be gone for a few days. George's leg was healed, he was off his crutches, and he was almost done with the book. He really didn't need me anymore.

"It's a family emergency," I said. That phrase had stopped Gavin from asking more questions, and it had the same effect on George.

"I'm really sorry to hear that," George said. "Is there anything I can do?" I shook my head. "Okay. Well, you'll be back by the weekend, right?"

"I think," I said, looking at the carpet.

"Because I was hoping you'd do an interview for me."

"For the book?" He nodded. For one quick second I wasn't thinking about Zack or Jules. "Like, a real live journalist interview?"

"Yes." He smiled. "A real live journalist interview."

"Who would I interview?"

"Paul Morgan. He's a friend of your mom's, right?"

"Yeah."

"I've been going through my notes, and his name comes up more than once. I think he and Boaty were pretty good friends at one point. He might have some unexpected treasure for me."

"How will I know what to ask?" I wanted to get out of there, but it would have been a shame to miss out on this. It was my chance to really be a part of the book.

"I'll help you," he said. "That is, if you think you'll have time to do it."

Forty

"FIRST OF ALL, THANK YOU SO MUCH FOR MEETING ME," I said to Paul Morgan. I'd called him right from the annex, and he'd agreed to meet with me the next morning before my flight. We were sitting in the living room of his house on Union Street. It had wooden floors and a mix of antique furniture and modern things. There were some paintings of boats on the walls, framed nautical charts, and also the kind of unexpected things that Nina would've picked out. A bright red rocking chair. A poster from a theater festival in France. The guy had style. Mom would like this place, I thought. I scanned the mantelpiece for pictures of a wife and family, but only saw people who looked like friends. I think it was safe to say that Paul Morgan was single.

"Oh, I'm happy to do it," Paul said. "My schedule on Nantucket is very open."

"Well, I really appreciate it. I know your time is valuable." I was remembering what George said about being polite. He told me how important it was to make the interviewees comfortable so that they'll reveal their own stories, hand them over like the keys to their house. George said that a lot of journalists were jerks in the way that they tried to get information. They tried to catch people off guard and make them uncomfortable, but George's philosophy was the opposite.

"If you don't mind, I'm going to record this," I said, and pressed the screen of my iPad. The chair I sat in was so big that I needed to sit on the very edge of it for my feet to touch the ground.

"I don't mind a bit," he said, laughing a little. "I've got nothing to hide. So, you're writing a book about Boaty Carmichael?"

"No, *I'm* not," I said. My brow furrowed. He thought that this was some kind of school project. "George Gust the journalist is."

"George Gust the journalist?"

"He writes for *The New York Times* and *The New Yorker*," I said. George had only been published once in *The New Yorker*, but it sounded so impressive to me. "The book is being published by Random House. It will be out in the spring." Paul Morgan nodded, making the "I'm impressed" frown. "I'm his intern," I continued, "and he thought since you were a *special friend* of my mother's that it would be okay if I interviewed you." I watched his face closely as I said "special friend." Sure enough, his eyes twinkled. More on this later, I thought. Even if I didn't come back to Nantucket, it didn't mean I couldn't arrange a meeting with Paul and Mom somewhere else. In Boston, maybe.

"Well, what would you like to know?" he asked, and clapped his hands once.

"I guess I'd like to know about any particularly fond memories of Boaty."

"Well, let's see. I met Boaty the summer after college. I've been coming here all my life, but it was Boaty's first summer on the island. After a month, he knew everyone. He was very charming. My own mother had a crush on him. I remember him bringing her a birthday present, and forget it, it's like he was already building his campaign. He had her vote for life."

"What was the present?"

"A bottle of Oil of Olay!" he said, as if he were realizing for the first time how funny that was. We both laughed. "He was kind of a hick when I first met him, but, boy, he got savvy fast."

And we were off. Paul settled back in his chair and spoke of a sailing trip they went on, and how Boaty made the best ham-and-pickle sandwich in the world by slipping potato chips under white bread slathered with yellow mustard, and the bonfire beach parties that lasted until dawn. George was right. People liked to talk. I looked at the grandfather clock. An hour had gone by, and with the exception of a few questions asking Paul to elaborate or "tell me more about that," I'd hardly been able to get a word in. It was almost time for me to go. I wasn't sure I'd gotten anything out of him that we'd be able to use, but my plane was leaving in a few hours and I needed to wrap it up.

"Thank you so much," I said at the first awkward silence. "This was very helpful." I closed my notebook and shut off my iPad.

"So," Paul said, gripping the edges of his armchair, "your mother and father must be so proud of you, an intern for a journalist and you're not even out of high school. Are they planning on visiting you?"

"I'm trying to convince my mother," I said. "But they won't come together. They're divorced."

"I'm so sorry to hear that," he said.

"It happens, I guess."

"If your mother visits, I'd love to take you two out to dinner."

"I'll pass along the message."

He smiled at me warmly as he stood from his chair and walked me to the door. I trailed him through the kitchen with the speckled floor and the old-fashioned-looking sink. Blue and white dishes were stacked on open shelves. Lemon-yellow curtains billowed in the breeze. I could definitely see Mom in this kitchen, if she would only give it a chance.

"Oh, here's a detail you might like," he said. "Everyone thought Boaty got his nickname because he loved boats so much."

"Yeah, there's a story that as a toddler he made a boat out of a laundry basket and insisted on sleeping in it," I said. Paul opened the front door and we stepped onto the porch into the perfect Nantucket morning—warm, breezy, sweet-smelling.

"That may be true," Paul Morgan said, "but that's not how he got his name."

"Oh. How'd he get it?"

"His little brother gave it to him. He had a big birthmark in the shape of a boat, on his lower back." I smiled and made a note in my notebook. This was exactly the kind of detail that George was after. I'd succeeded after all!

"You look just like your mother when you smile," he said. "I bet you're a real heartbreaker."

You have no idea, I thought as I shook his hand and thanked him one last time. *You have no idea.*

Forty-one

DAD PLANTED A KISS ON MY FOREHEAD WHEN I STEPPED
out of the cab. He handed the driver some money and took
my duffel bag. There were bunches of balloons tied to the
porch railing. In front of the house hung a big colorful banner
that spelled out HAPPY BIRTHDAY, ALEXI! in primary colors.

"Hi, Dad." I leaned into his shirt. He wrapped his arms
around me and gave me a squeeze. This is what I'd needed.
A Dad hug. I couldn't exactly tell him what had happened
(who wants to tell their dad the details of their love life?),
but I was hoping he might be able to sense my wound and
apply his special Dad Band-Aid. When I was little and I'd
fallen down and scraped my knee, he would sweep me into
his arms so fast that I'd actually forget to cry. The tears were

coming now, so I squeezed him back, hard, hoping to make them stop.

I hadn't told Mom I was coming home yet. I couldn't take her sadness. It was so dark and deep, I was afraid, now more than ever, that it'd pull me in and I wouldn't be able to get out. What if I was like her? What if I became permanently sad? What if the same cloud was destined to hover over my head?

Dad ended our hug with three pats on the back and guided me up the walkway. "Come on, the party is in full swing."

"Okay," I said.

"Your Aunt Phyllis is here," he said. "And so is Uncle Rob." I was about to ask why Aunt Phyllis, who lived in Maine and only visited at Christmas, was here in Providence, when Dad opened the gate to the backyard. There were llamas in my father's backyard. Llamas! There were other animals, too. There was a sheep, a goat, and a pig—an entire petting zoo. There was one of those jumpy castles. There was a guy in overalls sitting on a bale of hay playing songs for kids. There was a popcorn maker, like the kind they have in movie theaters. And who were all these people? Was that a waitress serving the punch? The only thing that had come close to this was Mom's fortieth birthday party, and even that hadn't included a waitress.

"Oh my god, Dad. This is amazing. What's all this for?"

"Alexi's birthday," he said. "He's six!"

"It's so cool that you did all this."

"Well, it made Polly happy for me to make a big to-do," Dad said, beaming. "And if Polly's happy, I'm happy." There was Polly in a sundress. She did look happy. Her hands were on Alexi's shoulder. He was watching the guitar guy, riveted. Polly waved to me and I waved back.

"So, Dad, do you notice anything?" I asked, and twirled around in my new jeans.

"A haircut?" Dad asked.

"No! I'm wearing the jeans you got me. My Clovers!"

"Oh, do you like them?"

"I love them!"

"Good. Polly picked them out," he said. I kept smiling, even as my thoughts were suddenly treading dark pathways. He hadn't met the Great Birthday Challenge after all. Polly had chosen my present. He had given up on the very last year.

A woman I didn't know approached us. She and Dad started talking about the special school Alexi was going to in the fall.

"Your father is an absolute saint," the woman said to me. "An angel!"

"I know," I said, my cheeks hurting from smiling. One of the goats bleated. Dad didn't even like zoos. He was allergic to all animals.

"Go put your bag inside, honey, so you can enjoy the party," he said, and gave my shoulder a squeeze.

"Okay." I headed into the house. I put my bag in the kitchen and looked for a glass to fill with water. I couldn't find the glasses. I didn't know where they were kept. So

I grabbed a mug and held it under the tap. As it filled, I looked out the kitchen window at Polly and Alexi.

I watched as Dad brought Polly a drink and put his arm around her. He tussled Alexi's hair. Polly called Dad her "knight in shining armor," her "dream guy." And I got it now. He would do anything for them. He would turn his yard into a zoo. He *loves* them, I thought as I watched Polly lean on him. He *really loves* them.

I took a sip of water and found my hand shaking. Dad had traded Mom and me in for Polly and Alexi. We were out and they were in, and it was just our tough luck. It wasn't fair. It wasn't fair at all. Those people, those *strangers*, stole my family. I drank the water. Then I spotted an open bottle of wine. With a shaky hand, I filled the mug to the top and downed it in just a few swallows. My empty stomach seemed to curl around it. A scream sat at the bottom of my lungs, waiting, like a crocodile.

"Hey, honey, you find what you needed?" Dad asked as the screen door slammed behind him.

I turned around and crossed my arms, glaring at him.

"You okay?" Dad asked.

"Eighteen is a much bigger birthday than six," I said. I hated how bratty I sounded, but the wine had gone straight to my head. I was dizzy and warm and certain I was right.

"Don't tell me that you wanted a petting zoo, Cricket." He was smiling, but he looked kind of scared. His eyes searched mine as if to ask, *Are you joking?*

"You couldn't pick something out for me, but you got

Alexi a . . . a . . . farm festival?" My voice was shrill, loud. I could hear it, but I couldn't stop it, like it was coming from a different person.

"I thought you liked the jeans." He put a hand on my back. I recoiled from it like it was a hot iron.

"That's not the point," I said.

"Well, what *is* the point?" he asked.

"I wanted *you* to pick them out. Only you."

"Well, Polly and I are a team now."

A team? Barf. "You know, maybe if you'd done something like *this* for Mom she wouldn't have gotten so depressed. But you never even tried."

"Yes, I did," he whispered.

"Not like this," I said, pointing to the party outside. Tears sprang to my eyes. "You never tried *this* hard!"

"Oh, honey." He opened his arms, but I took a quick step backward.

"Why didn't you fight for her? Why didn't you fight for us?" I pressed my fingertips to my chest so hard I left a red mark. Tears poured down my cheeks. I couldn't catch my breath. Dad tried to hug me, but I sidestepped him, turned away, and gripped the counter. "I don't even know why you love them. Polly's not that great and Alexi isn't even your kid. Who knows whose kid he really is."

"Cricket, that's enough," Dad said. His voice was low and angry.

I turned around. Polly was standing there, covering her mouth.

"You need to leave," Polly said. Dad wrapped his arms around her as if she were a little girl, as if she were his one and only daughter, as if she needed protection from some awful stranger who'd barged into their home.

"I didn't mean it like that," I said to Dad, pleading. My ears were ringing. "It's not fair. I didn't know she was there."

"Go to your mom's," Dad said, shaking his head at me. "Just get your things and go to your mom's."

I grabbed my duffel bag and ran out the back door.

I was at the Claytons' house in twenty minutes. Not the Nantucket house, but the real house. The Providence one. I knew where the key was hidden, under the stone mermaid in the backyard, and I knew the alarm code. I let myself in to the peacock-blue vestibule with the rustic coat rack and the dark wood table with the curvy silver bowl on it and the portrait of the woman with the green scarf.

I climbed the stairs, two at a time, and opened the door to Jules's room, which was stuffy and hot, familiar and safe. I kicked off my shoes, threw off the quilted coverlet, and crawled under the sheets—the cool, beautiful sheets that Nina had brought back from Italy. Nina, I thought. Nina would've known what to say and how to make me feel better. She would've given me words to hold on to as the world swung around. "Nina," I said aloud. "Please be a ghost, please be a ghost." I kicked my legs against the mattress and waited for the lights to flash. I listened for the house to creak, for footsteps to land, or a window to fly open, for the stereo to blare. I waited for a chill to pass over me, for her presence to be made known, but there was nothing but silence. Dead, empty silence.

I'm eighteen, I told myself. This divorce stuff wasn't supposed to bother me anymore. I was leaving for college next year. I'd even found a really nice guy for Mom. So why was I such a wreck? And why was this just sinking in? Why didn't this happen right after the divorce? Or when Dad got remarried?

Zack. It was sinking in because I had fallen in love. This was the thing about feelings. They find each other. You let one in and others follow. I pulled the sheet over my head, curled myself into a cocoon, and let the tears fall until I was tired and ragged and my eyes were raw and my stomach muscles hurt. An hour passed, and then another, and then I fell asleep.

It was dusk when I woke up. The light switched on. Mom stood in the doorway.

"Cricket," she said. She ran to the bed and opened her arms. "Oh, my sweetheart, I was so worried. Oh, my dear girl, here you are." She wrapped her arms around me.

"Mom," I said, and wept into her sweater. "Mom, I'm so alone."

"No, you're not. I'm right here." And for the first time in I don't know how long, I let her hold me. Really hold me. She smelled like Paul Mitchell shampoo and almond soap and a little bit like Cheerios. She smelled like home.

Forty-two

"DAD SAID YOU SAID SOMETHING TERRIBLE ABOUT THAT child, drank a mug of pinot grigio, and took off through the backyard like a bat out of hell. I didn't even know you'd left Nantucket. What happened? What's wrong?"

"You wouldn't understand."

"Try me."

I started at the beginning, at the memorial service. I told her about the party and Parker and the mean thing I'd said about Jay and his brother. I told her that Zack and I had started dating secretly, that I hadn't meant for it to happen, but that our relationship seemed to have a life of its own. I told her that it'd become serious.

"How serious?" she asked.

"Serious," I said.

"Serious serious?" She closed her eyes.

"Yes."

"I'm not ready for this," she said, now covering her entire face with her hands. "Were you safe?"

"Mom! I don't want to talk about that right now."

"As your mother, I have to ask. It's my job. Were you safe?"

"Fine. Yes."

"Good. Are you planning on getting serious again soon? We need to make you a doctor's appointment."

"Mom, not now."

"Okay, okay. We can talk about it later." She cleared her throat. "Are you and Zack still together?"

I told her about Jay and the picture in *The Inquirer and Mirror*, and how everyone on Nantucket hated me and I couldn't go back. I told her that we needed to look into boarding schools for the fall. Boarding schools that were at least two states away.

"You're not going to boarding school," Mom said.

"Why not?"

"Because you have to face this."

"Why?"

"Because you can't just run away. Do you love him?"

"Yes."

Mom smiled. "No hesitation there."

"I know I love him. But I don't know what to do."

"First we need to get out of here."

"Why?"

"Because we've broken into the Claytons' house, that's why," she said, a little amused that I couldn't see this for myself.

"How did you know where I was?"

"I had a feeling. You love this house."

"How did you get in?"

"You left the door wide open, and all the lights were on, leading right to this room. You may as well have left a trail of bread crumbs. Come on, now. I think we should get some dinner and talk it over." I shook my head. "I'm craving fried clams." I moaned. She knows how much I love fried clams. She took my hand and looked me in the eye. "You can handle this."

"I can't go back to Nantucket," I said.

"Right now I'm just asking you to get out of bed and splash water on your face. That's it." Okay, I thought. Okay. I can do that. "One leg on the ground," she said. I put one leg on the floor. "Now the other." Both feet were on the floor. Once I'd done that, it wasn't as hard to climb out of those soft Italian sheets. I opened the door to Jules's little bathroom and ran the cold tap. It'd been a long time since I'd heard that take-charge tone in Mom's voice. It'd been years.

"I do have *some* good news," I said as I brought a handful of water to my face.

"What's that?" she asked.

"Paul Morgan is still in love with you." I patted my face dry with a hand towel monogrammed with Jules's loopy initials.

"What? Who's Paul Morgan?"

"Your first love?"

"I have no idea who you're talking about." In the bathroom mirror, I watched her make up the bed. It didn't look like she was lying. She didn't seem to be having any emotional reaction at all. She was focused on tucking in the sheets.

"The name Paul Morgan doesn't ring a single bell?" I asked.

"Not one," Mom said. She fluffed the pillows.

"Maybe this will help." I dried my hands and pulled the Emily Dickinson book out of my bag. I fanned the pages until I saw the picture of Mom and the guy. I plucked it out. That's when I saw the boat-shaped birthmark on Lover Boy's lower back.

"Oh my god, Paul Morgan wasn't your first love. Boaty Carmichael was."

Forty-three

WE WENT TO SUE'S CLAM SHACK IN NEWPORT. WE ORDERED fried clams, coleslaw, and lemonade, the kind that's neon yellow and tastes wonderfully fake. We sat on the same side of the picnic bench so that we were both facing the ocean. I told Mom about working for George, and she told me about Boaty.

She said that they'd been in love. The relationship had only lasted six weeks, but at that time, it was the most exciting, romantic six weeks of her life. She felt like she was the star of her own movie. "He could light up a room with his smile. By our second day together we were making out in the broom closet and pledging our love under the moonlight. We were so happy, but our relationship was a secret."

This was because of their jobs. The employees at the

Nantucket Beach Club weren't allowed to date each other. The beach club had two locations. One in 'Sconset and one near town. Mom worked at both. She worked at the one in 'Sconset with Boaty during the week, and the one near town with Paul Morgan on the weekends. Even though Mom didn't recognize Paul yet, I knew this was true because Paul had talked about working at the club in town and so distinctly remembered her. I guess Mom had just been too gaga for Boaty to notice anyone else. The manager thought that employee dating, even between the two hotels, caused drama and distracted them from their jobs. "I was still in high school, but Boaty needed that money." Also, what they were doing was technically illegal. Boaty was twenty-two. Mom was seventeen. "But," she added, "I think the secrecy made it more exciting." I knew exactly what she meant.

"So what happened?"

"Lilly Francis," Mom said. "I knew her from my one semester at that awful boarding school. She was from one of the wealthiest, most powerful and well-connected families in the country. What Lilly wanted, Lilly got. And she had her eye on Boaty from the minute she saw him."

"Did he like her too?"

"Not at first. He used to call her pig nose because she looked like this." Mom used her index finger to push her nose up.

"That's mean," I said, laughing.

Mom shrugged. "But she was persistent, and as he came to understand who she was and the amount of wealth and connections she had . . ." Mom paused, ate a clam, and shook her head. She wiped her fingers on one of our stack of paper napkins. "Well, he stopped calling her pig nose and started calling her Lilly."

"But he was in love with you," I said.

"Yes, he was. I cut off his mullet and turned up his collar so that someone like Lilly would notice him in the first place. And I introduced them. I realized later he was dating us at the same time. But I guess the reasons I was so unbelievably attracted to him was the reason he left me: his ambition. When he met Lilly Francis, he found someone who could take him where he wanted to go, fast. The next time he came to Nantucket, he wasn't working at the beach club. He was a member, and he was married to Lilly Francis."

"You were the first one he stepped on, Mom. You were the first rung on his ladder to the top. You should talk to George."

"I'll think about it."

"I can't believe he left you for pig nose!"

"Can't see a pig nose in the dark," she said, and smiled.

"So, what happened with you? The journal just stopped."

She shook her head. "He stopped talking to me cold. He ignored me. I was so heartbroken. I left Nantucket. I came home. He erased me, so I tried to erase him. I buried it. I told no one. There's something about that first broken heart. In some ways, it's the worst one."

A father with his two little boys sat down across from us.

"Dad hates me," I said. "What I said was terrible."

"He doesn't hate you," she said. "But you do owe him and Polly an apology. He'll cool down. He loves you, honey. He's your father. And I love you. We're your parents. No more pretending that you belong to another family, deal?"

"On one condition. You make this family better. You go out on a date with Paul Morgan."

"I don't even know who this man is."

"You will when you see him. Come on, Mom."

"I told you. I'm not ready to date," she said.

"And I'm telling you that it's time. Come on. He's handsome and nice, and he thinks you're great. And he has a cool house on Nantucket." I studied her as I sucked down the last of my neon lemonade. She wasn't budging. "Will you at least promise to stop watching *Real Life Mysteries*?"

"That's my favorite show."

"It's on Saturday nights and it's meant for people who are a hundred years old. Or at least fifty-five."

"That's not true," she said.

"Then how come all the commercials are for adult diapers and Viagra?" I sighed. "It's time to get a life, Kate."

"You make it sound easy. And you may not start calling me Kate."

"Maybe it's not as hard as you think." We threw our garbage away, walked back to the car, and got inside. We sat there for a minute staring at the water. I checked my phone. Still no word from Zack. I didn't want to go back to Nantucket. I didn't even want to go back to Providence. I wanted to stay right here, at Sue's Clam Shack. Forever.

Mom spoke first, as if she could read my mind. "I can't force you to go back. But you only have one week left. If you just quit, you'll ruin your first job reference, and who knows if that writer will write you a letter of recommendation for college? Quitting right at the end doesn't look good. And don't you think it's better to talk to Jules while it's still fresh?"

"No. The thought of going there and talking to Jules gives me a stomachache."

"Sometimes you have to do things that make you uncomfortable."

"But you don't," I said, turning to face her. "You won't even go on one date."

"That's different," she said.

"Bullshit." I unrolled the window and stuck my feet out. "This apple has landed directly under the tree."

She leaned into her seat, rubbed her temples, and closed her eyes. Then she sighed.

"Put your feet in the car." I did, and she started the engine. "Okay. If I go on a date with this Paul Morgan, will you go back to Nantucket? Will you finish out this job and talk to Jules?"

"Yes," I said, and buckled my seat belt as we headed out of the parking lot. Then I leaned over and hugged her so hard we swerved a little onto the grass.

"Quick, turn on the radio," Mom said as she steered us back onto the road. "Before I change my mind."

I put on the '80s station and turned it all the way up.

That night, I heard Mom laughing in her bedroom.

"What are you doing?" I called into the darkness.

"I'm reading my diary," she said, nearly wheezing. "This thing is hysterical."

Forty-four

"I THINK THAT GUY WAS WORKING HERE THE LAST TIME I was on the ferry," Mom said under her breath about the unfriendly white-haired guy behind the food counter. We bought hot dogs, chips, an iced tea for me, and a white wine for her, and found two seats by the railing. It was cloudy and even a little cold today. I wished I'd worn my jeans. I told Mom that she didn't have to come, but now I was glad she was here. I was scared of seeing Jules and Parker and of being rejected by Zack, but it was the thought of having another one of the moments when I couldn't breathe or move that made me want her around the most.

I'd described the moment with the red Volvo to her back

in Providence. I was sitting on her bed with my laptop as she packed. I told her it felt like someone was choking me.

"It's called an anxiety attack," Mom said. "Now, do you think we can find a picture of this Paul Morgan person?" I Googled him and found a picture on his law firm's Web site.

"Oh, yeah, I think I do remember him. He was fun." She studied the picture. "Nice hair. He remembers me?" she asked.

"I already told you, he's, like, in love with you."

Mom smiled and tucked hair behind her ear. Then she looked in her closet and pulled out . . . oh my god . . . a pair of heels. They actually had dust on them.

"Cricket, you're back!" Liz was headed upstairs with an armful of clean towels. She put them on a table and threw her arms around me. "I'm glad to see you." She pulled back and mock slapped me. "Leaving me alone with Bernadette for two whole days, the nerve." She stuck out her hand to Mom. "You must be Cricket's mum. I'm Liz."

"Nice to meet you," Mom said.

"I'm Cricket's top advisor on matters of the heart," Liz said.

"We could all use one of those," Mom said, laughing.

"Especially this one," Liz said, blowing a loose curl from her eyes. "What room are you in, Mrs. Cricket? We'll make sure you get plenty of towels. Maybe even an extra bar of soap if you play your cards right."

"I think we can put her in room fourteen. I've got to check with Gavin," I said.

"You should visit Liz in Ireland, Cricket," Mom said. "That would be fun."

"That's impossible, actually, because I'm going to be living on Nantucket full-time." Liz beamed.

"What about college?" I asked.

"Shane and I decided we're happy here and want to stay. Why mess with a good thing? If we can avoid becoming raging alcoholics, I think we have a very nice life ahead of us."

"Cool," I said. Not going to college seemed crazy to me, but Liz just did whatever she wanted.

"The rooms aren't cleaning themselves, Liz." Bernadette glared as she passed us on the steps.

"Thank you for covering for me, Bernadette."

"Yup," she said, without looking back.

Liz leaned in and whispered, "And how could I part with such island charmers as Bernadette?" She picked up the towels and headed up the stairs. I showed Mom my room with the slanted ceiling and the rose wallpaper, and the kitchen and the backyard. I knocked on the annex door, which was halfway open. George, as usual, was inside typing away.

"George, this is my mother, Kate Campbell."

"Nice to meet you," George said, rising to shake her hand. "Your daughter is just terrific. She might have a future in journalism."

"Thanks," I said. Oh, George. It was good to see him. When I'm much, much, much older, I'd like to marry someone like him. I was glad I'd come back.

"Cricket told me about your book," Mom said. "I think I might have a story that interests you." So she'd decided to talk to him!

"Great," George said. He smiled at me, mystified.

"But I'd like to remain anonymous," Mom said.

"Absolutely." He clapped once. "I'm intrigued." They agreed to meet the next morning at the Even Keel.

We were walking back inside to find Gavin when I spotted him in the rosebushes with a pair of clippers.

"Hi, Gavin, I'm back."

"Hi, Cricket." Gavin turned around. He paused. He smiled at Mom. He put down his clippers and walked toward us, wiping sweat from his brow.

"This is my mom, Kate. What room should I put her in?" I asked. "Fourteen is free, right?"

"Yes, but the ventilation isn't that great in there. How about the Admiral's Suite?"

"She doesn't need a Jacuzzi and a canopy bed," I said.

"Actually," Mom said, shooting me a look, "I could stand a little pampering."

"It's like, four hundred dollars a night," I said.

"I can get you a discount," Gavin said, waving me away. "I kind of run this place." He smiled and wiped off his face with the sleeve of his T-shirt. "Kate, I'm just about done here. Would I be able to tempt you with a fresh piece of blueberry pie and a glass of iced tea?"

"Sounds yum," Mom said with a sly smile. Pampering? Yum? Yuck! She was flirting. With Gavin. I almost preferred her in her bathrobe with her mysteries. Almost.

Forty-five

I SHOOK AS I WALKED UP TO THE DOOR AT 4 DARLING STREET. I took a deep breath and knocked. After the longest thirty seconds of my life, Jules appeared at the door. She must've checked out a window or something, because she didn't look shocked to see me.

"What do you want?" she asked, a hand on her hip. "Or, *Oh, I'm sorry, are you looking for Zack?*"

"No, I want to talk to you." I handed her the bouquet of flowers that I'd picked from the backyard at the inn, but she didn't take them. "Please."

Jules sighed, stepped outside, and plunked down on one of the little benches. I sat opposite her and put the flowers next to her on the bench.

She crossed her arms and looked at me like she didn't know me, like our history had been wiped from her memory. I wanted to remind her of how I'd practically lived at her house for the past year, or how I'd taught her to drive a stick in the Dunkin' Donuts parking lot. Or how we'd danced in her old gymnastics leotards for hours to the same Rihanna song on REPEAT, laughing until we almost wet our pants. I wanted to find the notebook with all the notes we'd ever passed, tear the pages out, and cover her with them like a quilt. I wanted to play her the three-and-a-half-minute voice mail she left me when she got her period, in which she laughed and cried as she went back and forth between being excited and sad.

I wanted to remind her of the time I'd called her, frozen with fear, when I'd found a hair growing someplace it shouldn't, worried I was a werewolf or a late-blooming hermaphrodite, and she didn't laugh or make fun of me; she made me feel better. I wanted to thank her for that. I wanted to tell her how, even though it was funny now, in that moment I'd been as scared as I'd ever been. Or the time we drove to that boarding school outside Boston for their spring weekend and pretended to be Finnish exchange students. We called sodas "fizzy fizzy pop pop" and declared everything to be "extra cool" in weird, pseudo-European accents. I wanted to read our story to her like a book. In those moments, she'd made it feel like the world was ours. Now she was looking at me like any world I inhabited was one she'd flee.

"I'm so sorry," I said, my eyes filling. "I know what I did hurt you, and I'm sorry."

"I was trying to be nice to you at the Even Keel. I thought *I'd* been the bitch all summer."

"I should've said something then," I said, tears dripping into my lap.

"I told you I needed space from you, and you slept with my little brother." She shook her head. "He's a *sophomore*. Don't you think he's a little young for you? Don't you think he's a little young for anyone?"

So, Zack had told her that we'd had sex. I wanted to say that I wasn't his first, but that wasn't my information to share. It was Zack's. "I can't help how I feel. Besides, senior guys go out with sophomore girls all the time," I added quietly. I had to point it out. "Are you mad that I lost my virginity first?"

"You didn't." She smiled. "I had sex with Fitzy in like, June."

"Oh." It made me sad for Jules. Fitzy had flirted with me when I'd run into Jay and those guys just a few days ago. Maybe it was okay that they weren't in love. But I don't know. I wanted something else for her. "That's great."

She drew a deep breath. "Is there anything else?"

"Do you think you could accept my apology?" She looked away. "I hope you at least know that I wasn't trying to hurt you. Zack and I didn't mean to fall in love."

"Maybe you're in love with him, but he's really pissed off at you."

"I know," I said.

"And so is Parker. And Jay. He said you were a tease. You led him on."

"Do you know where Zack is?" I asked. "I need to talk to him, too."

"No. Anyway, tomorrow he goes to soccer camp. He'll be at Fitzy's party tonight."

"I guess I could try to find him there," I said. "Fitz lives on Cliff Road, right?"

"I wouldn't go if I were you. Nobody wants to see you, Cricket. Not Jay, not Parker, not Zack. And not me." Jules stood up and opened the front door, leaving the flowers on the bench. "Seriously, I'm telling you this as a friend. Don't go." She went inside and shut the door. And then she did something very un-Nantucket. She locked it.

Forty-six

MOM AND I MET PAUL MORGAN AT A FRENCH RESTAURANT on Broad Street. The hostess led us inside and I spotted him right away. He was seated at a table by the window. He looked clean and handsome in searsucker pants and a crisp white shirt. He stood up to kiss Mom on both cheeks, European style. I felt proud I'd found him for Mom. "You look just the same," he said, and pulled out a chair for her. He turned to me. "Your mom was kind of like a badass Gwyneth Paltrow."

"That was a long time ago." Mom blushed and ordered a white wine spritzer. As she and Paul reminisced about their beach club days, I sipped an Arnold Palmer, watched the passersby on Broad Street, and thought about my conversation with Jules. Losing her had me hunched with sadness, weighed down by a sense that the world had unraveled.

Jay thought I'd led him on. Parker thought I was desperate for going out with a sophomore. Jules thought I was a bad friend. And worst of all, Zack thought I betrayed him. I could already hear the names: Tease. Bitch. Slut. All the words designed to make girls feel bad and small. All the words I'd worked so hard to avoid could now be stuck to me like a name tag. And I would have to bear them with quiet dignity. I'd have to put the Jenna Garbetti method back into effect: lie low, look good, and learn. In order to restore my reputation at this point I'd have to lie so low I'd be subterranean. I'd have to learn so much I could operate a NASA spacecraft. I'd have to look as good as a supermodel. I ran my hand through my half-brushed hair, which Mom had encouraged me to put into a ponytail so it was off my face. And I noticed a coffee stain on my T-shirt. I placed my napkin high on my lap to cover it as I tuned back to Paul and Mom's conversation.

"Nantucket sure has changed," she was saying. "Was it always this upscale?"

"No," Paul said. "It happened in the past fifteen years when the mega-rich discovered our little paradise."

"I was in a shop today," Mom continued as she stirred her spritzer with the little plastic straw, "and I saw a pair of sandals for seven hundred dollars. I thought, What is this?"

"Some of these shops are ridiculous, but there are also some gems." His eyes widened and his voice rose. "I should take you shopping."

"I would love that," Mom said.

"We'll get some lattes and make an afternoon of it."

"That sounds like just what I need." Mom and I exchanged a smile. How had I missed it? Paul Morgan was gay. I thought I'd found her the perfect new husband, but maybe what she needed right now was a new friend.

I looked up and saw Zack through the window, from behind, walking up Broad Street. I didn't get a good look at his face, but I knew those shorts and that red T-shirt. I sat up. My heart slammed, pushing blood faster through my veins. Here was my chance to talk to him, in person and alone.

"I have to go," I said, sitting up straight.

"Where are you going?" Mom asked. Paul looked confused.

"I see Zack," I said. "And he's alone. And I really want to talk to him before he gets to that party."

"Okay," Mom said, her brow wrinkled with concern. "Be careful."

"What's happening?" Paul asked, a hand to his chest.

"I'll explain," Mom said as I stood from the table, letting my napkin drop to the floor.

The entrance to the restaurant was crowded. There were people trying to get in and people trying to get out, and the line by the hostess podium was thick and busy with people who smelled like perfume and cologne; laughers and chatters who were slow to move out of the way. It took me a while to get clear of them. When I did, I spotted Zack at the top of the street, about to turn up Centre Street. He was on his way to Fitzy's. It was a busy August night, and the sidewalk was crowded with amblers; couples holding hands; families walking in loose, lolling groups; and kids licking dripping, precarious ice-cream cones. "Excuse me, excuse me," I said as I wove though them to get to Zack.

"Hey!" I called when I'd almost caught up to him. "Hey, it's me!" He turned around. But it wasn't Zack. It was some guy with a baby strapped to his chest.

"Sorry," I said, a little breathless. "I thought you were someone else."

"No worries," said the man, and kept walking.

The man didn't look anything like Zack. He was at least thirty or forty. My wish to see Zack was so strong I'd erased an entire baby. But now the desire to touch Zack, to hold him and kiss him and tell him that I loved him was out of its cage. It was alive and wild, set free by a man with a baby. A strong breeze pushed against my back. I caught my reflection in a store window and stared at the girl looking back at me, breathing deeply, with her hands on her hips. Her ponytail was half undone and I could see she wanted something, and wanted it bad. Why, exactly, was I going to stop her?

I was afraid to go to Fitzy's. I was afraid of what other people thought. I was afraid of what other people would say and do. I wanted to preserve some idea of me. I was practically taking a page from the book of Boaty Carmichael, caring more about my public self than my private one. Was that who I was?

The only opinion that should matter to me was that of the girl in the mirror. Edwina MacIntosh had been saying this for years in the Rosewood School for Girls annual anti-clique speeches. For the first time, it felt true. It didn't matter what other people thought of me; it mattered what I thought of me. I'm not sure why it was at that moment that it finally sank in, except that maybe this is how wisdom works sometimes. You hear it, and some extra-smart part of your brain that you don't even realize you have grabs it. It stays there, hidden away, until it's needed. I looked at my self in the window again. I bet this was what I looked like when I played lacrosse. Strong. Determined. Self-assured. I felt glad I'd gone to an all-girls' school my whole life.

I turned up Centre Street and walked toward Fitzy's house. I wasn't going to lie low. Jenna Garbetti's method wouldn't work for me. I wasn't Jenna Garbetti. I was Cricket Thompson.

Forty-seven

AT FIRST NO ONE SAW ME WHEN I WALKED INTO FITZY'S backyard. I stood by the rose trellis and scanned for Zack, but I didn't see him. Fitzy, Oliver, and a few other guys were jamming on their guitars. Jay was standing nearby, alone, pumping a keg of beer. I took a deep breath and approached him.

"Hi, Jay," I said. He looked up. I'd caught him off guard.

"Hey," he said. I braced myself for him to call me a name, but he didn't. The moment hung in the air until finally he spoke. "You know, if you didn't want to go out with me, you should've just said so."

"I know," I said. "You're so right. But here's the thing. I've liked you for a really long time. I've dreamed of going out with you since the eighth grade. You kissing me and asking me to be your girl was literally a dream come true."

"Then . . . I don't get it." He looked a little nervous as he filled his red plastic cup with beer. I never imagined that I might make Jay Logan nervous. Jules, who was sitting next to Parker on a wicker love seat, had noticed me. She was whispering to Parker. My mouth went dry.

"Well, I really don't know you. When I said that thing about your brother being a loser, I didn't know you; and when I said that I would do anything to go out with you, I didn't know you. I just knew *of* you. I kissed you because I'd thought about it so much, because it's something I've wanted for so long that I just kind of got swept up in the moment. But the thing is, I love someone else, someone I actually know."

"This is a lot of information, C.T." Jay sipped his beer. "You're complicated."

"I'm sorry if I mislead you," I said. "Maybe you could see it as a compliment?"

"Hey, it's cool." To my surprise, he grinned. "I'm sorry I couldn't make your dreams come true." He shook his head. "And I guess it turns out Zacky Clayton has some moves." He wiggled his eyebrows. I did not like where this was headed.

"Do you know where he is?" I asked.

"He's inside," Jay said. The only problem with getting inside was that I had to walk by Jules and Parker and Fitzy and Oliver and a whole gang of other kids. Some were jamming on their guitars and some smoking weed and some playing a drinking game, and others were lounging on the lawn furniture like noblemen in a palace garden. Together they radiated a force field of confidence that required physical strength to pass through.

"Hi, Jules," I said as I walked passed her, holding my breath. Just as I climbed the steps, Zack emerged from the back door. Our eyes met. He still loves me, I thought.

"Zack," I said. "I'm so sorry, but I can explain this whole thing. I really want to talk to you, alone."

"Hey, desperado!" Parker called. I was standing on the steps, under a porch light. Parker was laughing, and I felt the attention of the party shift toward me.

"If you think I'm desperate, then you must not like Zack very much," I said. Parker closed her mouth. "And that's just stupid, because Zack is the best." Jules flashed me a quick glance. She wasn't smiling, but she was looking at me like she knew me again.

"Can we talk now?" I asked Zack.

"Yeah," Zack said. "Let's go."

Forty-eight

ZACK WALKED NEXT TO ME WITH HIS ARMS FOLDED OVER
his chest. I told him the whole story of how I'd liked Jay
since the eighth grade, and how when you go to an all-girls'
school you do a lot more imagining of boys than getting to
know them. I told him that in one way I was sorry that I'd
kissed Jay, but that it also helped me realize that my feelings
for him were made up and the ones I had for Zack were real.
In a weird way, I explained, the whole thing with Jay was
what let me fully open up to Zack.

"But it wasn't just the kiss. He asked you out and you
said yes," Zack said when we reached the Steps Beach rock.
We kicked off our shoes and left them by the twisty wooden
fence.

"It was what I had wanted for so long," I said, following

him down the steep staircase to the beach. "It was like I thought I had to. But as soon as I saw you, it was so clear how wrong I was. Does that make any sense to you? Can you understand that?"

"I don't know," he said when we reached the sand. I wanted him to take my hand, but he didn't. He kept walking.

"I wish you would've answered my calls," I said. "I wish you'd called me back. Or at least texted me." I stopped walking. I didn't want to chase after him. It took him a few paces to notice. When he did, he faced the water. "We had sex, Zack, and you didn't call me back. It was my first time and you didn't call me back. I don't even know how you felt about it. I mean, I don't even know if it was any different with me." I tried to gauge his expression, but he gave me nothing.

"I didn't know what to say," he said, and bent down to pick up a stone. "Jules showed me all those notes you'd written about Jay, and said you had this whole plan about getting some other guy to like you first so that Jay would notice you." He shook his head, skipped the stone. "That's messed up."

"I wrote that in, like, March." I walked over to him, my heels sinking into the cool, soft sand. "You could've at least given me a chance. Did you really think I was using you? Did it *feel* like I was using you?"

"No"—he looked into my eyes and sighed—"it didn't."

"So, can you accept my apology?" It felt like we were

staring at each other for hours, but it was probably less than a minute.

"Yes," he said. Finally, he wrapped his arms around me. I breathed in his T-shirt; I inhaled his Zackness.

"I'm sorry," he said. "I should've called." I stood on my tiptoes and rubbed his back, but when I looked up at him, he turned his face away.

"What's wrong?" I asked.

"I don't know, Cricket. You helped me forget about my mom. But in the past few days . . ." He shut his eyes. He held his breath. "I've started to think about everything I've lost." I pulled him closer. He was shaking. "I miss her. I miss my mom."

"Me too." I held him tighter. We stood holding each other for a long time. When his breathing seemed more even, I loosened my grip and looked up at him.

"Want to go swimming?" I asked.

"If we go swimming, I'm going to want you, and I just . . . Not right now. I know it's crazy." He pushed my hair behind my ear and stared at me.

"Do you want to just sit here?" I asked, trying not to let the rejection sting.

"Yeah," he said. We sat. He flopped back in the sand. A horn sounded.

"Last ferry of the night," I said.

"People are heading home. Summer's over."

I didn't want the summer to be over. I didn't want

Nantucket to be over. I was going to have to face my senior year without my best friend, without Nina, without the Claytons' house to run to when I couldn't deal with my own.

I was going to have to apply to college. This time next year, I'd be heading in a completely new direction.

I lay back next to Zack because, more than anything, I didn't want *this* to be over. I wanted to kiss him, but for the first time since we'd started this whole thing, I was unsure of what to say or do. His eyes were shut, and he was wincing against an invisible blow. For a moment I could feel him slipping away, into a heartbreak that was both enormous and private.

I put my hand on my chest. Was my heart breaking, too? I didn't know. I missed something, longed for something I couldn't quite name. I got up and walked into the surf up to my ankles. I stood still and quiet in the ocean mist. The water was warm, but a deep chill passed through me. Was it ghost girl making contact? Was it Nina trying to tell me something? Was it the part of me that she'd promised would stay on Nantucket leaving my body and stepping into the night air?

"It was different," he said. I turned, surprised to see Zack standing so close. I hadn't heard him approach.

"Good different?" I asked.

"Good different," he said.

"Oh," I said, smiling. "Well, that's good. Especially since, you know, the other girl was French and everything.

Historically speaking, I think the French are the best secret lovers."

"Well, she had nothing on you. With you, I was like, okay, this is it." He wrapped his arms around me and kissed my neck. There were those flutters. The sparking. The humming. This was not a broken heart. It was alive and jumping. I thought he was crying for a second, but when he pulled me closer I realized that he was actually laughing.

"What?" I asked. "What's funny?"

"I don't know," he said, facing me and brushing the hair out of my eyes. "A few minutes ago I was going to break up with you."

"Why?"

"I thought I needed to in order to, I don't know, deal with everything."

"I don't want to break up," I said. I had come this far. I had marched to Fitzy's house despite being told no one wanted me there. I had stood up to Jules. I wasn't about to hide my feelings now. "Do you?"

"No," he said. "I'm just so confused."

"What would the worry doctor say?" I asked.

He thought about it for a minute. Then he took a deep breath and said, "She'd say, *Zack, life is messy.*" He was speaking in a British accent.

"She's British?" I asked.

"Australian," he said, but continued in the British accent. "She'd say, *Life is full of conflict and complexity. The loss of your mother is going to be very painful, and I'm afraid you're going to have to go through it. And it will hurt."*

"Of course." I nodded. A twist of pain.

"But I'm also hearing that you're in love," he continued. *"And love is a rare and wonderful thing. There is nothing in the world that feels better."* He took my hands and dropped the accent. "So maybe I'll just feel both at the same time."

"I want to be your girlfriend, not just your secret lover." I had never had a real boyfriend before.

"Me too," he said. "I want that, too."

And then we kissed. Our kissing was urgent and sweet. It was mixed with laughter. We stumbled backward until we were up to our knees in the ocean, until the bottom of my shorts were wet. When we finally stopped kissing, I looked up at the sky. There were so many stars out there. Packs of them in swirling, looping galaxies. You can't see stars like this in a city, not like you can out here on a rock in the middle of the ocean.

Feelings find each other, I thought. Let one in and the others follow. At that moment it seemed that all our feelings were shimmering above us, around us, in a new and stunning constellation.

Acknowledgments

THANK YOU TO MY WONDERFUL AGENT AND FRIEND, THE incomparable Sara Crowe. I love being on this journey with you and am very lucky to have you on my side. I am so grateful to my editor, the excellent Emily Meehan, for believing in this book and challenging me to make it better. It's an honor to work with you. A special thanks goes to Elizabeth Holcomb for her careful copyediting, and the entire team at Disney-Hyperion for their hard work and enthusiasm.

Thank you to Kayla Cagan and Vanessa Napolitano for their friendship, wisdom, and guidance as, chapter by chapter, they helped this story grow from an idea into a manuscript; and to Elena Evangelo and Brandy Colbert for their assistance with revisions.

I am indebted to the people who educated me about beautiful Nantucket, especially Eileen McGrath. Not only does she know everything about the island, a half hour in her company is a tonic for the soul. Thank you to the Island Reef Guest House for providing an affordable place to stay on Nantucket while I researched, and to Bob Crowe for his hospitality and generosity. Thanks to Ethan Rutherford for our many conversations about writing and publishing, Richard Rushfield for his insight into journalism, and Melissa Pennacchia Nash for sharing her knowledge of lacrosse.

Thank you to my family: my mom, my dad, Gifford, Maryhope, Elizabeth, and Meredith. I also thank my aunt, Mimi Freeman, for her faith in me from the start. Thank you to all the teachers and friends who have supported my writing over the years, especially Hettie Jones, Alison Singh Gee, Gay Cima, Robert Florin, Jim Hines, Maria Collins, Larkin Hatchett Peters, Paola Fantini, Alice Johnson Boher, Kate Snow, Gina Hirsch, Lisa Bastoni Boucher, Patty Smith, and, of course, Izzy Smith Haring.

And to my husband, my sweetheart, Jonathan Davis. I value your brilliance, humor, and love beyond words. Thank you for everything.

TURN THE PAGE FOR A SNEAK PEEK AT

Nantucket RED

I NEVER LIKED THE LAST FEW DAYS OF SUMMER VACATION. Hot without the promise of beach days, heavy with the knowledge that a whole school year is ahead, and stuck in a muggy haze between summer and fall, they're the slowest days of the year. Today felt like the most in-between day of all. It was almost eleven o'clock and I was still in bed. The sun streaked through the blinds and made patterns on the walls. I stared at the ceiling, watching the fan go around and around. Zack was starting boarding school tomorrow and we still hadn't discussed whether we were going to stay together or break up. How was it that only a week ago we were at Steps Beach, kissing under the stars, with what felt like an ocean of time sparkling ahead of us?

A few days after we'd returned to Providence, Zack told

me he was going to Hanover Academy, an elite boarding school in northern New Hampshire. I understood why he was leaving. His mom, Nina, had died in June and his dad and sister, Jules, had completely shut down. Who could blame them?

Nina was the most alive person I'd ever met. I loved her, too. She taught me how to ice skate backward. She taught me how to make a perfect vinaigrette. She introduced me to Frida Kahlo and William Carlos Williams. She made the best paella. There was no one like her, and now she was gone. Mr. Clayton and Jules were shadows of their previous selves. Zack was living with ghosts.

Hanover would give him a chance to start fresh and be among the living. When he told me that a space had opened up at the last minute and he was taking it, I was happy for him. It didn't feel real. I still had Nantucket sand in my shoes. I was so dizzy-happy in love with him that nothing felt real, but it was starting to sink in: the boy I'd risked everything for this summer was going away. He was coming over in a few hours to spend the afternoon with me, and we had to decide what to do. Break up? I wondered as I kicked off the sheets. Stay together, I thought, and sat up.

I lifted my hair off my sweaty neck, twisted it into a bun, and turned on my laptop. When I logged onto Facebook, Zack's new profile picture was at the top of my feed. He'd taken down the photo of himself on the beach in Nantucket and replaced it with one of himself in a Hanover Academy sweatshirt. No, I thought.

Jules commented: "Don't forget your jockstrap!"

A flurry of "good lucks" and "have funs" and more specific comments followed, references to Hanover that I didn't understand. No, stay with me, I thought and felt myself contract and stiffen. My jaw tightened. My stomach clenched. I wanted to hold on to him and keep him in my world, our world. This feeling, this panicky collapse, was opposite of the sweet effervescence I felt when I was with him; it was foreign and unwelcome, and it didn't feel like love.

"Cricket, it's for you," Mom said with a girlie smile when Zack knocked on the door a few hours later. Mom had never been good with boundaries; my being in love gave her a contact blush.

Zack's eyes lit up as I walked toward him in the new white tank top Mom had bought me from the Gap after she saw the state of my clothes when I'd returned from Nantucket, and my old, worn-out cutoffs she couldn't have separated me from if she'd tried. My hair was still damp from a shower and I knew I smelled like the vanilla soap he liked. A slow grin spread across his face as he leaned in the door frame.

"Let's get lost," Zack said like someone from an old movie. He handed me an iced coffee just the way I liked it: extra ice, lots of cream, no sugar.

Mom lingered in the front hall and placed a hand over

her heart, slayed by Zack's charm. "Don't forget an umbrella," she said. "It's supposed to rain."

"That's okay. Thanks, Mom," I said as we walked to his car. I slid my fingers through his belt loop. "I know where we can get some privacy." I'd discovered this place on an away game in Newport. It was about a half hour outside Providence, off Route 24, past Dotty's Donuts, down a shady country road. You had to drive by the farm with the self-service strawberry stand and the Catholic school with its low, humble buildings, all the way to where the road ended at the Narragansett Bay.

The air-conditioning was broken in Zack's old station wagon, so we drove with the windows down. We listened to the college station, stopped for donuts, and even spotted one of the monks from the Catholic school talking on an iPhone. We held hands and kissed at stoplights, but we didn't talk about us.

After we parked, Zack headed down to the beach. I balanced on the abandoned train tracks that hugged the shore and watched him pick up a stone, examine it, and send it skipping into the bay. He was having dinner with Jules and his dad in an hour and a half, and then they were heading to New Hampshire, where they would spend the night at an inn so they could move him into his dorm the next morning. It was time.

I hopped off the tracks, walked down the rocky hill to the beach, and wrapped my arms around his waist. There was a pale band on his neck where his hair had been cut for school.

"What are we going to do?" I asked, breathing into his back.

"I don't want to break up," he said, turning to face me. The clouds collected weight and darkness above us. He pulled me close. "What do you think?"

"I think long distance sucks." Zack pressed his fingers into my spine, confusing my chemicals. Part of me was trying to shut down so that I could deal with this, but my blood spun under his touch.

"It's only a few hours away. We can switch off weekends."

"I don't have a car."

"You can take the bus. And there are so many vacations. For as expensive as this school is, I'll hardly ever be there."

"But I don't want to be someone you text or a face on the screen," I said as his hands left swirls of heat on my back. "We'll forget each other. Or fade away. Long distance will distort everything."

"I could never forget you," Zack said as a wave washed over our ankles. My shoes got soaked. I tossed them back on the beach where they landed in ballet third position.

"When I saw you'd changed your profile picture, I felt like this." I clenched my fists and gritted my teeth. He smiled. "Zack, I'm serious." I looped my arms around his neck and leaned in. "I don't want to feel that way about you. All tight and anxious."

"Let's not do long distance, then."

"So we're breaking up?" The words were so far from what I wanted that they didn't feel real—like I couldn't have possibly just said them. "No, no, no. I don't want that."

"I don't either."

"Maybe we can just . . . pause," I said.

"What do you mean?"

"I mean, we'll just stop here, right now, like this, and then pick up where we left off next summer." A few fat raindrops fell. "No Facebook, no Instagram, no texts, no phone."

"Okay," Zack said. "I can do that."

"But we have to stick to the rules, otherwise the pause won't work."

"I'm unfriending you right now." Zack slid one hand in my left back pocket while the other took out his phone. "Well, there's no reception out here, but I'm going to do it as soon as I get home." Then, before I knew it, Zack snapped a picture of us: me looking up as the rain started, eyebrows raised, him with his arm around my neck, smiling at me.

The rain started for real. We ran for the car and dove into the backseat. Rain splattered against the windows as if flung from a million paintbrushes.

"Paused," I said.

"Paused," Zack said. He pulled off my tank top and I slid his T-shirt over his head.

"Wait—the monk!" I said, covering myself with my hands.

"He's on his iPhone," Zack said, and we laughed, guessing whom he was talking to: His mom? A nun? God?

"I love you," he said as we slid back on the seat.

"I love you, too." It was the first time we'd said those three words in that order. I shivered. I knew in my bones that the words were as true and real as the vinyl seats in that wood-paneled station wagon, the rusted rails of the train tracks, the drumroll of thunder in the distance. My foot made a print on the cool, fogged-up window.

Forty-five minutes later, flushed and unable to stop smiling, we drove off. I'd forgotten all about my shoes, which had been left on the beach, waiting, in third position, for our return.